PREY NO MORE

A SHIFFY P.I. NOVEL (BOOK 2)

MICHAEL ROBERTSON, JR.

ISBN: 978-1-7360939-8-6

room 7 would be the one they'd get assigned. Easy-peasy. The spy camera, which Alexa had hidden between the room's ancient television and a dusty ice bucket (Alexa had yet to see an ice machine anywhere), was set to be triggered by motion.

Alexa drove back to East River, had a nice lunch (which would be billed to Michelle VanFleet, of course), did some shopping (buying a cute top for her girlfriend, Piper), and then drove back to the motel and parked in the back corner of the lot and waited. She had timed it almost perfectly. Fifteen minutes later, Adrien VanFleet had hurried from room 7 to his waiting Lexus SUV without even looking up. Kate Williams came out five minutes later and drove away in her white Toyota Camry.

Alexa retrieved her camera from the room that still smelled of sweat and sex, gave the key back to the woman at the front desk, who grunted something unintelligible when Alexa thanked her, and then drove home, satisfied that the job was done.

"I've also got normal pictures of the two of them arriving and leaving the motel. One with their cars parked out front at the same time," Alexa said. "You know, normal, legal stuff that would be admissible in court. But, well ... might leave room for argument." She tapped the picture of Michelle's naked husband. "Hard to argue these, privately. Take care of the special ones."

Across the desk from her, Michelle VanFleet sighed and looked around the office space, as if in search of an answer to her question: "What am I going to do now?"

Alexa, glancing to the clock again, ready to stand and escort Michelle out, stayed put and leaned back in her chair, crossing her arms and giving the woman a stern look. "You're going to go home, show Adrien that picture, file for divorce, milk him for every fucking cent he has, and then go do whatever you want. Don't think twice about it."

Michelle nodded, slowly, then gave the smile one gives when they're talking to somebody who doesn't fully understand where they're coming from. "It's not that simple."

"Bullshit," Alexa said. She lunged forward and snatched up the picture and held it up. Pointed to Kate Williams's naked body. "Your husband is fuck—sorry ... your husband is having sex with a young woman he works with. What's not simple about that?"

Michelle looked away again, staring into the corner of the room, her mind far from the Shiffy PI office. When she looked back to Alexa, the woman suddenly looked tired. "I have to think about the kids," she said. "And what's best for them. Do I want them growing up in a broken household? Figuring out schedules for who gets them at Christmas, for birthdays..."

Alexa sat dumbfounded. She thought about her own childhood, about the nightmare she'd lived through when she'd barely been a teenager and all the long, hard years that had followed until she'd landed in Silent Falls. She shook her head. "Michelle, there are a lot worse scenarios those kids could experience than joint custody. Trust me."

Michelle smiled politely. Nodded her head and pushed back from the desk and stood up. "Thank you so much for this," she said. She picked up the photograph and placed it back inside the opened blue folder with the others Alexa had printed. She flipped it closed and then tucked the whole thing into her purse, the top sticking out like a bookmark.

"You did great work, as weird as that sounds, given the circumstances."

Alexa didn't move. Watched as Michelle gathered her purse and the light jacket she'd been wearing. *She cannot be serious*, she thought. *There's no way she's going to stay married to that asshole.*

"You'll send me a bill?" Michelle asked, heading for the door.

She was gone before Alexa could say yes, leaving Alexa in the office with only the sound of the ticking hand of the clock, reminding her she was late, and a frustrating feeling that Michelle VanFleet wasn't thinking straight.

Alexa took a deep breath and sighed. *Not my problem*, she told herself as she locked her computer, shut off the lights, and then stepped out onto the stairway landing, the smell of coffee and baked goods rising up to her from the café on the building's ground floor. Alexa climbed the steps up to the third floor, which was the loft apartment where she lived, quickly changed her clothes, shot Ezra a text message letting him know she was on her way now, and then made it as far as the landing outside her office door again before she stopped in her tracks.

A tall man wearing black slacks and a neatly pressed white dress shirt with the top two buttons undone was leaning against her office door, one foot crossed over the other, looking as casual as if he were waiting for a bus. He was handsome, with a coffee from the café in one hand and in the other a large manilla envelope. He wore a thick gold chain around his neck that might have been tacky on anyone else, and even though he smiled at her, Alexa saw the seriousness in his eyes.

"Hello, Alexa. Got a few minutes to chat?"

Alexa wanted to say no. Would have said no to most anybody else.

But she knew this was not somebody you were supposed to say no to.

CHAPTER 2

"You have five minutes," Alexa said, unlocking her office door and stepping inside, catching a whiff of the lingering scent of Michelle VanFleet's perfume in the air, a pleasant scent for a suddenly unpleasant situation. The tall man waited outside the door while Alexa turned on the lights and walked across the room to her desk. Only then did he come in.

He's trying to act like he's no threat to me, Alexa thought. Which she knew was bullshit. The guy right here in front of her might not mean to cause her any harm, but the people he worked for were as dangerous and corrupt as they came. The man, of course, had not specifically told her who his employer was, but he didn't have to. He had the look. They all did. Plus the air of casual confidence, like they were in total control of any room they entered.

Taking the same seat Michelle VanFleet had sat in just minutes ago, the man crossed his legs and leaned back. Sipped his coffee and looked around the office space. "I like what you've done with the place," he said. "Business has been good?"

The way he spoke made it seem like he genuinely cared, like an old friend there on a social visit.

"Four minutes," Alexa said. "I'm already late."

Just over three months ago, when Alexa had arrived in Silent Falls, she'd been awakened on her first morning in town by the sound of a sheriff's deputy pounding on her door at the Silent Falls Inn. When she'd opened the door, she'd been instantly thrown into a murder case where she'd briefly been considered the primary suspect. The victim, Anthony Romano, had been found with his body dismembered and out on display on a ballfield in Collins Park. The night before, Anthony had tried a handful of embarrassing pickup lines on Alexa while she'd been enjoying her dinner at Smokey's, a local restaurant and sports bar, and he'd been shut down with vigor and Alexa's sharp tongue. This, apparently, in the eyes of the young sheriff's deputy, was enough to give Alexa motive.

He couldn't have been more wrong.

Anthony Romano had fallen afoul of a rogue member of the Abatelli family crime syndicate and had paid the price. In Alexa's attempt to clear her name and get to the bottom of who had really killed Anthony, three members of the Abatelli mob had been ambushed and killed. The Abatellis believed Alexa had something to do with those three dead guys.

They were right.

But Alexa would never confirm nor deny that.

In the end, an impromptu meeting held inside a black SUV with one of the Abatelli higher-ups had resulted in a mostly unspoken agreement. In the Abatellis' eyes, Alexa owed them a debt. On some level, she worked for them now, whether she chose to believe it or not.

The man across from her, who was just another Abatelli goon as far as Alexa was concerned, no matter his appearance and charm, smiled. "To the point. I respect that."

"Good," Alexa said. "You should try it, instead of acting like you actually give a shit about me or my business. Just tell me why you're here."

The man looked wounded, cocked his head to the side just slightly. "We do care."

Alexa said nothing. The "we" was her reminder that she was dealing with more than the man in front of her.

"Honestly," the man said, taking another sip of his coffee. "But I do apologize. I don't want to make you later than you apparently already are." He set the manilla envelope, which had been resting atop his knee, onto the desk and tapped it twice with his finger. "An invitation. We'd appreciate a prompt response."

Alexa eyed the envelope for a second, trying not to outwardly show her curiosity, and then looked back to the man. "Let me guess, your annual pancake breakfast fundraiser? Which shell company do you funnel the money into?"

The man laughed, a real laugh that carried no menace. He pointed at her. "Funny. I see why we like you."

Again with the "we."

He stood from his chair and pushed it back into place. Smoothed the front of his shirt and took another sip of his coffee. Smacked his lips, satisfied. "Good stuff. Must be dangerous working so close to a place that makes coffee like this. I'd be an overcaffeinated mess."

Alexa smirked. "Somehow I manage the risk."

He nodded. "I'm sure you do." Then he pointed once more to the envelope and said, "Twenty-four hours."

Alexa despised being told what to do. To say she had a problem with authority would be both accurate and a gross understatement. "And if I take longer, or, you know, don't respond at all?"

The man shrugged. "I guess I'll have to come back for some more of this delicious coffee." He smiled and waved goodbye. "I'll get out of your way now. Sorry for the intrusion. I hope you have a wonderful evening out ... wherever you're headed."

The way the man spoke, Alexa was beginning to have a hard time deciding which phrases carried subtext and innuendo and which did not. That's the problem when dealing with criminals ... they're *criminals*.

The man left, closing the door softly behind him. Alexa listened until she could no longer hear his footsteps on the stairway and then she stood and rushed over to the windows in the wall opposite her desk, which overlooked a one-way side street at the back of the building. A black SUV was parked behind Alexa's ancient Oldsmobile sedan, and its headlights flashed to life just as she saw the man with his coffee step out onto the narrow sidewalk and climb into the front passenger seat. The SUV signaled properly despite the lack of any traffic, then slowly pulled out onto the street and drove away, its brake lights casting a red glow across the brick buildings.

Alexa turned and eyed the envelope on her desk. She wanted to rip it open, wanted to see what was so damn important that the Abatellis had decided to send a messenger to visit. But the ticking sound of the clock reminded her of two things. One, she was already late. And two, the man had told her she had twenty-four hours.

Plus, she didn't want to take with her to dinner whatever burden might fall upon her from that envelope. It could wait.

For now.

CHAPTER 3

Alexa couldn't think of any reason why the black SUV might be following her as she drove to Ezra's farmhouse, but the conditioned cautious and cynical side of her caused her to do repeated checks in the rearview mirror, watching for any sign of a tail.

They'd followed her before, after all.

But that was different. Before, during the whole shitshow that had been her life in the days following Anthony Romano's murder, the Abatellis had been curious about her because they'd wanted to know if she was some sort of threat, itching to know who she was working for. But after that had been cleared up, and after that lovely meeting where she'd been held at gunpoint in the back of a black SUV—of which the Abatellis seemed to have an entire fleet; hell, she and Ezra had completely torched one and the damn things still popped up everywhere like weeds—Alexa had been under the impression that she was now less a person of interest and more like...

Just another goon on the payroll, she thought and rolled her eyes. *Except I'm not getting paid.*

Though the fact they'd let her live that day she'd been forced into the back of that black SUV and hadn't driven her to some abandoned warehouse and shot her in the head and then chopped her up and disposed of the pieces was maybe payment enough in their eyes.

Honestly, she'd pushed the thought of the Abatellis as a whole deep into a dark corner of a closet in her mind and had closed the door and locked it. For the first few days after their meeting, she would have been lying if she said she hadn't been a little on edge, constantly checking over her shoulder, watching the streets for black SUVs, double-checking all her locks at night. But eventually, the paranoia faded. She convinced herself that if the Abatellis had meant her harm, then they would have exacted it when they'd had the chance. Plus, they had made it very clear that they knew her secret—her *past*—or at least enough of it. Alexa, who had just recently chosen to finally move past the horrific events of her childhood and had shared the truth of what she'd experienced and witnessed as a twelve-year-old girl with only a handful of people over the years, had no desire for the Abatellis to go digging further into her history, or dragging any of it up to the present.

That was the grip they had on her. And it was a subtle reminder to Alexa that no matter how much progress she had made over the last few months, no matter how much happier and productive and full her life felt, deep down there was still a part of her that was fucked up.

Even if her father's body was one day found and identified and his decades-old disappearance suddenly became a confirmed death, even if this somehow caused the authorities to begin looking for Alexa again and by chance they found her, she had nothing to fear except exposure of the truth.

But the truth can be a strange and powerful thing, and Alexa planned on keeping it buried along with her father's rotting corpse. She'd worked hard to detach herself from every aspect of him, especially the demon of his memory that haunted the attic of her mind. Even having somebody speak his name aloud was more respect than the monster deserved.

So, no, Alexa did not currently fear the Abatellis, but she was wary of them. She'd resigned herself to accept the unspoken agreement they'd made in the back of that SUV and had then thrown herself into her business—Shiffy PI *was* doing very well, thanks for asking, Mr. Tall Man—her new town, and her new friendships.

Speaking of friendships, she was well outside of town now, buildings and neighborhoods replaced by fields and dense clusters of trees and forest, and she had just turned into the nearly hidden driveway. After she broke the tree line, the warm lights from Ezra's farmhouse were a welcoming sight, one that would forever make her smile.

Alexa felt a pang of guilt as she parked next to his truck in front of the porch. She had never told Ezra about the backseat meeting she'd had with the Abatellis. She told herself lots of reasons why, but the most prominent one was that she didn't want him getting protective and deciding to wage a war against the entire mob. He had already done so much for her; she was afraid of what else he might do.

A brown ball of fur was suddenly framed by the window

next to the farmhouse's front door, and in the blink of an eye, all thoughts of the Abatellis and her father were swept away and Alexa's heart was filled with joy. She killed the engine and then half-jogged up the porch steps and opened the door.

Ezra had picked Barlow up from her office around lunch, when he'd headed home for the day, as was their normal Wednesday routine. The acres of open land behind Ezra's home gave the dog plenty of exercise and fun. Now, Barlow's tail was a blur of speed as it whipped back and forth. His entire body was shaking with happy energy, his long pink tongue dangling from his mouth as he smiled his greeting to her. Alexa knelt and buried her face into the dog's fur, rubbing him down and then kissing him on top of his head. "Have you been a good boy?" she asked.

Barlow stepped back and sat down with a look on his face that said he was insulted she even had to ask.

"He's been his usual charming and lazy self," Ezra called to her from down the hall, his tall and lean silhouette appearing in the entryway to the kitchen. "He takes after his mother."

"Very funny," Alexa said, standing and following the aroma of spices and grilled meat to the kitchen. "You know I'm not charming." She punched Ezra playfully on his shoulder, and he turned sideways to let her by.

"I've been keeping it warm," Ezra said, moving toward the oven and then opening the large door to reveal a rack of pork ribs, the sauce caramelized and bubbly. The smell that had greeted Alexa in the hallway rushed at her like a gust of wind and her stomach groaned in appreciation.

"Sorry I'm so late," Alexa said. "A client had to find a babysitter and ... well, I got here as fast as I could."

She hated lying to him, even by omission.

Ezra, the amber light from the oven casting a golden hue across his dark skin, plated the ribs and then scooped large helpings of coleslaw from a dish on the expansive kitchen island. Everything in the kitchen, and most of the rest of the home, was modern and expensive. All the luxuries needed to almost make you never want to leave. Which, Alexa guessed, was sort of the whole point of the renovation Ezra had done after he'd purchased the farmhouse. He had wanted his secluded paradise, an escape from the world ... and his own past, and he'd gotten just that.

Until Alexa had shown up.

But, no, she wouldn't blame herself for that. In reality, they were exactly what each other needed. In fact, Alexa was certain that the Universe had brought the two of them together for that very reason.

Plus, despite his efforts, Ezra hadn't *completely* abandoned his past. The rack of computer servers and other high-tech cyber-gadgetry he kept in his basement office/man cave was evidence enough of that. It was those tools, plus Ezra's connections and skills from his previous life as an agent for a secret government agency (which he still hadn't told her the name of) that had allowed the two of them to track down and eliminate the three Abatelli members who had caused all of Alexa's problems from her first day in Silent Falls.

The three members whose deaths were now the reason she had a manilla envelope sitting on her desk.

"It's no problem at all," Ezra said, carrying the plates to the table while Alexa filled two glasses with water from a pitcher in the fridge. "If you ever need to cancel, you know that's completely fine, right? Barlow certainly wouldn't mind a sleepover, I'm sure."

Alexa and Ezra had implemented their weekly Wednesday night dinners the very first week after Alexa had moved into her new apartment and office space above the café, and they'd yet to miss one. Ezra did the cooking on most nights, but sometimes Alexa would pick up takeout on the way over. Even though they saw each other in town frequently throughout the week and spoke on the phone often, the Wednesday night dinners still felt special. It was always just the two of them—plus Barlow—and the intimacy of their friendship carried with it an aura that seemed to simultaneously energize and calm them both.

"I wouldn't dream of it," Alexa said, taking her seat and digging into the meal. She really was starving.

"So how is everything with my favorite investment?" Ezra asked, sipping his water and laying his napkin across his lap. Barlow had trotted into the kitchen and was sitting patiently at Ezra's side, playing the waiting game for scraps—which he knew would come. Ezra spoiled him badly.

"So far, another profitable month," Alexa said. She ripped a chunk of meat off a rib and popped it into her mouth.

Ezra nodded, apparently satisfied. It was because of him that Shiffy PI existed at all. Alexa, after deciding she was going to stay put in Silent Falls after over twenty years of being on the move, had come up with the idea for the business, but it was Ezra who had agreed to bankroll the whole thing—*Only until it's self-sustaining*, Alexa had insisted—and had also used his previous life's connections to fast-track a private investigator license for her with little red tape or questions asked. Very little digging into her past. Just the way she liked it. The way they both liked it.

"I told you people would pay those prices," Ezra said. "It's a luxury service, in my opinion."

"I am *not* a luxury."

"You're very good, and worth every penny you charge."

Alexa felt the warmth of his compliment spread through her chest. "Well, don't forget that you do help me out from time to time."

Ezra nodded. "I'm also very good, and grossly underpaid."

They laughed and raised their glasses and clinked them together. "I agree," Alexa said.

They ate in silence for a while then, enjoying the food, before Ezra asked, "So, do you want to tell me what your meeting with your late client was about, or shall I humor you with what ridiculous thing I heard Herb tell a family of four today?"

Herbert Little, one of the few other employees of the Silent Falls Inn, was a Vietnam veteran. He was short and stocky and possessed almost zero filter between his brain and his mouth. Alexa loved him, and from what Ezra had told her, the man adored her, too.

Herb had also been there the day the three Abatelli goons had gone down and had put a bullet through one of their chests.

"Oh God, the Herb story, definitely," Alexa said.

But as she listened and laughed, she couldn't quite keep her mind from drifting back to her office. Back to the manilla envelope waiting for her.

Ezra, damn his perception, must have noticed from the very beginning, because as they were cleaning up after dinner, with Alexa putting their plates into the dishwasher, he dried his hands with a dishtowel and casually asked, "So are you going to tell me what's bothering you?"

Alexa closed the dish washer and stood. "What makes you think something's bothering me?"

Ezra stared at her, said nothing. She watched as his sharp jaw clenched and unclenched.

I can't tell him, Alexa thought. *Not now and not like this.*

"I'm just pissed about what happened with my client today, the one that was late."

Ezra leaned against the counter, stuck his hands into the pockets of his jeans. His blue button-down shirt was still neatly tucked in, and in the elegant kitchen lighting he looked like a model posing for a photo shoot. Sometimes Alexa hated how naturally gorgeous he was.

He eyed her quietly for what felt like a beat too long. "Bad news?" he asked.

Alexa sighed and leaned against the granite island to face him, crossed her arms. "Her husband's having an affair. I showed her naked pictures of him and his side chick."

Ezra grinned and shook his head. "I'm guessing that got the point across."

"See, that's what frustrates me," Alexa said, using his statement to her advantage, happy to have something else to blame for her apparent mood. "I mean, aside from being pissed that another asshole out there is screwing around behind his wife's back while she's at home taking care of the kids and cooking the meals and washing his fucking boxer shorts, I ... I'm not sure she's going to do anything about it."

Now Ezra crossed his arms, cocked his head to the side. "What do you mean? What is she supposed to do?"

"Before she left the office, it seemed like she was actually considering staying with him. When I questioned her on it, she said it wasn't that simple. Said she had to consider the kids. Can you believe that bullshit?"

Ezra was quiet for a moment, looked across the kitchen to the sliding glass door that led out to the back porch. Finally, he looked back to her and said, "I get why you're upset. It doesn't make any sense to me either, for somebody to want to tolerate something like that from their spouse, but..."

Alexa rolled her eyes. "You always have a 'but.'"

"But this is not your problem, Alexa. You did your job, the job this woman hired you for. You gave her the information she needed and now it's up to her to figure out what she's going to do with it. You can't—"

"I can't save everybody, yes, I know." She sighed. "You're right."

"Remember what we talked about? You need to be able to compartmentalize. Mixing your personal feelings with work is always a bad idea. It's tough for you, because you're a passionate person, but it's the only way. Especially in your line of work."

She nodded, looking down, trying to appear somber. "I know. I *know*."

But the truth was, even though the situation with Michelle VanFleet wasn't the thing that had made Alexa distracted during dinner, Ezra was still right. She had let herself get too upset about whatever decision Michelle was going to make. Alexa had done her job and provided the info Michelle needed. She would send a bill and get paid. End of transaction. If she was going to start playing the role of therapist, she would have to start charging even more than she already did.

"Wine?" Ezra asked, breaking the quiet tension.

Just like Barlow had looked at her when she'd asked if he'd been a good boy, Alexa looked at Ezra as if she was offended that he even needed to ask.

CHAPTER 4

Alexa had left Ezra's at a little after eleven, and Barlow had promptly curled up and fallen asleep in the back seat, leaving her alone with nothing but the moonlight and the rattling sounds from the car's engine and her thoughts.

In the darkness, her thoughts were much louder, refused to be ignored.

Before she knew what she was doing, Alexa had pulled her cell phone from her jacket pocket and popped in her Bluetooth earpiece. She instructed the smartphone digital assistant to call Piper, and it obeyed. As the phone rang, Alexa was certain she was going to invite her girlfriend over to spend the night, suddenly aware that she did not want to go back to her apartment alone. Not because she was afraid, but ... unsettled.

The odd thing was she couldn't quite put her finger on *why* she felt this way. Sure, the appearance of an Abatelli asshole was enough to knock a few points off the day, but whatever was in that envelope certainly wasn't going to jump out and bite her ... or chop her into pieces. The Tall Man had told her it was an invitation, which, after having some time to think, Alexa was beginning to suspect might mean they had a job for her. She wasn't thrilled at the idea of doing the dirty work for a crime syndicate, but she highly doubted they would expect her to actually kill anybody—they had their goons for that—so nothing about the scenario seemed to really warrant the sick feeling she had in her gut.

My gut...

Instinct. Hers had always been strong. And right before coming to Silent Falls, she'd met a very special friend who had taught her she should always trust it.

"Hey, sweetie. Are you okay?" Piper's voice filled her ear, and Alexa could tell she'd woken her. She quickly remembered that they were meant to have an early breakfast together in the morning and then Piper was leading a livestreaming workout class from her apartment studio right after.

There was no way Alexa could invite her over. If she asked, she knew Piper would say yes, but Alexa didn't want to do that to her. Piper was good at her job, and it was important to her. Alexa would not be so selfish as to potentially ruin her girlfriend's performance the next day just because she was feeling a little spooked. She was a big girl and she could take care of herself. Had dealt with much worse than mysterious envelopes delivered by well-dressed men.

"Yeah, I'm fine. Sorry, I didn't realize it was so late. I'm on my way home from Ezra's and just wanted to say goodnight."

"And how is our tall, dark and handsome friend?"

Alexa smiled. "Still all three of those things."

"What an asshole."

Alexa grinned. "I know, right?"

"Still good for seven thirty in the morning?"

Alexa groaned playfully. "You know, it's a good thing I only have to walk down two flights of stairs to get there."

Piper yawned, and Alexa knew she needed to let her go. "If you want more exercise after, you could join my livestream."

"Why would I stream you when I can have you in person?"

"Hmmm." Another yawn. "You make a good point."

"As always. Look, go back to bed. Sorry, I shouldn't have called so late. I'll see you in the morning."

In response, Piper made a kissing sound and then hung up the phone.

Back at her building, Alexa forced herself to walk past her office door and continue up the stairs to her apartment. Barlow trotted slowly behind her, looking like a grumpy teenager who'd been awakened against their wishes.

Compartmentalize, Alexa thought. *Work is done for the day. You can tackle the envelope in the morning. It's fine.*

But it wasn't fine.

She managed to take a quick shower and then tossed on a baggy t-shirt and crawled into bed just as the clock ticked over to midnight. Barlow snored on the bed beside her, and as Alexa switched off the bedside light and laid her head down against the pillow, she knew what she would see the moment she closed her eyes. That damn envelope.

She lasted five minutes before she sat up and tossed off the covers, clicking the light on again. "Fuck it," she said. "It's technically tomorrow now."

Barlow opened one eye and watched her pull on sweatpants and her shoes. "I'll be right back," she told him, and then she slipped out the door and down the stairs to her office.

The envelope contained three large photographs, all roughly the same size as the photo Alexa had shown Michelle VanFleet, plus a scrap of paper with a phone number handwritten across it.

Alexa was still fighting down the revulsion rising from her gut while she stared at the photos spread out across her desk and used her cell phone to dial the number. She knew it was late, but she also knew somebody would answer.

They did, on the second ring. "It's Alexa," she said. "I've seen the pictures."

She listened carefully for the next thirty seconds. When the call was over, she sent Piper a text message: **Sorry, I can't make breakfast.**

CHAPTER 5

At the ungodly hour of five thirty in the morning, her normal wake-up time, Piper didn't ask any questions about Alexa's breakfast cancellation other than: **Dinner instead?**

Alexa, who'd finally managed to fall asleep after ending the phone call with the Abatelli Hotline and returning all the photographs to the envelope and carrying it back upstairs to her apartment, heard the chime and groaned, reaching for her phone and reading the message through one squinted eye.

She probably thinks I'm just being lazy, Alexa thought, sitting up in bed and contemplating what to say back. She didn't like the idea of Piper thinking that she was blowing her off because she couldn't drag her ass out of bed. Nothing could be further from the truth. She respected her way more than that.

It's not just respect, Alexa's thoughts crept up on her. *It's love.*

Shut up.

Dinner would be great!, Alexa sent. And then: **Sorry about this morning, but a client sent an email while I was at Ezra's and I need to head out of town this morning to follow up on something. Smokey's at six? Meet here first?**

Alexa felt her stomach do something funny as soon as she sent the second message, and she realized it was because it was the first time she'd ever directly lied to Piper. But what was she supposed to say? *Sorry, I can't make breakfast because I have to meet up with the mob?* She glanced at the envelope full of photos, which was sitting on her kitchen table where she'd dropped it the night before. *And trust me, you don't want to know why.*

She hadn't even told Ezra, the man who had risked his life for her just months ago, about any of this, so she certainly wasn't going to tell Piper.

Yet. If ever. Maybe.

Ugh. She knocked her head back against the headboard a few times. She was tired of secrets, and had hoped that Silent Falls would help her move past them.

Sounds good, Piper sent back. **Go save the world! (But be careful, please. You're too cute and I think I'd miss you if you were gone.)**

Alexa read the message and felt even worse about the lie.

But at least I know she'd miss me. That was the thought Alexa held on to as she got dressed and fed Barlow and took him out to do his business, and also as she made her way down to the café and ordered her usual Americano. The place had just opened for the day, but there was already a line to the door as morning commuters came for their fuel.

"You're here early," Mal, the café's owner, said as she handed Alexa her drink. The two of them had become sort of friends over the last few months, given Alexa's frequency as a customer since she literally worked and lived above the place, though they really didn't know much about each other once you got below surface level.

"Trust me," Alexa said, "I know."

AN HOUR and fifteen minutes later, Alexa was passing by the same motel outside of East River where Adrien VanFleet liked to make his deposits with the young bank teller. The GPS had her continue on for another eight miles before turning left and following a series of rural roads that eventually brought into view a high black wire fence surrounding a huge industrial building and parking lot. A big black sign with red lettering read Xpedited Xchange. The lot was only half-full, but there still had to be over a hundred vehicles parked there, and along one long side of the building, tractor-trailers were backed up to what appeared to be an endless line of loading bays. Alexa drove through the main entrance gate and up to the guard shack positioned beside a mechanical traffic arm.

"Help you?" a young Hispanic woman asked, leaning out from the shack's window. She wore a rent-a-cop security uniform and an untrusting face. The only things on her belt were a walkie-talkie and a large key ring, but Alexa would have bet all the dollars she had that the woman had at minimum one firearm in there with her. Probably just out of sight, right below the window. Easy access. One quick raise of the hand to put an end to any threats.

"My name's Alexa," Alexa said, smiling for some reason. It

wasn't like she needed to be polite. "If you've got a list or something in there, I guess I'm on it. They're expecting me."

The woman did not say anything back to her. Slid the window closed and picked up a cheap-looking cell phone—not the walkie on her belt, Alexa noted—from a shelf below her desk and proceeded to have a brief conversation with somebody on the other end, glancing at Alexa once and nodding in agreement to something. She ended the call and then slid the window open again. "Drive around back, there's a trucker's lounge entrance. Hit the buzzer five times." Then the window was slid shut and the mechanical arm was raised and Alexa drove past the long line of sleeping semis and around to the back.

She found a spot and parked. Stepped out of the car and pulled on her leather jacket and then walked toward the building, its enormous shadow spreading out across the ground like a giant curtain. HVAC units from up on the roof hummed like a swarm of giant angry bees. The trucker's lounge door, with frosted glass and black stenciled lettering, was on the far right, last in a long line of other doors, these all solid metal with no identification except numbers. Alexa found the intercom installed into the wall and pressed the buzzer five times in a row, staring directly into the camera mounted above the door as she did so.

Thirty seconds passed. Then a full minute. Alexa was about to play the buzzer song again when one of the metal doors two down from the trucker's lounge door opened and Mr. Tall Man stepped out. He'd traded his white dress shirt for a royal blue one, the top two buttons undone, the gold chain dipping below the fabric. In the shade of the building, it looked more bronze than gold, almost fake. But Alexa knew it wasn't. Faking was something she figured these people did not do.

"Glad you could make it," the man said. Just like yesterday, he sounded genuine. It pissed Alexa off.

He held the door open for her and when Alexa stepped inside she found herself at the bottom of a dim stairwell. No windows, no other doors. Dirty beige walls. It smelled like mildew and pizza, and something faintly sweet hidden beneath it all that Alexa couldn't quite put her finger on, and when Mr. Tall Man let the door swing shut, sealing out the sunlight, it took a moment for Alexa's eyes to adjust. On the other side of the walls, she could make out the sounds of machinery, maybe forklifts, clangs and beeps and whirs, and the occasional shout of muffled words she couldn't make out. People at work. Loading and unloading trucks. An operation this large, Alexa knew most of it was probably legitimate business, but the curious part of her desperately wondered what *other* things were getting loaded and unloaded, wondered how much cash was getting passed under the table. Kickbacks delivered and favors called in. A black market enterprise hiding in plain sight, staffed with mostly unaware employees who were happy to collect their paychecks and get their 401(k) matches and occasionally look the other way if they happened to see something they shouldn't.

She wondered how many bodies, or, well, parts of bodies, might have been packaged up and shipped off on one of those waiting trucks over the years.

"Right this way," the man said, heading up the metal stairs. "Watch your step. These things are a bitch to bump your shin on."

On the third-floor landing the man opened another solid metal door and waved her through. He led her down a corridor of offices, all with their doors closed, most looking abandoned, until they reached the end, which was capped with a door that looked exactly like all the rest, except there were voices coming from behind this one.

"Are you okay?" the man asked, not yet opening the door. "You've been awfully quiet."

Alexa looked at him for a moment, tried to see if he was playing some sort of game. She asked, "You knew what was in the envelope you gave me, right?"

The man nodded. "Yes."

"And you know why I'm here?"

He nodded.

"So what exactly is it you think I should be saying right now? Asking you how your night was? What you had for dinner?"

He smiled. His teeth were very white. "I see your point."

He knocked twice on the door and then opened it, stepping inside. Alexa followed, and at the last moment was hit with the fear that she might never leave.

CHAPTER 6

The office perched on the corner of the building, directly above the trucker's lounge, and had a row of large windows along the left-hand wall. Probably luxurious at one time long ago, spacious and welcoming and comfortable. Meant for executive meetings and leisurely lunches and talks of the weekend golf match. Now it was just big and sparsely furnished. Nothing fancy. Scuffed and long-faded linoleum flooring, peeling at the corners, wood-paneled walls, a wooden desk that looked like something salvaged from a secondhand furniture store or an estate sale, big enough to cause Alexa to wonder how in the hell they even managed to get it up here, and six metal folding chairs scattered around the room in nothing even resembling an organized pattern except for the one sitting directly in front of the desk. The air was like a cloud of cologne and grease and cigarettes. Thick, like you might have to peel it off you when you left.

Nothing about the office itself gave any indication that the massive man behind the desk was high up the totem pole of an extremely dangerous and wealthy crime syndicate. It was the rest of the people in the room that gave that away. The dynamic of some sort of hierarchy was palpable, everyone playing their role. Two beefcakes with buzzcuts leaned against the wall directly behind the desk with their arms crossed and their eyes leveled at Alexa. They wore tight-fitting sweaters and blue jeans and reminded Alexa of two of the men who had died that day behind the abandoned factory. They were the muscle. The protectors. The ones who got their hands dirty, not just because it was their job but because they liked it. By the windows, two more guys dressed like Mr. Tall Man, neither of whom were as good looking or as tall, gave Alexa a lingering glance when she entered the room, but then both turned and looked out the windows, down to the parking lot. They were there, but they weren't really there. Observing, but pretending they weren't. Waiting to be used, called upon.

At the center of it all, behind the desk was the same man who had been in the front passenger seat that day that Alexa had been forced into the back of the black SUV. He had appeared large then, and now, even in the open office space, he seemed even bigger. His mountainous frame was squeezed into what must have been the world's biggest executive chair, several cows' worth of leather straining against the bulk. Just like that day in the van, he was wearing a black windbreaker overtop a white t-shirt, zipped halfway up, his gold chain glinting in the light from the windows, part of it swallowed by one of his neck rolls. The only thing different was that, instead of sporting the combover he'd worn before, his head was now shaved, traces of stubble peppering his olive-skinned scalp. Droopy eyelids hooded intelligent eyes, eyes that were waiting patiently. In front of him on the desk were a laptop computer and five cell phones lined up in a neat row. Alexa wondered if it had been one of those phones that had rung when she'd placed the call just after midnight, wondered who she'd spoken to.

Mr. Tall Man moved next to the desk, pulling up one of the metal chairs and taking a seat. Pointed to the empty seat in front of the desk and nodded for Alexa to sit.

"It's nice to see you again," the big man behind the desk said. "I didn't get to formally introduce myself last time we met." With little effort, telling Alexa there was more than enough strength left inside his otherwise creampuff exterior, the man rose up just enough to lean forward and offer her his hand. "Francis Abatelli."

Alexa shook the man's hand, which felt like shaking hands with a bear, her flesh and bone swallowed by his the same way the man's neck swallowed part of his gold chain.

Francis released his grip and lowered himself back into the chair, springs and coils and fabric all groaning at once.

"So tell me, Francis," Alexa said, "how is the Tatooine underworld these days?"

The men behind Francis Abatelli stiffened, their muscles tense. Alexa was surprised they had the brain cells to pick up on the Jabba the Hutt reference. Maybe they didn't. Maybe they figured if they didn't understand it, it must be an insult. Maybe they were just conditioned for violence, waiting and hoping for their next chance to beat somebody's skull in.

But when Francis smiled and his shoulders bounced with a chuckle, the two bodyguards eased back against the wall again. They looked disappointed.

"I see your sense of humor has not changed," Francis said.

He spoke slowly, as if each word that came out of his mouth was analyzed before being delivered. He looked over to the two guys who were still staring out the windows. "Bobby, Sal, didn't I tell you she was a funny one?"

Both men turned and nodded. "Sure did, boss," one of them said. The other offered his own chuckle, like the joke had just managed to reach him across the room.

Francis looked back to Alexa. His smile had vanished. "You saw the pictures?"

Alexa nodded. "I'm here, aren't I?"

"What did you think of them?"

Alexa gave the man a look that asked if he was as dim-witted as the two goons standing behind him. There was only one answer to his question. "I thought they were extremely disturbing and proof that evil not only exists but is thriving in the world. Not that I needed any more evidence of that."

Francis nodded but said, "Evil is subjective."

"No, it's not."

His lips twitched, a quick, tiny smile. Gone before Alexa had hardly registered it. "Are you telling me that you've never done something that someone else might consider to be evil?"

"I didn't say that."

"So you have."

She shrugged. "Sure."

"But you consider yourself a good person, yes?"

Alexa was quiet for a moment, realizing the trap she'd fallen into. Finally, she shook her head. "No," she said. "But I'm trying to be better."

She was surprised at the sympathy she saw in Francis's

face when he said, "I understand completely. Unfortunately, the world often forces our hand."

"Fucking A," Alexa said. But what she was really thinking was, *Just like you're about to force mine.*

Mr. Tall Man's eyes flicked back and forth between Francis and Alexa as they spoke, a verbal tennis match.

Francis asked, "So, the photographs ... do you think the murder was random or planned?"

"What am I, a homicide detective? An FBI profiler?"

Francis waited, his eyes still patient.

Alexa sighed. "It wasn't random. Well, at least not the act itself. That was planned for sure, had to be. The victim?" She paused, thought. "Hard to tell. Might have been the first girl they saw walk out of a gas station alone somewhere, or might have been somebody they'd selected ahead of time. Maybe they'd been stalking her, waiting for the right time. It might have even been somebody they knew personally, somebody who wouldn't second-guess getting into a car with them or maybe even going to their house.

"Oh, and since we're debating what's evil or not, look me in the eye and tell me that whoever did those things to that girl isn't the very definition of the word."

The room fell silent. Alexa wasn't sure, but it seemed like everyone had stopped breathing, like a change in pressure before the tornado touched down. A new sense of realization crept up her spine, a remembrance that she had been asked here for a reason. She looked at Francis and asked, "Who was she? Who was the girl in the pictures?"

Francis swallowed, and the room waited. "My niece," he said. "Somebody killed my sister's little girl."

Oh shit.

The room let out a collective breath as the truth was spoken. The two men by the windows turned and looked outside again, and Mr. Tall Man adjusted the cuff of one of his pant legs, looking down and away from the desk. The goons behind the desk were staring straight over Alexa's head, toward the door, focused on nothing. It was a bubble of faux privacy, and only Alexa and Francis were inside it.

"I had *nothing* to do with this, Francis," Alexa said, somehow managing to keep her ass in her chair and not run for the door, suddenly electric with the absurd idea that the man across from her thought she could have ever done the things that had been done to that poor girl in the pictures. Francis knew Alexa had something to do with why three of his men were dead, but that was a completely different situation. Then, she had been provoked, attacked. She and Ezra had settled the score and that had been the end of it. Why would—

"I know," Francis said. "If I thought you had anything to do with Victoria's murder, do you honestly think you'd be sitting here with me?" He shook his head. "Come on, you are smarter than that."

Alexa felt her heart begin to settle in her chest. "Okay, sure. You're right. But why did you ask me to come all the way out here? Why show me the pictures at all? I mean, I'm very sorry for your family's loss, but what does any of this have to do with me?"

Francis Abatelli leaned back in his chair and crossed his arms. "I'd like for you to find Victoria's killer."

CHAPTER 7

Alexa felt all eyes in the room land on her, all waiting for her response as if Francis had just proposed marriage.

"Why me?" she asked. The relief she'd felt at realizing that Francis did not actually suspect her to have any involvement in his niece's murder had quickly faded when Alexa had also realized that, despite any objections or questions she might have, there was no way Francis was going to take no for an answer.

He wasn't a man you said no to without potential repercussions.

But still, she was curious and felt she deserved answers.

"You're a private investigator, are you not?" Francis answered her question with a question. "Fully licensed, legitimate business."—He smiled—"Five-star rating on Google. Why wouldn't I want to hire you?"

"Wait, you want to pay me for this?" This took Alexa by surprise. She'd been expecting strong-arming, threats, blackmail, some sort of tit-for-tat situation: *Hey, you killed my men, now find the killer and we'll call it even. Otherwise...*

Francis reached down to the floor and picked up a nylon duffel bag that had been hidden from view. He placed it in his lap and unzipped it, reached inside. Even though Alexa knew it was a ridiculous thought, her mind flashed to images of Francis pulling out a gun and aiming it at her face. Instead, his baseball mitt of a hand came out clutching two wrapped stacks of cash, which he slid across the desk to her. "Is ten thousand enough for a retainer?"

Alexa's pulse quickened again as she processed the amount, but outwardly she showed no emotion. Didn't even look at the cash on the desk except for the quick first glance. "Why me?" she asked again, narrowing her eyes at him.

Francis leaned back in the chair, rezipping the bag and tossing it onto the floor. "Why not you?" He tried on an aloof expression. "I must not understand what you're asking."

Alexa didn't buy it. "For starters, murder is a bit out of the scope of my business. Let the police handle it. They've got the resources and the authority, and well, it's their fucking jobs. I also know, though not in great detail, I'll admit, that you all have your hands in the Silent Falls Sheriff's Office, so it would make sense to me that you're probably finger-banging other departments throughout the state where it behooves you. I'd imagine the murder of a family member would be enough of a reason to call in big favors for all of those checks you've been writing, work the system the way I'm sure you've perfected. Law enforcement is obviously the better choice over me."

Given Alexa's hatred of police officers—*most* police officers, that was—the words coming off her tongue tasted bitter,

regardless of their truth. Despite her biases, she was not ignorant enough to believe that not trusting somebody equated to
them not being able to do their job.

"Also," she started again, "don't you all ... I don't know,
have your own sort of guys for this?" She nodded to the two
goons behind the desk. "Like them. Isn't that kind of what
part of your whole business is, finding bad guys and
breaking legs or whatever?" She remembered their conversation from the black SUV, how Francis had let her know that
they knew who she was and enough about her past to cause
her concern. "You've clearly got the resources to do your own
research and track people down," she said. "I guess I don't
see how I'm better than anything you all could do on your
own."

The entire time she was speaking, Alexa felt herself
crossing some sort of the line with the man across the desk
from her. Pushing back against somebody who was not used
to being pushed against. She looked around the room to
gauge the reactions of the others, all of whom were ignoring
her, Mr. Tall Man picking at the cuff of his pant leg once
more, and when she looked back to Francis, she was
surprised to see he was smiling.

"That right there," he said, pointing a bratwurst finger at
her. "The way you think, your logic, your gumption, all part
of why I want you on this."

"The police? Yes, we have friends there, but..." He leaned
his head from side to side, searching for the right words. "The
police have rules. Too many rules. In the end, if they catch
the person who did this, worst case is they arrest them and
they are tried for murder and spend the rest of their life in
jail. Better case, they resist arrest, maybe pull a gun, make

some threats, and end up with a police-issued bullet through their chest.

"But *best* case of all," Francis continued, "is that we find Victoria's killer first, and we make them understand what a terrible mistake they made when they decided to end the life of an Abatelli."

Alexa was pretty sure the room suddenly felt about five degrees colder. She digested everything Francis had told her and then asked, "What are the police saying now? Do they have *any* leads?"

"The police do not know."

"*What?*"

"Victoria's body was found on my sister and her husband's property by one of their groundskeepers. He alerted my sister, who was home at the time, and she in turn immediately alerted me. I took care of the rest. Nobody knows outside the family, and now you. And we will keep it that way."

Alexa nodded but asked, "Why wouldn't you at least want the police trying, even if you are too?"

Francis sighed, like this part of the conversation was boring him. "We have enemies. I'm sure you can understand that."

"I can't imagine why," Alexa said before she could stop herself.

Francis didn't seem to care, but Alexa made a mental note to try not to be such an ass, at least until she was no longer in the man's office, surrounded by his entourage. "If Victoria's death was supposed to be a message delivered by one of such enemies, we will not give them the satisfaction of even acknowledging it publicly, or within our own business channels. Alerting the police would do just that and more. I have no intention of doing so."

"I see," Alexa said. It made sense, even if it was fucked up.

"Which is another reason we want to hire you for this job," Francis said. "You're a nobody."

"And you're a real charmer, let me tell you." *Dammit, Alexa...*

Francis didn't even flinch. "What I mean is that we are known. Our faces, our names, our businesses, our interests. Our enemies, if they are smart at all, will know the moment we start poking around and looking for answers, even if we are extremely careful." He held up his hands. "To be honest, they might even be wary of you. I won't pretend to know all the information they've managed to gather over the years, so with the whole thing at the end of last year ... since you were on our radar, it's possible you might have shown up on theirs as well. I don't think that's the case, but I can't guarantee that for you."

Alexa shrugged. "Sure." What else was new?

"But statistically, you are the better stealth option for us at the given time."

"Uh-huh."

"And since you brought it up," Francis said, "murder is not out of the scope of your business. Murder is exactly what brought you to us in the first place. If it wasn't for the scheme you and your black friend who owns the inn managed to pull off, we wouldn't even be having this conversation."

The mention of Ezra might be another subtle scare tactic Francis was using, another unspoken threat, but the man might also just be stating the facts as he saw them. Again, it might be fucked up, but it was the truth.

She was also pretty sure that if they knew the whole truth about Ezra, it would be him sitting in the office right now and not her. Whatever change-of-identity voodoo his agency had performed to essentially wipe away Ezra's past must have been a spotless job. No trace left behind.

Alexa thought about it all for a moment. One of the men by the windows sneezed, and then apologized like he'd disrupted a eulogy. "What if it's not an enemy of yours?" she asked. "What if, by chance, this killer had no idea who Victoria was ... or who her family is? They just needed to get their rocks off with another kill?"

Francis shook his head. "I still want him for myself." Then, after a brief pause, he added, "You said 'another.'"

"What?"

"Just now. You said this person needed to get their rocks off with *another* kill. You think they've done this before?"

Alexa thought about the photographs still in the envelope back at her apartment. Nodded her head. "I'd bet my life on it."

Francis stared at her from beneath those droopy eyelids for a long time, and Alexa couldn't tell if this opinion of her had improved his mood or worsened it. Finally, he reached down and slid one of the cell phones out of line and across the desk to her, parking it next to the stack of cash. "Take this. Joey's number is programmed into it," he said, nodding toward Mr. Tall Man.

Ah, finally he has a name.

"He is the only person who you are to discuss the specifics of this with. Understood?"

Alexa nodded.

"Anything you need, he'll get it."

"Got it," Alexa said, realizing she'd somehow accepted the job without actually doing so.

"Questions, you ask him."

"Didn't you already say that?"

Joey laughed. Francis shot him a look, but when Joey shrugged, the man only shook his head and rolled his eyes. An action that looked comically out of character. To Alexa, he said, "You'll be receiving an email later today with some information that will hopefully be helpful in your investigation."

"Great," Alexa said, and she meant it, because right now she had absolutely nothing to start with other than a name. And if Victoria was Francis's sister's kid, she might not have the Abatelli surname.

"Anything else?" Francis asked. Apparently the meeting was over, which was fine by Alexa. Her skin was starting to crawl sitting there.

She stood from her seat. "Not right now." She picked up the cell phone and pocketed it.

Francis stood too, towering almost a foot over her head, and again stuck out his hand. "I appreciate you very much for this," he said.

When their handshake was finished, Francis picked up the two wrapped stacks of cash and held them out to her. "Don't forget this."

Alexa turned and headed for the door, leaving the money behind in Francis's outstretched arm. "You can pay me when I find this fucker."

CHAPTER 8

Alexa stripped off her jacket and tossed it onto the passenger seat as she got into the Oldsmobile. Drove away from the building without even glancing at the woman in the guard shack as she waited for her to raise the mechanical arm and let her out of the parking lot. Tried not to think about Bobby and Sal standing by the windows and watching her right now. Would watch until her car was nothing but a speck on the horizon. She rolled down her window and hoped the cold air would wash away the stink of Francis Abatelli's office as she drove, her hair whipping around her face as wildly as her thoughts.

Did that really just happen? she asked herself. *Did I just agree to work for a mob boss?*

If you had asked her two days ago what her thoughts about the Abatelli family were, she would have told you they could all burn in hell. She would have told you they were scum, bottom-feeders. She would have told you they were exactly the type of people she would have felt no remorse about killing.

She knew this last part as fact. Because Francis Abatelli might not have known all the specifics, but he knew enough to understand that Alexa and Ezra had laid and then sprung the trap that had killed his three men. Alexa hadn't hesitated for a moment through any of it. Had felt nothing but relief and satisfaction when Herb had put the bullet through the last man standing that day.

So why had she agreed?

I didn't have a choice, she tried to tell herself, but she wasn't quite buying that.

No. She'd had a choice. Whether she had chosen to politely decline the job offer with a shake of the head and a smile or had caused a scene and flipped over chairs and stormed out in an offended rage, she always could have said no.

But in doing so, she'd have run the risk of consequences, the gamut of which was sprawling. A roulette wheel of outcomes: exposure of her past, threats to her friends, or her own death and dismemberment. None of these seemed pleasant in Alexa's book, and she would like to avoid them.

And that was what it boiled down to, wasn't it? Fear. Despite her own confidence and resolve and sharp tongue, despite everything she'd fought against and survived over the years, when it came to the Abatellis, Alexa found she did have fear after all.

Why?

Because I don't want to die yet, she thought. *Not now. Not when I'm finally getting my life together. Not when I finally have a life.*

She thought of Barlow and Piper and Ezra, of Herb and all the other friendly faces she'd met in Silent Falls these past few months. She thought of her Wednesday night dinners at the farmhouse, of wing nights at Smokey's, of hiking in the mountains and Herb's promise to take her fishing when the weather warmed because he knew all the best spots. She thought of her business and her apartment and the fact that they were *hers*—the first things that had been hers since she was a twelve-year-old girl who'd yet to have her entire world upended.

Alexa had always been a fighter, and now ... she'd fight like hell to keep it all.

She turned off the last of the rural roads and accelerated onto the highway that ran toward East River. Rolled up the window as the wind became too fierce at such a high speed. As she drove, she dug deeper into her decision, replaying the meeting in her head.

Thinking back, Alexa realized that the office and the men inside it had not seemed to exude danger so much as power. And Francis Abatelli, the most powerful of them all, had treated her with nothing but respect, acting almost as if he and she were...

Partners.

He'd made no threats—at least not directly—and had seemed genuinely interested in Alexa's thoughts and opinions, listening patiently, wanting to understand her mindset.

Maybe he just wants to understand his enemies better, so he'll know how best to strike.

Or maybe he was a man true to his word, one who could fully separate business from personal and was concerned with nothing other than doing everything he felt was best to find out who had killed his niece.

The photographs of the dead girl flashed across Alexa's

mind and she shook them away, disgusted. When you stripped everything else about this away, all you were left with was a girl who had been brutally murdered, and a killer who hadn't been caught. The family wanted justice, and Alexa knew she'd be lying to herself if she didn't admit that she did too. Because Victoria probably wasn't the first, and if the killer wasn't stopped ... she wouldn't be the last.

Her cell phone chirped from its spot in the cupholder, and Alexa saw a new email had come in. Her office phone system was a cloud-based digital service that Ezra had set up for her, and right now she had all voice mails that were left on the main office line forwarded as sound files to her email. She popped in her Bluetooth earpiece and hit the button to play the message.

Her eyes widened in surprise.

The message was from Adrien VanFleet. He wanted to see her at the Shiffy PI office as soon as possible.

He sounded upset.

CHAPTER 9

A drien VanFleet had left his personal cell phone number in his voice mail, so Alexa dictated a text message through her earpiece telling Adrien she could meet him at the Shiffy PI office in two hours. She got a response within a minute: **I'll be there.**

How ominous.

But ... was it?

Alexa had figured that eventually a PI job would result in her royally pissing somebody off, especially if the task she'd been given was to expose somebody's wrongdoings or deceitful ways. And boy did Adrien VanFleet fit that mold. But, as she replayed Adrien's voice mail again, her instinct was telling her that his tone wasn't that of somebody who was angry; it sounded more like somebody who was concerned, or even afraid.

Alexa smiled, proud of Michelle VanFleet. The woman had obviously decided to confront her husband, and the repercussions must have been sinking in for Adrien. The dismantling of his life playing out in his mind in all its sad, pathetic glory. He was realizing that he'd gambled and lost.

Instead of taking the highway around it, Alexa decided to drive through East River, passing by the bank building where Adrien worked. The bank occupied the first four floors of one of East River's tallest buildings, the front facade all mirrored glass and stonework, and as Alexa slowed down for the stoplight at the intersection, she wondered if Adrien had gone to work today in order to keep up appearances, if he was in there staring down at the traffic through one of those big windows like Bobby and Sal had stared out the windows back in Francis Abatelli's office. Only Adrien's face would be that of a man who was on the cusp of losing everything. His wife, his kids, hell, maybe even his job, depending on how Kate Williams decided to act. When the truth came out, would she admit her complicity, or would she call Adrien out for his threatening behavior and sexual advances, telling everyone how he'd promised her promotions and one of those upper-level offices with the big windows as long as she'd suck his cock for just a while longer?

Alexa didn't know her truth, didn't know the real story behind Kate and Adrien's repeated hookups at the sleepy motel, but whatever that truth was, it didn't excuse any of Adrien's actions. And you could take that to the bank.

She got lucky and found a parking spot on the street and ducked inside a coffee shop for another Americano. As she stood in line to order, she realized that her anger at Adrien VanFleet had temporarily derailed her real question: why was he coming to see her at the office?

If it was fear and concern that were prompting the meeting, Alexa figured maybe he was in damage control mode.

Maybe, even though Michelle had confronted him, Adrien had somehow managed to talk his way out of things, promise her it was a stupid mistake, that he'd never do it again, all the tried-and-true bullshit. Maybe they had agreed to move on from the whole thing, start fresh. Maybe the photographs Michelle had shown him were now ashes in the fireplace or crumpled strips at the bottom of a paper shredder. All the evidence destroyed, so that the slate could be wiped clean.

But Adrien would need to make sure there weren't copies, wouldn't he? Because even though he might have been able to convince his wife his days of infidelity were behind him, what would stop a PI with an axe to grind from, oh, I don't know, emailing the digital files to everyone who worked at Adrien's bank, or maybe sneaking copies into this week's church bulletin? Or maybe using them for something as boring as simple blackmail?

Alexa laughed as she sipped her coffee and drove onto the highway. Adrien wouldn't threaten her for the files, she knew that. It was too risky on his part. But he'd offer to pay for them, of that Alexa was positive. Hell, he might even convince Michelle to come along with him, to show their newfound solidarity in the matter, let Michelle ask for the files, woman to woman.

Alexa didn't really care anymore, as much as it pained her to say so. Because Ezra had been right last night. She couldn't save everybody. She could only give them the information they asked for and let them make their own decisions, live their own lives.

Whatever the reason for Adrien VanFleet's visit, Alexa was sure it would be terribly boring when compared to meeting with a mob boss. She smiled and took another sip of her Americano, drove in silence back to Silent Falls.

BY THE TIME Adrien VanFleet walked into the Shiffy PI office, Alexa had returned home, taken Barlow for a quick jaunt down to Collins Park for a walk, and had just managed to get herself seated at her desk with three of the more tantalizing photographs she'd captured of Adrien and Kate opened and minimized on her computer screen, ready to be pulled up if she might need them for dramatic effect. During those last several miles of her drive from East River, Alexa had decided that after enduring the stress of meeting Francis Abatelli, she would have some fun with Adrien VanFleet. The bastard deserved it, after all. Deserved a lot worse.

But when Adrien walked through the door and closed it softly behind him, Alexa temporarily forgot all thoughts of tormenting the guy, because he looked like a man who'd already been put through the wringer and then back again.

During Alexa's initial and essentially unneeded hour or so of online research for Michelle VanFleet's case, she'd come up basically empty on finding any social media presence for Kate Williams aside from a private Instagram account and the girl's LinkedIn bio. Alexa had silently applauded the girl for not exposing her entire life to the world. Somebody must have raised her right. But Adrien VanFleet had all the usual fixin's of a social media meal. In all the pictures of the man Alexa had seen online, he'd always been the definition of confidence and comfort: standing tall, hair neatly combed, a big smile showing white teeth, always neatly dressed. The photo of him that accompanied his bio on the bank's website showed a man who could both stare down adversaries in a board room and joke with ease during a business luncheon to close a deal. The family photos on Facebook and Instagram showed a man proud to be on top of the world, snapshots of the American dream—the family and the big house with a picket fence, tropical vacations and sun-kissed skin, golf outings with his buddies.

His entire online persona exuded success.

The man walking across the office floor to Alexa now was a bag of dirty laundry.

Adrien wore gray sweatpants with scuffed white sneakers, probably the ones he wore while doing work around the house, and a blue long-sleeved t-shirt with the name and logo of a health club in East River that Alexa had seen advertisements for online. He looked exhausted, his body hunched over like his own weight had become too much to bear. His graying hair, usually neat, was sticking up in the back and strands hung down into his eyes. He swept them out of the way as he greeted her, trying to put on a smile but only managing a sad grin.

"Hi," Adrien said. "Uh, thanks for seeing me on such short notice." He sat down in the chair. "This probably could have been a phone call, but..." He trailed off and looked around the room. "Something told me I should come in person."

Alexa was still processing the scene of the man before her. "Sure," was all she managed to say.

"Oh"—Adrien stuck out his hand—"I'm Adrien VanFleet. Nice to meet you."

Nice to meet me? What the hell is going on here? Whatever

Adrien's angle, Alexa figured it was best to play it cool and play along for now. See where this was all going and only break out the claws once provoked. Adrien was obviously an intelligent man; maybe he had enough sense to keep this all civil. Or maybe it was all a tactic, an act. Maybe he figured Alexa would be more prone to negotiate with a man who looked broken and repentant of his sins than a man who came in kicking and screaming and making demands.

Alexa slowly extended her own arm and shook Adrien's hand. "Alexa," she said. Adrien's hand was soft and cold.

Adrien nodded, tried and failed at another smile, and then looked around the office space again in a way that reminded Alexa of the way that Mr. Tall Man—aka Joey—had done yesterday. She thought maybe he'd make a small-talk comment now, something like telling her what a nice place she had here, or asking her how business was. Instead, when Adrien turned back to her and met her stare, all pretense had left his eyes.

Here it comes, Alexa thought.

"Have you ever met my wife?" he asked. "Has Michelle ever been here?"

Alexa was slow to react, taking her time to think ahead, as if she were playing chess. She nodded and decided to keep things simple, vague. "Yes."

"Was she here yesterday?" Adrien asked. He shifted in his seat, as if the question was making him uncomfortable.

He doesn't know, Alexa then realized. Something about this entire meeting had felt off from the moment Adrien had walked through her door, and right now Alexa's gut was telling her that man sitting across the desk from her had no idea what job Alexa had done for Michelle.

Curious, and still seeing no harm in being honest, Alexa again said, "Yes."

Adrien leaned forward now, resting his arms on the desk and causing Alexa to lean back, away from him. "What time?" he asked, more hurriedly. "Was it late in the afternoon? Five or five thirty or thereabouts?"

Alexa was suddenly tired of answering questions. If Adrien VanFleet wanted something from her, she was going to make him come out and say it and stop dancing around things. "Mr. VanFleet," she said, "do us both a favor and tell me why you're sitting in my office on a Thursday afternoon when you should be at work. Today's not a bank holiday, is it?"

She had expected her knowing where he worked to have had some sort of impact on the man, the first official jab in this little boxing match they had going. But instead of showing any reaction at all, Adrien VanFleet just sat back in the chair and looked at her with eyes full of worry.

"Michelle never came home last night," he said. "You might have been the last person to see her before she went missing."

CHAPTER 10

Alexa was quiet for several seconds after Adrien VanFleet's proclamation that his wife was missing. His words hung suspended in the air over her desk, and Alexa pulled them apart, dissecting and rearranging and examining their every meaning, considering the possibilities. When she added in what she knew about Michelle having proof of Adrien's infidelity, Alexa kept coming to the same conclusion. She'd hoped Michelle would leave Adrien, and now it looked like she had.

"Why do you think your wife is missing?" Alexa asked, trying to sound uninterested, like the whole thing was a waste of time.

Adrien narrowed his eyes at her, and the loose hair around his forehead fell across his lashes. "Because she didn't come home last night. How's that for starters?"

Alexa nodded but said, "That doesn't mean she's *missing*. It only means she's not home."

Adrien's face warmed with frustration. "I don't see the difference."

Trying to sound as pedantic as possible, Alexa said, "Missing would imply that nobody knows where Michelle is. Her not being home only means that you don't." When Adrien stared at her with a disbelieving look, she added, "Are you sure she didn't text you or leave a voice mail or a note or ... *anything* to say she was going somewhere? Maybe a night out of town with a girlfriend? Do you guys have a family calendar or something? Did she maybe have something planned that you simply forgot about?" Alexa grinned. "I'm sure the bank keeps you busy, so nobody would hold it against you if you lost track of your days every now and again."

Adrien's face turned to stone, and he blinked three times, slowly, studying Alexa after she'd finished. Finally, he said, "Are you being serious right now?"

"I'm only laying out all the possibilities. I understand you being worried about your wife, but we need to look at the entire picture before jumping to any conclusions."

"She's missing," Adrien said. "That's the entire picture."

"What makes you so sure?"

"Our fucking *children*, that's why!" Adrien's timidness melted and his words echoed around the office. He took a few deep breaths and then held up a hand. "I'm sorry," he said. "I shouldn't have yelled. But I'm finding it frustrating that you don't seem to believe me."

Alexa was surprised at how genuine he sounded, and she had to remember the picture of the man naked in a motel room with Kate Williams to keep herself from feeling bad for him.

"We had children late in life," Adrien said. "We weren't

sure we really wanted them for a long time, and then once we realized we did, it was ... a struggle. Then, because life is funny like that, we were blessed to have two. Phillip wasn't planned, but boy, talk about a happy accident." Adrien's face flickered with the light of a smile before falling again. He shook his head. "Anyway, those kids mean more to Michelle than anything in the world. So yeah, her not coming home last night to kiss them goodnight and tuck them in, or, if you'd like me to even entertain your, forgive me, ridiculous theory that she went off for some me time with a friend, not even calling them to say goodnight ... to me it only means one thing. She's missing. She's either had an accident of some kind or—" His voice suddenly broke, and he put a hand to his face. He took another deep breath and cleared his throat. "Or somebody took her."

Alexa gave the man a moment to compose himself. He was either genuinely hurting, or one hell of an actor. She decided to stop dragging things out. "I'm sure I already know the answer to this question, Mr. VanFleet, but have you tried calling? Texting?"

Adrien nodded. "Both. Calls go straight to voice mail."

"What about GPS? Do you all use any of those family tracking apps?"

"No." He laughed, but it was a sad sound. "We didn't trust those things. You know, all the stories you read about apps selling your personal information. What even is privacy anymore, right?"

Alexa bit her tongue, trying to keep herself from asking if the real reason Adrien and Michelle didn't use any smartphone location tracking apps was because he didn't want

Michelle to see his little dot parked outside a certain motel. She glanced at the computer screen, to the three minimized pictures waiting to be clicked and expanded. But when she looked back to Adrien VanFleet, his eyes were soft and pleading again.

"I logged into our cell phone account this morning and checked her call logs. Aside from babysitters, she placed calls here yesterday and that's it. And you've already told me she was here. So"—he sighed again, and it was heavy and desperate—"I guess all I'm asking is why was she here, and do you have any idea where she might have gone when she left?"

Alexa said nothing for a long time, weighing her options, her next move.

"Please," Adrien said. "My children are asking where their mommy is and I don't know what to tell them."

Shit. Alexa thought. *Fucking kids.*

She sat up straight and got down to business. Adrien VanFleet had come for answers, and she would give them to him. Because, let's face it, unless Michelle VanFleet never returned home, which Alexa knew was extremely unlikely, he was going to find out one way or another.

"Your wife hired me to investigate you, Mr. VanFleet. She stopped by the office yesterday so I could share with her the results of that investigation."

Adrien slumped back in his chair, creased his brow and shook his head, looking down at the floor. "I don't ... investigate me how? Why?"

Alexa raised an eyebrow. "Really? You want to play dumb on this?"

Adrien's head darted up, and fresh anger burned in his eyes. "Why do you keep acting like I'm some sort of villain here? What have I ever done to you? Christ, I just met you a few minutes ago. What is *wrong* with you? My wife is *missing!*"

"Has your wife ever met Kate Williams?"

All air, all sound was sucked out of the room. A split second of nothing as Alexa's question hit Adrien in the chest. She waited patiently for his response, unable to suppress the smirk that wormed across her lips.

Adrien shook his head, as if now he was the one who found he was only wasting his time. "Kate has nothing to do with this."

"Mmm-hmmm. Even though you're fucking her?"

Adrien's closed his eyes, swallowed. Sighed and said, "You have no idea what you're talking about."

Alexa slowly reached for her mouse and clicked one of the pictures, making it full-screen before swiveling her monitor around for Adrien to see. He looked at the screen, taking in the sight of his naked self, the motel room, the young girl slicked with sweat on the bed. But instead of anger or outrage, instead of shame, which was what Alexa had been betting on, Adrien only looked further confused. He looked away from the screen and met her eyes. "How did you ... never mind. This is what Michelle hired you for?"

Alexa nodded. "Your wife saw these yesterday, so..." She shrugged, letting her shoulders imply the rest. *She left your cheating ass.*

Adrien VanFleet remained somber. "But I don't..." He took one last look at the picture on the screen, then stood from the chair and looked Alexa in the eyes. "My wife is missing," he said. "Please let me know if you hear from her. That's all I'm asking."

He left the office, closing the door as softly as he had when he'd entered.

CHAPTER 11

Alexa stared at her office door for a full minute after Adrien VanFleet had left. Part of her expected the man to return, to explode through the doorway carrying all the anger and aggression she'd expected from him when he found out he'd been caught cheating. She had been nearly certain that the photograph she'd shown him would have caused a more severe response. Now, sitting at her desk during the aftermath of their meeting, Alexa realized she'd actually been hoping for things to get heated. She wanted Adrien VanFleet to know she had the upper hand on him, and she wanted him to be pissed about it. Pissed because he and all the other arrogant cheating scumbags out there didn't rule the world the way they thought they did, and that in the blink of an eye—or the snap of a camera shutter— they could be toppled from their throne, cast down into a pit of disgrace from which they'd never be able to climb out.

But those things hadn't happened. Instead, the picture seemed to have had almost zero effect on Adrien's stance, on his mission. He'd come because he was worried that something had happened to his wife, and while Alexa had figured the photograph would have proven her point that maybe Michelle had simply run off after learning that her husband was sleeping with a young bank teller, Adrien had seemed, at best, confused by the information that Michelle had hired Alexa to spy on him, and at worst, completely unfazed.

The fact that he'd been caught cheating hadn't diminished at all his resolve that something bad had happened to Michelle.

Denial, Alexa thought, finally looking away from the door and back to the photograph on her computer screen. *His God complex won't even allow him to consider the idea that his wife could leave him. The fact he's been caught has no bearing on his own delusion of control over her.*

Alexa sighed and closed the picture file, along with the other two that were still minimized.

Prick.

But something still felt off. There was a feeling of uncertainty that Alexa found herself unable to shake. Despite all her preconceived notions about Adrien VanFleet, and her evidence-backed knowledge that he was an unfaithful bastard, something about the way he'd acted in her office still worked its way under her skin, searching for the soft spot that was sympathy.

Alexa shook her head to clear away the ridiculous idea that she could ever feel bad for the man. *It was the part about the kids,* she thought. *It was meant to be a sob story and it worked.*

Alexa didn't particularly like kids, but she did empathize with them. After the childhood she'd had, it would be impossible not to. As a child, your entire existence is essentially dictated by the adults in your life, and Alexa understood better than most what a crapshoot that could be. Some kids rolled sevens and thrived, some watched as the dice formed snake eyes and braced for the bite.

She heard Ezra's voice in her head. *Compartmentalize, Alexa. You did your job.*

She decided to change gears, pulling up her email on the computer and checking for anything important. She had two new inquiries submitted via the form on her website, a notification that a customer invoice had been paid, and there at the top, right above a piece of junk mail that had managed to worm its way through the filter, was an email with the subject line: You have received an encrypted message. The sender address was a random series of numbers and letters, followed by the domain of a well-known secure messaging service.

Alexa already knew what it was and who it was from. Had been hoping for it, since it would give her something to do other than spend any more mental energy on the VanFleets for the time being. She opened the email and clicked the link to authenticate and verify her identity. As soon as she did, she was prompted to enter a six-digit code. Her jacket was draped over the back of her chair, and from its pocket her cell phone buzzed. She reached behind her and fished it out, but there was nothing on the screen. Confused, she once more clicked the link, and again there was another buzz. But it didn't come from the phone in her hand. It came from the other jacket pocket. From the cell phone that Francis Abatelli had slid across the desk to her before she'd left his office. Alexa pulled the phone free and typed in the code she saw in the notification, unlocking the message.

Which was completely blank.

There was no text in the email body, but there was one zipped file attached, its file name nothing but random numbers and letters, just like the email sender. But still, the fact that the authentication code had come in on the Mafia Hotline phone told Alexa all she needed to know. As odd as it was to say, since the Abatellis were well-known crime lords, she trusted whoever had sent this message. Besides, even if the file contained some sort of spyware or other malicious code, the computer and all the other devices that Alexa owned were protected by top-of-the-line antivirus and encryption programs courtesy of Ezra.

She downloaded the file and then extracted its contents.

Alexa whistled as she scrolled through the files, which all amounted to a digital treasure trove painting the picture of Francis Abatelli's niece's life: links to her social media profiles, credit card statements, cell phone records, names, addresses and phone numbers of friends, a list of frequently visited locations, such as her gym, favorite coffee spot and restaurants, and more. As Alexa grew more and more impressed with all the information that had been provided, another darker realization settled in. This wasn't only data that had been cobbled together since Victoria's death ... they'd been monitoring the girl since before her murder, keeping tabs on her and who she associated with.

Alexa shook her head, wondered if the higher-ups in the Abatelli food chain committed such invasions of privacy against all their loved ones, probably justified in the name of protection, or if Francis Abatelli's soft spot in his artery-clogged heart for his niece had caused him to treat her differently.

Or... Alexa considered. *Maybe it was Victoria herself who warranted being kept tabs on. Maybe she was a wild one, a liability of some sort. Maybe Francis wasn't as worried about protecting* her *as about protecting himself and his business.*

It was possible, but it didn't quite add up. Unlike Adrien VanFleet's genuine confusion over his wife having him investigated earlier that had made Alexa feel like something was off, like she was misreading something, Francis Abatelli's anger over his niece's murder had been unmistakable and sincere. If the man had had any concern or doubt about Victoria's actions that might have been helpful in tracking down her killer, Alexa was sure the man would have told her, or the information would be prominent in the files she'd just downloaded to her computer.

It was too early, and Alexa knew too little to start making assumptions.

She checked the time and saw she still had a couple hours until she had to get ready for her dinner with Piper. Alexa locked the computer and left the office, retrieving Barlow from the apartment and taking him for a quick lap around the building so he could do his business, and then grabbed another Americano from the café before heading back upstairs to the office. She brought Barlow with her, and he curled up on his bed in the corner behind her desk while she sipped her coffee and prepared to get to work.

CHAPTER 12

Alexa had set the alarm on her phone to go off at five thirty, and when it did she pulled herself out of the digital graveyard where Victoria Jameson's past was buried. Yes, Victoria's last name was Jameson because Francis Abatelli's sister, Collette, *had* taken her husband's surname. There was a part of Alexa that was depressed about this, honestly. That the patriarchy had won out and Collette had swapped such a vanilla surname to replace her powerful one. Well, powerful to those who were in the know enough to recognize it.

But maybe that was the whole idea. Maybe Collette didn't want the recognition, didn't want to be associated with the power. Maybe she despised her family's business and wanted no part of it. Alexa couldn't blame her there, she supposed. She wondered if Collette's husband knew the truth about his wife's family. Wondered how much dirty money had been spent to buy the massive house they lived in—Alexa had looked up the address online and even the Google Street View of the home was imposing.

The caffeine was wearing off and Alexa's left eye was starting to twitch from squinting at the screen for so long, so when her phone alarm went off, she was glad for it, closing all the open documents on her computer and locking it. Tossing her empty coffee cup into the trash, she told Barlow it was time to go home, and he stretched long and hard as he got up from his bed and followed her to the door. Alexa shut off the lights, locked the door behind her, and climbed the one flight of stairs to her apartment.

She showered, washing away the day's travel and the stink of Francis Abatelli's office that still seemed to be clinging to her nostrils, and then dressed in tight black jeans and a black blouse. She fed Barlow and was about to take him outside when Piper arrived. Barlow pranced away from Alexa, his tail going into overdrive as he danced circles around Piper, who leaned down and gave him all the rubs and attention that he desired.

Alexa closed the space between them and said, "Okay, dude. Save some love for me."

Piper stood and brushed the dog hair from her hands and pulled Alexa close. "Oh, don't worry. There's plenty left for you. Wanna skip Smokey's and order in pizza?"

Alexa kissed Piper on the lips and squeezed her tight in a hug. "Tempting," she said. "*Very* temping. But I've been staring at my computer screen for the last three hours or so and I need to get out of here for a while."

There must have been something in Alexa's voice, because Piper pulled back, held her at arm's length and studied her face. "Everything okay?"

Alexa smiled, looked at Piper, who was wearing black leggings with a light brown sweater and black knee-high boots. Her amber hair framed her face and fell to her shoulders, and Alexa felt a warmth in her belly as she conjured the memory of the way that hair looked in the morning as it created a golden fan across the pillows. She smiled. "Yeah, I'm good. Just a long day at work." It wasn't until right at that moment that Alexa realized how much of a toll the day had taken on her. *It's the pictures*, she thought. The images of Victoria Jameson's punctured body—*and those fucking quarters*—were not something you easily forgot. And the fact that it had probably happened to other girls, and would continue to happen to other girls unless the killer was stopped...

This is too big for me. This is for the police, or for the FBI or... She thought of Ezra and his connections. But no, she wouldn't involve him in this. Doing so would be admitting she had involved herself with the Abatellis, and she wasn't ready to rip that Band-Aid off yet.

Piper nodded. "I get it. Smokey's it is. You can tell me all about it at dinner."

No, I can't, Alexa thought as she said, "Sure," and hooked Barlow's leash to take him outside quickly before they headed to the restaurant. No matter how much she told herself she was done with the lies, they only seemed to keep piling up.

PIPER DROVE them the five minutes it took to get to Smokey's, which was just outside of town, a quarter mile past a rundown car wash and laundromat. The long cinderblock building sat off the road with nothing but field on either side, as if dropped and left behind by accident, but its looks were deceiving. It was maybe the most popular restaurant and hangout in Silent Falls, not that there were a ton of options, and would always have a special place in Alexa's heart. It was the very first place she'd stopped when she and Barlow had rolled across the city limits line, and was where she'd met the dearly departed Anthony Romano and had gotten pulled into the whirlwind of events that had ultimately led to her deciding to make Silent Falls her home.

The food was also great, and the atmosphere was all you could hope for from such an establishment.

Piper parked her Tesla Model 3 (yes, Alexa had quickly, and shockingly, learned that filming and posting videos on YouTube was a real job, and if you were good at it you could make a lot of real money) next to a jacked-up pickup truck with a muffler the size of a Civil War cannon. The juxtaposition, both physically and ecologically, was picture-worthy, and Alexa wondered how many likes and shares and comments and all the other seemingly meaningless metrics Piper would get if she posted the image on her accounts. The girl was smart, that was for sure, and Alexa wouldn't have been surprised if Piper could find a way to make the picture generate her enough income to damn near buy another Tesla.

They held hands as they walked across the parking lot, a warm and gentle breeze letting them know that spring was trying hard to make its entrance. Another couple exited as Piper and Alexa reached the door, and the man held the door for them with a smile and nod. *Friendly.* That had been another reason that Alexa had decided to stick around. The town, for the most part, had always seemed genuinely welcoming. Ironic, considering she'd been accused of murder the very next morning after she'd arrived. Oh well ... it had all worked out, right? That murder accusation had led her to the best friends she'd ever had and the life she'd only recently decided she wanted. A life she had been certain would be forever out of reach.

Speaking of Alexa's first night in Silent Falls, Clara Wanamaker greeted them from the hostess station. She smiled big and her eyes lit up when she saw the two of them approach, and she pulled two menus from a pile and said, "I just *cannot* get over how adorable the two of you are! Seriously, do you have any idea what a gorgeous couple you make?"

Alexa rolled her eyes. Piper squeezed her arm and laughed. "Oh, we know," she said and winked.

Clara led them to a booth in the back corner. "This is my section," she said, setting the menus on the table. "Drinks?"

"Water, please," Piper said, sliding into the booth.

Alexa shook her head. "Miss Health Nut over here always knows how to have a good time. I'll have a sweet tea, Clara. Thanks."

"Oh, that's so much better, you party animal," Clara said, turning to leave.

Alexa grinned and slid in across from Piper. "I love that girl. She reminds me of myself when I was younger. Spunky as hell. Oh, and minus the whole 'fucked up in the head and living on the streets' part."

Piper reached across the table and took Alexa's hand, gave it a gentle squeeze. Turned her head and watched Clara head to the waitress station to get their drinks. "She's so sweet."

She was. And it still pissed Alexa off every time she remembered what had happened to the girl.

Clara Wanamaker was twenty-two years old, and a lifetime resident of Silent Falls. She'd been Alexa's waitress that very first night at Smokey's, and the two of them had instantly hit it off, but that might have been mostly due to the fact that Clara had fallen in love with Barlow at first sight. Unfortunately for Clara, her and Alexa's friendship had been noticed by the group of rogue Abatelli goons who'd taken interest in Alexa after she'd gotten involved in the Romano killing, and they'd used the girl to send Alexa a back-off message.

Clara had been abducted right from Smokey's back parking lot, tossed into the back of an SUV, driven to a garage, and had her pinky finger broken as a warning.

Alexa had hated herself for allowing such a thing to happen to the girl, knowing that if she'd not shown up in Clara's life, she wouldn't have had to endure such a horrific experience—plus carry the memory of it with her for the rest of her days.

But Clara had taken the whole thing like a champion. The experience had not frightened her but instead fueled her, elicited a primal desire to take charge and dominate and to always fight back. To never let anyone take control of her again.

Another thing she and Alexa had in common.

The two of them had remained friends since, frequently texting and having lunch together, or hanging out some evenings so Clara could show Alexa the latest binge-worthy series on Netflix. Alexa found that she genuinely cared for Clara, enjoyed listening to her and giving advice or suggestions when needed, when asked. And even though on the surface their relationship was that of two adult female friends, with only about twelve years separating them, part of

Alexa felt like Clara was the grown-up daughter she'd never have.

Their drinks came and they ordered their food and the country music played from above and several NBA games were being shown across the televisions all around restaurant. They laughed and joked and chatted about nothing in particular until their food arrived, and it was when Alexa was nearly finished with her burger that Piper asked the question Alexa had known would be coming.

"So," Piper said, cutting the last bit of her grilled chicken breast into bite-sized chunks. "What happened at work today that had you down earlier?"

Alexa said nothing. Popped a french fry into her mouth and chewed.

"Oh, come on," Piper said. "I could tell. Something was bothering you. Was it because of whatever you had to run off to this morning? It must have been important since you canceled our breakfast date." Piper winked at her. "You know how hungry I am for you in the morning."

God, Alexa wanted to tell her. Wanted to tell her everything. *Craved* somebody that would let her get this off her chest. But even though she was confident that her and Piper's relationship was healthy and strong, and possibly headed for the long term, she wasn't sure she trusted it enough to casually mention over dinner that the reason she had canceled their breakfast date was to drive over an hour to an industrial shipping depot that was partially a front for an organized crime syndicate's, shall we say, "off the record" business dealings. And that she had taken a meeting with one of the top brass of said crime syndicate and had, in fact, accepted a job offer to help track down the killer who had butchered a young woman.

Alexa swallowed her french fry. "I think I know the answer to this," she said, "since I'm pretty sure today isn't your cheat day. But do you want dessert?"

Piper leaned back in the booth. "What I want is for you to talk to me."

Alexa felt her heart sink. This wasn't how she wanted things to go. After all those years of being alone, of having nobody that cared what she did or where she was or whether she lived or died, to have somebody as beautiful inside and out as Piper seated directly across from her, showing real concern, real compassion, wasn't something she was going to give up on so easily. So...

More lies.

Alexa sighed. "I can't talk about where I went this morning."

Piper's eyes narrowed to slits. It was a look Alexa had never seen on her before, but you didn't have to be an expert in deciphering the subtleties of human body language to determine Piper was not pleased with this answer.

"I signed an NDA, okay!" Alexa blurted. She was both proud of her quick thinking and embarrassed at the deceit. "This is a big job. I mean, a *big* one. Huge corporate client that needed some"—she searched for the right words—"hush-hush preliminary investigative work done to gather some evidence before they might have to get law enforcement involved. It's a big payday, Piper. My biggest yet. But it's also a little nerve-racking, you know? I mean, they could swallow me whole if they wanted to. So ... I'm sorry. Maybe I can tell you everything when it's over, but for right now, I just ... and look, you know I trust you, but I just ... I can't risk it."

Alexa waited, braced for whatever reaction was coming.

Piper cocked her head to side and gave Alexa a mischievous grin. "Oooooh, look who's playing with big boys all of a sudden." The grin morphed into a bright smile. "Damn, girl, I'm proud of you! How exciting! If I guess who the company is, will you tell me? No, you don't have to say anything, just blink twice if I'm right, okay?"

They laughed together in the booth, the sound echoing around them before getting scooped up and drowned out by the music playing overhead. Alexa felt great relief at having defused the situation, but the stone of regret in her stomach lurched at the sound of each of Piper's laughs.

In an attempt to feel as though she could share *something* real with her girlfriend tonight, pull back the curtain just enough to tease, Alexa said, "My second meeting today was definitely interesting, though."

Piper raised her eyebrows and ate the last bite of her chicken. "Do tell."

Without using any names—she was a professional, after all, dammit—Alexa explained how the wife of a banker had hired her to spy on the man because she'd suspected he'd been having an affair, and how Alexa had gotten several scandalous photos of the man in the act.

"Ugh, nothing worse than dick pics," Piper said, making a face.

"Tell me about it. Anyway, I showed the wife the pictures yesterday evening, and today the husband calls me and wants to meet. I figured he was pissed and was going to try and buy the pictures from me, try to hush the whole thing up, but the cheating bastard showed up looking like he'd just gotten off a three-day bender. He didn't even know his wife knew he was having an affair because she never came home last night and he thinks she's missing. He went through her call logs and saw that I was one of the last calls she made and he wanted to know if she'd come to the office. He says I might have been the last person to see her before she vanished."

Piper leaned back again, looked worried. "You don't sound concerned by that."

Alexa shook her head. "I'm not." *Yes, you are, but you're lying to yourself. See? More lies. Lies, lies, lies.* "I showed him the pictures and told him she probably left him." Alexa shrugged. "I figure she'll come back when she's ready to hash things out."

"What did he say to that?" Piper asked.

"He doesn't buy it. Said she'd never just up and leave their two kids at home like that. But the thing that I found the oddest, and the thing that I can't quite shake, is that he didn't even care that I had caught him cheating. He acted like I showed him a picture of a cute puppy instead of him and his mistress during the act. He's an arrogant asshole, Piper. I'm thrilled she left him."

Piper looked down at the table and didn't say a word, looked lost in thought. Alexa waited, suddenly worried that she'd said something wrong and had made her mad. Finally, Piper looked up and said, "A banker's wife with two young kids ... are you talking about the VanFleets?"

Alexa opened her mouth to say something, to ask how? But then closed it. *Small towns ... everyone knows everyone. What even is a secret?* Oh well, this was a secret she didn't mind exposing. She'd shout it from the top of the actual

Silent Falls if she had the chance. So what was the harm in admitting it? "Yeah," she said. "I am."

Piper suddenly looked sad. "Oh, that poor woman. I don't know her super well, but she watches my videos. She works from home—something in the travel industry, I think she told me once—so she can manage to show up to some of the midday livestream workouts from time to time. Is always friendly, says hi when I see her in town, jokes and thanks me for helping her pretend like she's staying in shape." She shook her head. "What an asshole. I can't believe he'd do that to her."

Alexa took a sip of tea. "I can. It happens every day all across the world."

Piper eyed her for a moment, thinking again, as if trying to work her way through Alexa's cynicism. She asked, "So you really don't think Michelle VanFleet is missing?"

"Wait, what? Michelle VanFleet is missing?" Clara said, appearing at the side of the table with a pitcher of water to refill Piper's glass.

Both Piper and Alexa turned to her. "Her husband thinks so," Alexa said.

"Michelle just found out Adrien was cheating on her," Piper added.

Alexa smiled as the small-town gossip train started its engine. By sunup tomorrow the whole county would know Adrien VanFleet was dipping his wick somewhere other than home.

"I just saw her last night," Clara said.

Alexa and Piper exchanged a quick glance before turning back to the girl. "When?" Alexa said, already feeling her heart do something funny in her chest.

Clara thought for a moment. "Maybe close to six thirty? She placed to-go orders on our website for her and the kids. Came in to pick them up."

The kids. The damn *kids.*

Alexa tried to keep herself calm. Cleared her throat. "You're sure she picked up orders for more than one person?"

Clara looked at her funny, like maybe she was missing out on the joke. "Uh, yeah. I mean, unless she was eating a Cobb salad and two full orders of chicken tenders and french fries all by herself."

Alexa leaned back in the booth.

Shit.

CHAPTER 13

The five minutes it took them to drive back to Alexa's apartment felt much longer, the weight of the new information they'd learned from Clara slowing them down as if it were strapped to the top of Piper's Tesla like a mattress, bulky and screwing with the aerodynamics.

"How was she?" Alexa had asked Clara. "How was Michelle when she came in to pick up her food?"

Clara had looked up to the ceiling, trying to remember. "Normal, I guess."

"You guess?"

"She was in and out in less than thirty seconds, so I didn't exactly get to psychoanalyze her," Clara shot back. "She prepaid by credit card online. I saw her walk in, so I went and grabbed her order from the kitchen and brought it out to her at the hostess station. She took it and left. That's it."

"You didn't speak?" Alexa asked.

"I mean, yeah. But not really."

"What?"

Clara sighed. "I said 'Here ya go,' and she said 'Thanks' and then she was gone."

"Was anybody in the car with her?"

Clara laughed, and then caught herself when she saw how serious Alexa's face had gotten. "I mean ... how would I know that? I'm not Superwoman, I can't see through walls. Why? Is she really missing? Did something happen to her?"

Piper, who'd been watching the exchange quietly from her side of the booth, reached out and patted Clara on the arm. "We don't know what's true and what's not right now," she said, her voice reassuring. She nodded toward Alexa, grinned at Clara. "You know how she is, those gears in her head always turning. She can't turn the job off. All we know for sure is that Adrien was cheating and Michelle didn't come home last night."

Clara got called away by another table in need of refills, and that had been the end of the discussion, except for Clara adding, "Let me know if I can help with anything," as they paid their bill.

Alexa stood and gave the girl a quick hug goodbye. "You've already helped."

Now, as Piper parked behind Alexa's Oldsmobile on the street, a country club behind a landfill, Alexa spoke out loud for the first time since they'd left Smokey's. "So he says."

Piper turned toward her, the glow from the car's big center screen lighting her face. "Who says what?"

"Adrien VanFleet. Back at Smokey's you told Clara that all we knew for sure was that Adrien was cheating and Michelle never came home. Only part of that is true."

Alexa was staring straight out the windshield, her eyes unfocused, thinking, scenarios dancing through her head.

"You think she *did* come home?" Piper asked, also turning to look out the windshield, as though if she could only see what Alexa was seeing everything would become clearer.

Alexa was careful with what she said next, knowing that she shouldn't allow herself to jump to conclusions and start flinging accusations. *But didn't you jump to the conclusion that Michelle wasn't missing but had just left her husband?*

Yeah, and it might have been a big mistake.

"All I'm saying," she started, "is when Adrien came to my office, the way he was acting ... I was having a hard time reconciling the person I was seeing with the person I had expected. Especially when I showed him the picture of him and Kate."

"Who's Kate?"

"The bank teller he's fucking who's literally half Michelle's age."

Piper scoffed and rolled her eyes. "Scumbag."

Alexa nodded. "Exactly. Which is why I was convinced that Michelle not coming home was just the start of her sticking it to him, and Adrien's whole innocent and depressed act was only to try and get my sympathy vote. In my head, things were playing out exactly the way I'd hoped they would, but I forgot the most important thing."

"The kids," Piper said. "She wouldn't just leave the kids."

"What? No. I mean, yeah, there's that. The kids. Sure." *You keep forgetting the damn kids...* "But I'm talking about the thing that brought Michelle VanFleet to me in the first place."

Alexa paused and shuddered at her own thoughts.

"Which is?" Piper asked.

Alexa turned and looked at her. "That Adrien VanFleet is a liar. He's been deceiving his wife for months. Who's to say

Michelle didn't really go home last night, confront Adrien, and then...?"

So many things could have happened in the VanFleet house last night.

"You think he did something to her?" Piper asked.

Alexa was quiet again for a moment, then shook her head. Didn't want to be right. "I'm saying it's a possibility I should have considered earlier."

Piper squinted, thinking. "If he truly thought something had happened to Michelle, why did he come to you and not go to the police? Wouldn't that be the first thing you'd do, instead of playing amateur sleuth and tracking down the last people your wife had called?" Piper paused, added, "Well, okay, maybe *you* wouldn't do that. But the rest of us would, right? And why even say anything so soon? It had been less than twenty-four hours at that point. Michelle was a stay-at-home mom ... it might have been days before anybody had noticed she was missing, if you think about it."

"Hey," Alexa said, "I'm the investigator here." She tried to smile but faltered. She thought about what Piper had said, realized there were a lot of good points there. But... "It's always the husband, right?" she said. "Isn't that what they say? Maybe Adrien thought the quicker he got out ahead of it, the faster everyone would start looking somewhere other than at him. I'm serious, you should have seen the way he was acting earlier. Like he was on the verge of a complete breakdown, and also completely innocent. Even *after* the pictures. And as to why he came to me, I actually had a thought about that earlier; I think he's faking some sort of denial. I think there's a lot of moving pieces to all this in his head—at the time I thought it was just his affair—and he's pretending things aren't as bad as they really are. I'm just not sure why yet. All I know is he was acting strange to me, and I don't think I'm just being paranoid."

Other than the heat blowing from vents, the car was silent. Up ahead at the intersection, the traffic light went through its cycle, splashing the darkened asphalt with color.

Finally, Piper asked, "But, if Michelle did go home last night, do you ... do you think he'd really hurt her with the kids there?"

Alexa knew firsthand the terrible things adults would *do* to kids, never mind with them simply being around to bear witness.

Piper realized what she'd said and quickly followed with, "I'm sorry. I shouldn't have…"

"It's fine," Alexa said, suddenly very ready to get out of the car. She'd had a long day, to say the least, and a headache was beginning to build behind her left eye. "Come on, let's go upstairs."

Compartmentalize, she heard Ezra's voice in her head. It was a word she was starting to like. Because when Alexa had gotten back upstairs to the apartment after taking Barlow out, she found Piper on the bed, naked and on her knees, waiting, her trim and fit body looking goddess-like in the warm glow of the bedside lamp.

Alexa forgot about her headache as she stripped out of her own clothes.

When Piper put her mouth on her, Alexa forgot everything else.

Later, with the lights out and Piper asleep on her stomach beside her, that amber hair appearing black in the darkness but splayed out across the pillow just the way Alexa liked,

Alexa did not sleep. Instead, she lay on her back and stared at the ceiling. Every time she closed her eyes, she would see the pictures of Victoria Jameson's corpse, and after a while, right before exhaustion finally took her into sleep's arms, the pictures began to change. Instead of Victoria's face smeared with blood, it was Piper's.

No! Alexa cried into the blackness of that space between wakefulness and dreams. *I won't let that happen. I'm going to find out who did this.*

And then a new image conjured itself, a flower of color blooming in the emptiness. A picture that took on motion and came to life.

The inside of an abandoned warehouse. A man tied to an old office chair, screaming as Francis Abatelli worked the hacksaw across his forearm, blood splattering in rhythmic spurts as the saw's teeth ripped and chewed through flesh.

We caught him, Alexa thought, with a giddy tingle of satisfaction.

The man stopped screaming, probably passed out. When Francis Abatelli dropped the saw and stepped to the side, Alexa saw that the man in the chair was Adrien VanFleet, and he hadn't passed out after all. He was staring straight at her, his face ghostly white, his eyes pleading. "Help me," he whispered.

Francis Abatelli started to laugh, the noise too loud, echoing throughout the cavernous space as the scene faded and then vanished, leaving Alexa with nothing but the dark.

The sound of somebody knocking on the door caused her to jerk awake, upset that she'd only just gotten to sleep. But the morning light streaming through the blinds and the sound of the shower running in the bathroom caused her to glance at the clock and see that it was just after seven in the morning.

Barlow grunted once, then barked under his breath, stretching as he got up from his bed and cautiously padded over to the door.

Another knock. A little harder this time.

"Who is it?" Alexa called, pulling on her clothes from the night before.

"It's Colin," a voice called back.

Colin Wanamaker. Clara's older brother, who was also a local sheriff's deputy.

The last time he'd knocked on Alexa's door first thing in the morning was when somebody had been found dead.

CHAPTER 14

Alexa opened the door and found Colin Wanamaker standing back from the threshold, in uniform, and with two to-go cups of coffee from the café in his hands.

"Colin, I swear to God if you ask me if I killed anybody last night I will throw you down the stairs," Alexa said.

Colin, only a couple years older than Clara, was baby-faced with a mop of curly blond hair that made for the least intimidating police presence Alexa could imagine. But despite he and Alexa getting off on the wrong foot a few months ago when Alexa had first rolled into town, they'd been amicable when their paths crossed ever since. Colin had apparently decided that Alexa was not a criminal, for the most part, and Alexa had learned that Colin's main flaw was only that he was still wet behind the ears—both as a sheriff's deputy and, quite frankly, as an adult living in the world today. But she had determined that Colin was honest and somebody who always tried to do the right thing, which she respected, and that he loved his sister very much, which she admired and respected even more.

The two of them stared at each other through the doorway for a beat, their eyes locked, their faces stone, before Alexa's lips finally twitched with a smile and Colin's cheeks reddened and his body relaxed. He shook his head, sighed and grinned. "Fair enough. I suppose I had that coming. But look, at least I brought coffee this time." He held out one of the cups. "Americano, right?"

Alexa took the cup from him, examined it briefly as if inspecting it for booby traps. "How did you know?"

"I asked Clara," Colin said. He sipped his own drink. "By the way, when I told her I was coming to see you, she also told me to try not to accuse you of murder."

Alexa laughed. "She's a smart girl."

Colin nodded. "Too smart."

Barlow, apparently satisfied that Colin was friend and not foe, wagged his tail and stepped out onto the landing, sniffing at Colin's black boot. Colin leaned down and scratched the dog behind the ear, looking up at Alexa and asking, "Do you have a couple minutes to chat?"

Here it comes, Alexa thought. *The real reason he's here.* She took a sip of her coffee and then crossed her arms, leaning against the door frame. "Is this police business, or a personal chat between friends?"

Colin stood and Barlow retreated into the apartment, jumping onto Alexa's now-empty bed and curling into a ball next to her pillow. "Honestly, a little of both."

Alexa rolled her eyes. "Do I need my attorney present?"

Colin cocked his head. "You have an attorney?"

"Kidding, Colin. Kidding. Give me a minute and I'll meet you down at my office."

She closed the door and then walked over to the bathroom, which had a sliding barn door design entrance. Alexa slid the door open enough to pop her head in, steam billowing out. The glass shower stall was fogged over, but she could still make out enough of Piper's naked body to put a goofy grin on her face. "Hey," she called out, "I have to run down to the office for a few minutes. Want me to get you anything from the café before I come back?"

Piper stuck her head out from the stall, her hair soapy and wet, her perfect shoulders peppered with water droplets. "Almond milk latte, please. But are you sure you don't want to join me first? Plenty of room in here."

Alexa compared the image before her with that of Colin Wanamaker waiting outside her office door. It wasn't even a contest. It was an act of tremendous willpower for her to shake her head and say, "Believe me, there's nothing I'd love more right now, but I can't. Be back in a bit." She slid the door closed, pulled on her boots, and headed down to the Shiffy PI office.

Seated across her desk from Colin, Alexa leaned back in her chair and sipped her coffee. Since she'd arrived, Colin seemed to have suddenly fallen shy, taking his time looking around the office, making small talk, and apparently having a hard time remembering why he was there.

"Colin," Alexa said, "I left my naked girlfriend in the shower alone to come down and chat with you. I like you, but I don't like you *that* much, so please, spit it out."

Colin blinked three times, and Alexa could only imagine

the thoughts running through his head. "Sorry," he said. "It's just, now that I'm here, I realized how it might seem."

"How what might seem?"

Colin leaned forward and set his coffee on the desk, resting his elbows on his knees. "Look, I'm not accusing you of anything, alright? Please understand that. I still feel terrible about what happened with us during the whole Romano case, and—"

"You were only doing your job." Alexa waved her hand dismissively. "I'm over it."

Colin stared at her for a moment, as if trying to decide if she was serious. Finally, he leaned back again and said, "Adrien VanFleet filed a missing person report late yesterday evening."

Alexa's stomach did a somersault, first sinking low in her belly like a dropped stone at the increased possibility that something very bad had happened to Michelle VanFleet, and then flipping over again as she thought about how sure she'd been yesterday that the woman had simply taken a night away from her husband to begin the first steps in leaving him for good. How much time might have been wasted by Alexa not taking Adrien seriously? And then ... there was Adrien himself. A man with something lurking beneath his skin, a hidden truth buried under all his external concern and worry for Michelle.

"His wife," Alexa said after collecting herself, keeping her voice calm.

Colin nodded. "Michelle."

Alexa now saw were this was all going. "Did Adrien tell you to come talk to me? Does he think I know where Michelle is?"

Colin suddenly looked uncomfortable, shifting in his chair. He nearly grimaced when he asked, "Do you?"

Alexa narrowed his eyes at the guy. "No," she said coolly. "What did that fucker tell you?"

Colin held up his hands. "Whoa, *nothing*. He didn't tell me—or anybody, as far as I know—anything about you at all."

Alexa tried to add this up. Didn't believe it. "Then why are you here?"

Colin seemed to be making some sort of internal decision, staying quiet for a few seconds before admitting, "I was parked on the street behind your building yesterday, eating my lunch, and I saw Adrien VanFleet come out, looking like hell. Most folks don't come out the back if they're coming from the café, so I thought there was a possibility he was leaving after visiting you. It didn't really matter yesterday, but now that he's filed the report..."

Alexa said nothing.

Colin raised his eyebrows. "Was he here?"

"Yes."

"Was he hiring you to find his wife? Did he come to you first before he came to us?"

Alexa thought about Piper's question last night, about why Adrien would have come to Alexa first after seeing his wife's phone logs instead of heading straight to the police, if he was really as concerned as he had seemed.

"No," Alexa said. "He didn't hire me to find his wife. But he did come to ask me about her."

Colin looked confused. "Why? Were you and Michelle friends?"

"No," Alexa said again. "Michelle had hired me. She came

to the office the same evening that Adrien says she didn't come home."

"Why did she hire you?"

"Are you asking me in an official police capacity?"

"I ... yes?"

"Was that a statement or a question?"

"I ... statement. Yes. I'm asking in an official police capacity."

Alexa nodded. "Alright, then. Short version: Michelle thought Adrien was having an affair and wanted confirmation. I was able to provide that confirmation, and I showed it to her the evening Adrien says she went missing. She left here and, according to your sister, drove to Smokey's to pick up dinner for herself and her kids. The next day, Adrien shows up here asking me why Michelle had visited. I told him and he left."

"Why is *Clara* involved in this?" Colin asked, his cheeks growing a light shade of red again, his body language shifting into something slightly more imposing. Alexa was seeing him morph into Protective Colin, the same way she'd seen him morph into this alter ego the day he'd stormed into the Silent Falls Inn's office and nearly attacked her on the day of Clara's abduction. He'd blamed her, and Alexa was honest enough to know that he'd had every right to. She'd blamed herself.

Now Alexa raised her hands, gesturing for him to take a breath. "Easy there. She's not involved at all. She overheard me and Piper chatting about it at dinner last night, that's all. The end."

Colin sat still for a moment, then seemed to deflate a little, settling back into his chair. He looked at Alexa, then raised his eyes to the ceiling, thinking, the same way Clara did. Still looking up, he said, "So Michelle VanFleet doesn't come home one night, and the next day her husband waits until lunchtime to come see you, the private investigator his wife had hired to catch him in his affair, you two chat, he doesn't hire you, and then he leaves and waits until almost nine that night to come into the sheriff's office to file the missing person report."

Alexa waited.

Colin looked away from the ceiling and met her stare. "Does that timeline seem strange to you?"

Alexa nodded. "Damn straight it does."

And it's nice to know somebody else thinks so too.

"Thoughts?" Colin asked.

Alexa was taken aback. She'd had her coffee halfway to her lips and paused, eyes growing big. "Seriously? You're asking my opinion?"

Colin shrugged. "Why not? Clara says you're smart. And hey"—he gestured around the room—"you're an investigator, right?"

You're alright, Colin, she thought. *You're alright.*

Alexa's head spun again with scenarios, all bad, but none with any true evidence to support them. Finally, she sipped her coffee and then said, "It's always the husband, right? Start with him, maybe take a visit to the VanFleets' house." Then, because it was the best way she could explain her feelings about the man, she added, "I don't trust his ass one bit. There's something off with him, I just don't know what it is."

CHAPTER 15

Alexa pushed through her apartment door carrying the almond milk latte she'd promised and found Piper seated at the small table by the windows, a plate of egg whites and a cup of yogurt in front of her. Her hair was damp and, much to Alexa's disappointment, she was now dressed, wearing sweatpants and a long-sleeved t-shirt. There were eggs and yogurt set out across from her, too, and when Alexa entered, Piper pointed to them and said, "You brought the coffee, I made the breakfast."

Seated at Piper's side, a puddle of drool forming at his feet, Barlow looked over his shoulder quickly to acknowledge Alexa's entrance but then went back to dutiful begging. Alexa stepped around him and sat down, handing Piper the latte, which she took and sipped and then smiled, saying, "Bless you, child."

"I'm the older one, don't forget," Alexa said, ripping the top off her yogurt cup. She wasn't really hungry, her anxiety stripping away any thoughts of food, but she spooned the yogurt into her mouth anyway. Among the many things Piper had taught her was the importance of nutrition, and giving your body what it needed, regardless of your own desires.

Most of the time, Alexa ignored this. She still scarfed down fast-food burgers and fries when she was out and about, and she never said no to pizza. The only reason the yogurt and egg whites were in her fridge at all was because Piper insisted on going grocery shopping with her. Alexa's exercise routine consisted mostly of the stairs between the café and her office and apartment, and her walks with Barlow. But she did want to try. Wanted to do better, to *be* better. For Piper, if not for herself. Alexa had so little to offer the beautiful woman seated across from her, the least she could do was order a salad from time to time and let something other than anger elevate her heart rate on occasion. She had to admit that she always felt great after doing one of Piper's workouts, after she'd been resuscitated, of course. And she could understand why people would want to chase that feeling, keep it with them on a daily basis. But it was just so hard, and she was so damn busy.

That's bullshit. You spend most days sitting at your computer doing research. You could at least get a standing desk.

Despite all of Alexa's not-so-health-conscious lifestyle choices, she was still blessed with a slender frame and had always been somewhat muscular. She didn't have gym muscles, she had life muscles. Earned by circumstance, not fitness routines.

Her father had been slender. Lean, with ropy muscles coiled like wire beneath his skin. Alexa hated the thought of having any of his features, would have rather been obese than catch any sort of glimpse of him when she looked in the mirror.

Fucker. Oh how she wished she could erase any memory of him, so he would never be able to creep unexpectedly into her thoughts ever again.

"So what did Colin want?" Piper asked.

Alexa looked up from her yogurt.

Piper pointed out the window. "I saw him leave a few minutes ago. He was parked on the street out there. I figured that's who you were meeting."

"Didn't I tell you I was the investigator?"

Piper smiled. "I can't help that I see things."

Alexa had in fact placed the small dining table against the wall by the windows for that very reason. The people watching. She could sit in the mornings or at night and sip coffee and eat her dinner and have her eye on the entire side street. Watch every car and person, every stray animal. She could watch the lights in other buildings turn on and off, learning schedules and routines. It was better than television. Quieter too.

Alexa finished off the yogurt cup and started on her eggs. "He came to tell me that Adrien VanFleet filed an official missing person report for Michelle last night."

Piper had finished her own food and leaned back in the chair, sipping her latte and stroking Barlow's head while he continued to eye her empty plate, more than willing to help dispose of any crumbs. "Why did he come to tell you that? Did Clara tell him something about our conversation last night?"

"God, no," Alexa said. "She knows better than that. He got pissed the moment I even mentioned Clara's name in conjunction with Michelle. No"—Alexa pointed out the windows, down to the street—"Colin happened to be parked out there on his lunch break yesterday and saw Adrien VanFleet leave the building. He assumed Adrien had been here to see me, so he wanted to know if Adrien had hired me to try and find his wife before he went to the police."

Piper thought for a moment. Asked, "So Adrien didn't actually mention anything to the police about Michelle having hired you, or coming to see you the same day she supposedly disappeared?"

Alexa smiled, shook her head. "Nope. Colin thought it was strange too. I tell you, I don't know what's going on, but Adrien VanFleet doesn't seem to be doing himself any favors."

"But this is good, right? I mean, this is what the police are for. Now that Adrien has made Michelle's disappearance official, they can start looking for her."

Alexa sighed and nodded. "I told Colin to check out the VanFleets' house first. But..."

"But what?"

Alexa looked out the windows, watched as a woman got out of her car, checked her hair in her reflection in the door's window, and then disappeared around the corner of the building. "He waited so long," Alexa said. "Hours went by between when he came to see me and when he went to the sheriff's office late last night. What was he doing in all that time?"

Piper's eyes narrowed. "What do you think he was doing?"

Alexa shook her head, met Piper's gaze and gave a half-hearted shrug. "Covering his tracks? Getting rid of—"

"Don't."

Alexa did. "Getting rid of a body."

Piper reached across the table, knocking her yogurt cup

to the floor, which Barlow pounced on as if it were a live animal and began licking away any indication that yogurt had ever existed inside it. She took Alexa's hand and squeezed. "You don't know what happened. You don't know she's dead, and you certainly don't know that Adrien killed her if she is."

"But he's being so *weird*, Piper. He's hiding something."

"*Men* are weird. They're always hiding something. Doesn't mean they're killers."

Alexa said nothing. The ball of anxiety in her stomach was growing in size. She pushed away the plate of egg whites.

"You said it yourself yesterday," Piper said, trying to sound reassuring. "She might have just run off for the night."

Alexa shook her head. "I was wrong."

"You don't know that."

"Yes, I do."

"*How?*"

"Because now it's not only one night. Now it's been two. Michelle VanFleet ordered takeout dinners for her kids and then didn't come home *two* nights in a row."

The room fell silent except for Barlow's licking, tongue flicking against plastic. Alexa said, "He sat in my office, Piper. He sat right across from me. What if the whole time I thought I was sitting across from a cheater putting on an act of remorse, I was really sitting across from a killer?"

Piper shot back, "Then be happy he didn't kill *you*." She scooped up both their plates and carried them to the kitchen sink. Turned on the water and stood with her back to Alexa for a long time. Alexa sat and waited, patient. Barlow left the discarded yogurt cup and came over to put his head on her lap.

Finally, Piper turned and said, "I'm sorry. I didn't mean for that to sound so ... selfish. I understand why you're upset. If something really has happened to Michelle, that's terrible. And if Adrien is who did it, that's even worse. But at the time, you didn't think him to be anything except a dirtbag who was having an affair. You were doing your job. You can't kick yourself for not seeing something that you weren't even looking for. I know you say the whole meeting with him felt off, but that doesn't mean that your mind should immediately think he's a killer, right? Your initial theory was a good one. A wife found out her husband is cheating, so she skips town for the night to blow off some steam and stick it to him. Make him sweat for a few hours. Nobody is going to fault you for this if the truth is as bad as you're thinking."

I'll blame me, Alexa thought but did not say. Instead, she did what she knew was the best thing to do right then: she nodded and stood and joined Piper in the kitchen, leaning against the counter. "You're right. It's in the sheriff's office's hands now. I've told Colin what I know, and if they have any more questions I'll be happy to answer them. I'll do anything I can to help find Michelle—*alive*, hopefully—but it's their case, not mine." She couldn't help but add, "But you'll have to somewhat excuse me if I don't have the most confidence in the Silent Falls Sheriff's Department."

Piper stepped forward and kissed her, quick and light on the lips. "I know. I *know*. But you can't get in their way, and you can't let your own worry about Michelle keep you from doing your own job." She pointed behind Alexa. "Like that, I'm guessing. Is that from your big secret client meeting yesterday? All it needs is a red Top Secret stamp on top and it couldn't be more obvious."

Alexa felt a chill run through her, turned and saw what Piper was pointing to. The large manilla envelope containing the photographs of Francis Abatelli's dead niece was on the kitchen counter. Alexa had been so wrapped up in everything VanFleet that she hadn't even noticed it.

"I moved it when I brought the food over to the table," Piper said. "What's in there, schematics for some new military warhead? It was heavier than I expected."

The thought of Piper even touching the envelope, forget actually seeing the photos inside, made Alexa's stomach full of yogurt churn with revulsion. She should have locked it away somewhere, out of sight, out of easy reach. "I..."

"I know," Piper said, smiling playfully. "You signed an NDA." She grabbed her bag from the floor by the bed and double-checked what was inside before zipping it up. "I'm headed out. I have brand sponsorship meetings through lunch and then two streaming classes this afternoon. I'll call you when I'm finished." She stopped in front of Alexa before heading to the door. "You're okay, right?"

Alexa nodded. "Yes. As okay as I'm going to be."

Piper considered this for a beat, then nodded and kissed her. "If you need me, call me. Or better yet"—she winked—"join one of my workouts later. A little sweat might do you good."

Then she was gone. Alexa watched out the windows after Piper had left and a minute later saw her pop out onto the sidewalk and walk around the driver's door of her Tesla. Piper looked up and caught Alexa watching and then blew her a kiss before climbing inside and driving away.

What am I doing? Alexa thought, stepping away from the windows and picking up the empty yogurt cup from the floor.

She's too good for me. She's got her entire life together and I'm just figuring out how to begin. She tossed the yogurt cup into the trash and finished cleaning up the kitchen.

When somebody knocked on the door five minutes later, Alexa's first thought was that Piper had forgotten something. But when she opened the door, it wasn't Piper standing on the landing but once again Colin Wanamaker.

"I just heard on the radio," he said. He was slightly out of breath, like he'd run up the stairs. "They found Michelle VanFleet's car."

CHAPTER 16

Alexa took one hand off the steering wheel and tapped her Bluetooth earpiece, answering the call. "Hello?"

"Colin said to stop following him," Clara Wanamaker's voice giggled into Alexa's ear. "He said he'll get in trouble if they find out he's why you're there."

Alexa saw the brake lights of Colin's sheriff's cruiser flash ahead of her, along with the left turn signal, and she eased onto her own brakes, matching his speed and flipping on her blinker. They were fifteen minutes outside of town, cautiously navigating the curving county roads that led into the mountains and the parkway. "I have no idea what he's talking about," Alexa said. "I felt like going for a drive and happened to end up going the same direction he is." She leaned forward and looked up through the top of the windshield, saw the sun slicing through the clouds. "It's a beautiful day," she said as Colin made the turn into the picnic area and campsite, "I thought maybe I'd go for a hike."

Clara gave a sarcastic "Uh-huh" and then added, "Just

keep playing dumb if anybody asks, alright? Colin's trying. He told me he brought you coffee this morning."

"He did," Alexa said as she turned into the picnic area. "It was very kind of him. I have no problem with Colin, Clara. I won't do anything on purpose to ruin his career."

"It bothers me you said 'on purpose.'"

Alexa smiled. "You know me too well."

"Why did he come see you, anyway? Was it about Michelle VanFleet?"

"Gotta go," Alexa said, following the tree-lined road as it curved around an outcropping of rocks and then led to the parking area beyond. "Time for that hike. I'll call you later. Promise." She hung up.

Alexa slowed a bit to create a little more space between her Oldsmobile and Colin's cruiser. Ahead, she saw two other sheriff's cruisers parked perpendicularly behind a white Lincoln Navigator. Michelle VanFleet's SUV. Alexa knew this because from the windows of the Shiffy PI office, she'd watched the woman climb into the vehicle after leaving their first meeting. It was a habit of Alexa's, to watch her clients or potential clients when they left. She liked to watch their body language, and the looks on their faces. She liked to see if they were already scrolling through apps on their phone when they pushed out the building's door and stepped onto the sidewalk or if they were already texting or on a call. It all meant nothing, mostly. But one day, Alexa figured it would mean something, maybe everything: a small tell that would expose a truth that would reveal a secret.

Nobody had ever looked back up toward her office while she spied on them, all of them ignorant to the fact that anybody in the world could be watching their every step, waiting around each corner. Nobody, that was, except Piper. The first time Alexa had watched her girlfriend leave the office, Piper had seemed to sense it almost immediately. She'd stopped and craned her head up and shielded her eyes and when she'd seen Alexa watching, she'd done exactly as she had done this morning. She'd blown a kiss. Alexa had felt her cheeks flush and she'd embarrassed herself by quickly turning away.

The blown kiss was nice, of course, but the act of catching Alexa watching carried more weight. To Alexa, it meant Piper was more aware of the harsh reality of the world, less naive. She was confident and assured, but wary of any dark spots hiding behind the bright exteriors of people and places. Her intuition was strong, and like Alexa she trusted her gut more often than not.

That first blown kiss, carried up from the sidewalk to Alexa's second-story office window on a cold winter's breeze, had symbolized the budding connection between the two of them, the first serious sparks of energy that would light the fire of their relationship.

Alexa hung back for a few more seconds while Colin drove ahead and added his cruiser to the conga line. As soon as he stepped out of the car, two more men in uniform came into view from the other side of Michelle VanFleet's Navigator. One of the men, a heavyset deputy with a flat face that reminded Alexa of a pug dog, waved at Colin and made some sort of remark that caused Colin to laugh and nod his head. The second man was tall and powerfully built, his silver hair cropped close to his scalp, and he wore big sunglasses that looked like black mirrors over his eyes. His entire look and stature were imposing, and Alexa figured that was exactly the way he liked it.

The man was none other than Sheriff Brooks Byrd.

Alexa had first had the pleasure of meeting Sheriff Byrd after she'd been knocked unconscious while chasing down a suspicious photographer in the woods around Collins Park the day after Anthony Romano's murder. When she'd come to, Byrd had been standing over her, offering his assistance. Alexa had thanked him by vomiting on his shoes and refusing his offer of a ride back to the inn.

Ezra had told her the guy was mostly alright, from what he could tell. But there was still a dense fog of mistrust between Alexa and Sheriff Byrd, like they both knew the other held secrets, and each was only waiting for the other to slip up. After she'd opened the Shiffy PI office, Byrd had stopped by the first week with a small gift basket full of fruit, congratulating her. Alexa had thanked him and then remained silent until he'd left. When she'd opened the card attached to the basket, the typed inscription had read: *Here's to a fruitful future of working* together *to keep our town safe.*

The fruit pun had caused her to groan, but the subtext was clear. Byrd wanted her to know that the sheriff's department was not her enemy. He wanted her to trust them. But Alexa also knew he didn't want her keeping secrets from them or...

Alexa parked in the first space at the beginning of the parking lot, as far away from the SUV as she could get. Stepped out.

Or getting in the way.

While Colin and the sheriff and the pug chatted behind the barricade their cruisers had created, Alexa walked briskly through the grass in front of the parking lot. A creek babbled from her left, and the last remnants of the long-dead fall foliage crunched under her boots. Several picnic tables and grills dotted the space between the parking lot and the creek, along with a few pavilions, and were shadowed by the rising landscape that grew into the mountains looming beyond. There were picnic areas and campsites like this one all around the county, trailheads and fishing spots and wildlife abundant. But as Alexa reached the space in front of the SUV, she thought: *You know what nature doesn't have? Cameras.*

Which reminded her...

She pulled out her cell phone as she closed the gap between herself and Michelle VanFleet's SUV, opened the camera app and started recording a video. Then she held the phone up in front of her face, as if she were immersed in reading something.

While recording, she walked right up to the driver's side window of the Navigator and stopped, angling the phone down to see inside.

"Miss Shifflett, what exactly are you doing?" Sheriff Byrd's voice was loud, but not at all surprised. Alexa figured the guy had seen her the moment she'd arrived in the parking lot. Her car was basically a boat on wheels, after all, and the engine coughed more than it purred. The only reason he hadn't stopped her before now, Alexa guessed, was his own inherent curiosity in her. Though curiosity was the nice way of putting it.

Alexa would bet good money that Sheriff Byrd was exactly the type of person who would look up to her office windows after he left. They did have that in common.

Alexa looked away from her phone, and she *did* act

surprised. "Huh? Oh, Sheriff Byrd," she said with a showbiz smile, "I didn't even see you all there. I was using this new app"—she held up her phone, careful not to show the screen —"that shows all the trails, and I guess I wasn't paying attention where I was going."

Sheriff Byrd stared at her with the deadpan expression of a world-class poker champion. The pug was looking up to his boss like an expectant child, and Colin was looking anywhere but Alexa's direction, as if mere eye contact would implicate him.

"This is a potential crime scene," Byrd said. "I'm going to have to ask you to step away from the vehicle." He raised his hand and pointed behind her. "The trails are that way."

Alexa stepped back, acting like she was suddenly shocked at the sheriff's revelation, but really she was just trying to get a camera angle through the gap of the front seats and into the back. "Oh, shit," she said, "I had no idea. So sorry." But then she acted as though she was seeing the vehicle for the very first time—*really* seeing it—and said, "Hey, isn't this Michelle VanFleet's Navigator?"

"It is," said the pug.

"*Marston.*" The sheriff's voice was a gut punch to the pug, aka Marston, and then the man's mouth shut so fast his lips made a smacking sound.

Alexa had gotten all she knew she was going to at the moment. She would let the men do their jobs for now, knowing that once Colin told the sheriff what she'd told him, she'd probably get a visit, sans fruit basket this time, or an invitation to come down to the sheriff's office for a chat.

Which she'd gladly do. Until then...

"Well, I certainly hope she's okay," Alexa said, turning to leave.

Byrd called to her as she headed toward the trailheads. "How do you know Mrs. VanFleet?"

"Church," Alexa called over her shoulder.

She heard Byrd mumble something that might have been *Bullshit*.

ALEXA DID GO FOR A HIKE, but only a short one. She found the closest entry point into the woods and walked just far enough to be out of sight from Sheriff Byrd and his band of Merry Men. Then she stepped off the path, her boots crunching and cracking through the leaves and twigs, and leaned against a tree, pulling up the video on her phone she'd recorded of the inside of Michelle VanFleet's SUV.

Beneath the canopy of trees, the light had dwindled and the temperature had seemed to drop ten degrees. Alexa zipped her jacket and shivered before she hit play, instantly lowering the volume so she wouldn't have to hear Byrd's voice again. She paused the video once the front inside of Michelle's Navigator was clear and in frame on the screen.

Her eyes went straight to the passenger seat, where a plastic takeout bag from Smokey's sat tall and full. Too tall for just one meal, but the perfect height for three—a Cobb salad and two orders of chicken tenders and french fries.

Alexa had never doubted Clara, but seeing the evidence with her own eyes solidified the truth: Michelle VanFleet had planned on going home that night, but she'd never made it.

Alexa's eyes caught something else, and she pinched the

screen to zoom in on what was sitting on the passenger floorboard. The bulk was somewhat hidden in the shadows, so
Alexa tapped to enable the video editing features and raised
the exposure until Michelle VanFleet's purse was easily visible, if not a tad washed out. Upon seeing it, Alexa's mind
flashed back to the last time she'd seen that purse, when
Michelle had picked it up from Alexa's desk along with her
jacket as she'd turned to leave the office. Which had been
right after she'd tucked the blue folder containing the incrim-
inating photographs of her husband and Kate Williams
inside.

Alexa remembered the way the top third of the folder had
stuck out like a bookmark, marking the point in Michelle
VanFleet's life where she'd have to make some tough
decisions.

In the video now, there was no blue folder.

Alexa zoomed and scrolled and swiped, checking every
pixel, looking for any sign of blue, thinking it possible the
folder had fallen out, or been pulled out and tossed aside,
perhaps in a struggle. She saw no sign of it.

A bird cawed somewhere above, and Alexa jumped and
fumbled the phone before it tumbled from her hand and
landed in the dirt. The rest of the woods came back into
focus, the smell of earth and pine, the sounds of unseen crea-
tures skittering and taking lazy strolls through the trees.
Alexa picked up her phone and brushed it off, slipping it
back into her jacket pocket. She stood and scanned the forest
with determined eyes, like a predator searching for prey.

"Are you out here, Michelle?" she whispered to herself,
imagining the woman's corpse, cold and blue—*blue like the
folder*—and half-hidden in a pile of leaves and dirt, dull and

lifeless eyes open and staring out, watching, waiting for somebody to discover the truth.

A phone buzzed in Alexa's pocket. Not her phone. She gave the trees one last knowing look and then pulled the Abatelli Hotline phone out of the other pocket and answered the call.

"Where are you?" the voice on the other end of the line asked.

"Hi, Joey, I'm fine. Thanks for asking. I'm currently in the woods, hiding from the sheriff and wondering if I'm about to accidentally step on a dead body. So, you know, normal day."

"Been there, done that," Joey replied, his voice that effortless cool. Alexa surprised herself when she laughed.

"You strike as more of a desk guy," she said. "Not really the field agent type."

"Have you made any progress?"

"What, with Victoria? Hell, I just got the email yesterday."

"You said it yourself," Joey said, "he's probably done this before, and he'll likely do it again."

Alexa felt a chill slice through her, and suddenly Michelle VanFleet's lifeless eyes stared at her from all throughout the forest.

Or maybe he already has.

"Francis isn't the most patient man," Joey said. "He likes you, but..."

Alexa sighed. She did a quick flip through the mental catalog of all the information she'd read about Victoria Jameson yesterday evening. She'd spent most of the time on the girl's social media accounts, which were your boilerplate examples of an average healthy and intelligent college student, but overall not that helpful unless Alexa wanted to track down any and every friend who'd been tagged in Victoria's photos. "I'm on it. I think I know where to start," she lied.

"That's great to hear. Keep me posted."

Joey ended the call, and Alexa suddenly felt very alone. She turned and jogged back to the picnic area and straight to her car. When she drove away, she glanced into the rearview and saw Sheriff Byrd standing beside his cruiser, staring right back at her.

CHAPTER 17

Alexa parked her Oldsmobile behind her building and headed inside, thinking she'd take Barlow on a quick lap around the block.

She'd lied to Joey on the phone when she'd been standing in the woods and imagining Michelle VanFleet's lifeless eyes staring out at her from somewhere in the forest. Alexa hadn't yet been sure where she was going to start, or even *how* to start, with tracking down who'd murdered Victoria. She'd been so mentally wrapped up in all things VanFleet that she hadn't yet allowed herself to really get down to work, other than her initial afternoon poring through all the files she'd been sent.

It was on the drive back from the mountains, while she tried to keep the VanFleet situation in the rearview where it needed to stay for the time being, that Alexa had realized what her most obvious first task should be. But before she proceeded, she needed to ask Joey to clear things with Francis. The last thing Alexa wanted to do was cross any boundaries and piss off Francis before she even really got started.

She hated asking for permission. After a lifetime of ignoring the rules, playing by them could be extremely frustrating.

But when the alternative might be having somebody take a hacksaw to your limbs, a little more patience than usual was required.

Alexa climbed the first flight of stairs, resisting the tempting smells coming from the café, but never made it up the second flight to her apartment. Adrien VanFleet was seated on the floor next to her office door, his knees pulled up to his chin like a small child pouting in the corner after being scolded for not sharing his toys. He wore a charcoal suit with a solid navy necktie. His shoes were shiny but scuffed on the toes. When he looked up at Alexa as she came onto the landing, she saw that his hair was combed today but his eyes betrayed any semblance of him having put himself together. The whites were tinted red, and half-moons of the same charcoal as his suit hung beneath them, seemed to drag his entire face toward the ground with the weight of exhaustion.

Alexa was surprised to find the man waiting for her, but more than her surprise, she was curious as to the look he was giving her. It wasn't a look of anger or malice, nor the look of somebody seeking retribution. It was the look of somebody pleading for answers.

"Why?" Adrien finally said, his voice a whisper, using all its energy to reach Alexa's ears. "Why did you do it?"

Alexa cleared her throat. Steeled herself against any sympathy her mind might trick her into feeling for the sad figure seated on the ground in front of her. He looked helpless, he looked devasted, but at the end of the day, he was still a cheater … and in Alexa's book, he was still suspect number one.

"Your wife hired me for a job, and I did said job," Alexa said. "Haven't we already been over this? You know, before you finally decided to go to the police. Oh, which reminds me, why didn't you tell them about me? Why didn't you happen to mention that I might have been the last person to see your wife alive when you were filing your missing persons report?"

She stopped. Forced herself to take a deep breath, waited for Adrien's reaction, figured the anger would come now, a crack in his fake woe-is-me attitude he'd been carrying around.

But no anger came. Instead, Adrien looked away for a couple of seconds, staring into the corner where a fire extinguisher and a smoke alarm were mounted on the wall. When he looked back up to her, the pleading was still there, but it was coupled with something else, as if he was seeing something new, something he hadn't expected.

He pushed himself off the ground and stood, his knees cracking.

Alexa took a step back.

Adrien sighed and cocked his head, staring at her. "I can't tell if you're being purposely obtuse or if you really have no idea what I'm talking about ... with any of this."

Alexa remained silent. Stared back. She wasn't going to give him an inch. Didn't trust him.

"My life is crumbling around me," Adrien said, crossing his arms and leaning against the office door. "My wife is *missing*. I had to ship my kids off to their grandparents' house this morning while lying to their faces, telling them everything was going to be fine, that mommy would be back from her special trip soon and she couldn't wait to see them. And now..."

For a moment, Alexa thought the son of bitch was actually going to produce some tears, get himself nominated for some fucking acting award. Not an Oscar, but maybe a Daytime Emmy.

Adrien took a breath and composed himself. Said, "And now I've lost my job. Thanks to you."

"Me?" Alexa asked, genuinely startled by the accusation. "I didn't do anything."

"The pictures," Adrien said, his voice losing its muster, falling back into a resigned desperation. "That's why I'm here. I had to ask you. I had to look you in the eyes and ask you why you would do such a thing. What have I ever done to you?"

The real question, Alexa thought, *is what did* you *do to Michelle?*

"I have no idea what you're talking about, Mr. VanFleet. Like I said, your wife hired me, and I did the job."

"Was part of the job sending naked photos of Kate and me to the entire bank? Did Michelle specifically make that part of your job description? How did you do it, anyway? Forget the *why*, the real question is how you got into my email. Michelle couldn't have given you the password, because she never knew it. I'm sure of that." He stopped, gave her a stare with eyes that suddenly looked as dead as the ones Alexa had imagined from Michelle's corpse. "I'm pretty sure hacking into a financial institution is some sort of federal offense, so..." He shrugged.

Was that some sort of thinly veiled threat? Alexa's head was spinning. Sure, she'd fantasized about ruining Adrien

VanFleet's life with those pictures, had joked to herself about all the possible options to mass distribute them and publicly humiliate the man, but she hadn't actually *done* any of those things.

She had to slow down, had to learn everything. Because whatever had happened with Adrien's email and those photos, it was suddenly the most important thing in the world to her.

She held up her hands, a gesture of innocence. "Mr. VanFleet, I promise you I did not send those photographs, and I've never been in your email."

He scoffed, but it sounded halfhearted. "Why should I trust you?"

"Because right now you don't have any other options, bud. I'm telling the truth. I've got more important shit in my life to do than sitting around sending your dick pics to your coworkers." *Okay, not really. It sounds like a great idea.* "And, honestly, hacking into a bank's email? Who do you think I am, some Silicon Valley expat with an axe to grind against horny middle-aged men?"

Adrien eyed her, quiet.

She could see the reluctant acceptance eventually spread across his features.

"Then who?" he asked. "Who else had the pictures?"

Alexa thought back to the video on her cell phone, the one that showed the inside of Michelle VanFleet's Navigator. The purse spilled on the passenger floorboard. The fact that there was no blue folder.

"Nobody else had them except Michelle," Alexa said. "She took copies when she left my office the night she disappeared."

"I don't..." Adrien started. He shook his head, clearly confused.

"Me either," Alexa said, and she meant it. She nodded toward her office door. "Let's go inside. I want you to tell me everything about what happened this morning, and if there's anybody—other than your wife, obviously—who would want to see you burned."

CHAPTER 18

A drien VanFleet had been thorough and detailed and would have made a great witness if he hadn't been Alexa's number one suspect. He talked for a long time, and Alexa hadn't interrupted once.

Adrien's parents lived two hours to the north, just across the West Virginia border, but were at their son's house at seven sharp that morning, scooping their only two grandchildren into their arms and loading their little suitcases into the trunk, promising they were all going to go get a big breakfast together.

Adrien watched them pull out of the driveway, and then, in what was becoming a habit, he pulled his cell phone from the pocket of his dress slacks and dialed his wife. The call went straight to voice mail, the same as it had been doing now for what felt like an eternity. He grabbed his travel coffee mug and got into his SUV and drove to work, leaving the house at just past seven fifteen.

He arrived at East River and drove through the busy morning streets of downtown, parking in the garage a block away from the bank. He pushed through the bank's big glass doors at just past eight and walked hurriedly across the lobby floor, head down and not greeting anyone. He hadn't told anyone at work about Michelle yet and planned on keeping it that way for now. He was afraid of the truth they might see in his eyes if he so much as glanced at them. He took the elevator up to his office on the third floor and closed the door behind him, locking it. The police had told him to try and go about his life as normal for the time being while they checked into things—whatever that meant. They told him not to assume the worst. But how could he not? He stood behind his desk and stared out the window, watching people down below on the sidewalks, the lazy procession of traffic through the stoplights. Miniature humans all with miniature problems compared to him.

And then his problems got worse.

At exactly nine a.m. the chime of an incoming email sounded from his computer, and almost immediately after, his desk phone rang. The noises jolted him from his stupor and he answered the phone. He'd barely said hello before two more of his phone lines lit up with incoming calls, and his cell phone began to buzz in his pocket.

At first, despite the police's advice, Adrien had assumed the worst about what the moment had meant. *They've found her*, he'd thought while his phones were screaming all around him. *They've found her body and it's all over the news and everybody has seen it but me. My wife is dead and I'm the last one to find out.*

The phone calls were not about Michelle. They were about the explicit photos sent from Adrien's email account that had just gone out to the bank's entire employee directory.

After that, everything happened in a blur of confusion. HR and IT both showed up at his office, with security lurking behind them in the hallway.

Intraoffice relationships were not forbidden, but they were to be disclosed to HR. The fact that Adrien was married and the woman in the picture was clearly not Michelle VanFleet would be a large black spot on an otherwise clean reputation and work record, but an affair might have perhaps been overcome, at least professionally. What was forbidden, however, was the consumption, storage, or distribution of pornography on company devices and systems. And with the subjects in said pornography both being bank employees as well, it was a zero-tolerance situation, and with a swift signature on a stack of documents HR had slid in front of him, Adrien's career was over and he was escorted from the building, carrying a literal bank box of personal belongings back to the parking garage and trying to begin to figure out what the hell had just happened.

"That's when he remembered me," Alexa said to Ezra, who was seated across from her at the small table in the Silent Falls Inn's dated employee kitchen and break room. "He knew I was the one who took the pictures, so naturally he assumed I had been the one to send them."

"Sure," Ezra said. His arms were crossed, and he'd listened without saying a word as Alexa had recounted the story that Adrien VanFleet had told her back at the Shiffy PI office less than an hour ago. "I think we both could see how that would make sense in his head."

Alexa nodded. "Yeah. Honestly, I had briefly allowed myself the fantasy of doing something like what actually happened to him—make the photos public somehow and knock him down a few pegs."

"But..."

Alexa grinned. "But I chose to be a professional instead. I'm doing like you keep telling me, I'm *compartmentalizing*. I told myself I had done my job and whatever happened next was up to Michell VanFleet."

"My little girl's growing up," Ezra said.

Alexa rolled her eyes. "Why does everyone act like I'm a child? I'm older than you, asshole."

Ezra shrugged. "Age is just a number."

"What does that even mean?"

Ezra waved her off, shifted gears. "What about the girl? The bank teller who was in the photos with Adrien? I'm guessing she got fired too?"

"Kate Williams. I can't confirm it, but Adrien thinks so. Apparently she called out sick Monday morning with the flu and hasn't been back in since. Adrien's tried calling and texting, but he hasn't gotten an answer. My guess is she's pissed and never wants to see or talk to him again. Oh wait, did I say guess? I meant hope. I hope she's pissed like hell and never talks to him again."

Ezra nodded. "She's collateral damage. Her immaturity didn't warn her this might be a possible outcome."

"Maybe. But what was Adrien's excuse?"

"Arrogance. Hubris. Same old story."

"Men are pigs?"

Ezra sipped his coffee. "I think we're saying the same thing. So do you believe him?"

"Which part?"

"Any of it. All of it. What's your gut telling you?"

Alexa leaned back in her chair, took a sip of her own coffee, needing the afternoon pick-me-up for the drive she had ahead of her. "Right off the bat, I was convinced he knew where Michelle was. Actually, I had all but decided he had done something to her. That she'd gone home that night I showed her the pictures of Adrien and Kate and when she'd confronted him, he'd..."

"Hurt her?"

Alexa nodded. "Or killed her."

"You don't think that'd be a bit of an overreaction to getting caught with your pants around your ankles?"

Alexa shook her head. "You said it yourself. Arrogance. Hubris. In my head I have Adrien pegged as a guy who was on top of the world and liked it that way. He probably walked around like he was wearing a suit of armor. If you get delusional enough to think you own the world, what might you do if somebody tries to steal it all away from you?"

Ezra was quiet for a moment. Said, "I don't disagree with you, I just wanted to hear your logic. Wanted you to work it out in your head again. It's always the husband, right?"

"Bingo."

"But now something's changed. You're not so sure."

Alexa studied him, tried to emulate his blank expression. Finally, she gave in and said, "Am I that easy to read?"

"No. But to me you are."

Alexa smirked. "Oh, right. I forgot I'm friends with the Black-Ops Batman."

"Can you put that on a t-shirt for me?"

"What, and blow your cover?"

They laughed together, and the noise caused Herb to poke his head in through the door that led back to the inn's lobby. "I thought this was supposed to be a damn serious and important meeting? What's with the giggles?"

Alexa choked off her laughter and smiled at Herb. "What gave you the impression it was a serious and important meeting?"

"The look on your damn face when you walked in!" Herb said, stepping into the kitchen. Barlow trotted in after him.

Alexa looked at Ezra. "Well, shit, I guess I'm easier to read than I thought."

This got them going again. Barlow cocked his head at the sound of their laughter and then made his way back into the lobby, apparently unimpressed. Herb shook his head and followed the dog out and saying, "Come on, Barlow, back to our chess game. It's your move."

Both Ezra and Alexa turned to each other, eyes wide, each making sure the other had heard what they thought they'd heard. This only got them laughing harder, to the point that Ezra had to stand up and get them both a paper towel from the roll on the counter so they could wipe the tears from their eyes.

When the laughter finally ramped down and the tears were all wiped away, Alexa looked to Ezra and saw he was once again stone-faced and stoic. "So..." he said. "Adrien. What changed?"

Alexa sighed, tried to get back in the right headspace. After thinking about it all over again, she said, "At first, I thought all his concern and worry was an act. I thought he was trying hard to jump the gun on anybody pointing the finger at him in regard to something having happened to Michelle, like he was trying a little too hard to make himself appear innocent."

"But now you think it's genuine?"

Alexa hated to admit it, but... "Maybe? You should have seen the way he left my office today when he got the call about them finding Michelle's car."

Adrien had just finished telling Alexa about his awful morning at work when his cell phone had rung. She'd watched what little color had been left in his face drain away as he'd listened to whoever was speaking on the other end. "I'll be right there," he'd said, standing up so fast the chair had toppled over. "They found her car," was all he'd said to Alexa before he'd rushed out.

"He looked ... hopeful," Alexa said. "Like maybe he'd finally start to get some answers."

"Or maybe he panicked," Ezra offered. "Maybe he's the one who hid the car and he was surprised they found it so quickly. Maybe he's doing like you said, reacting fast to make it look like he's the innocent one."

Alexa considered this. "Michelle's SUV wasn't exactly hidden, remember? It was abandoned at one of the picnic sites in the mountains. Right in the parking lot."

Ezra crossed his arms again, and Alexa watched as he clenched and unclenched his jaw. "So if he's not lying about knowing where Michelle is, what's he lying about?"

Alexa's mind went instantly back to the first time she'd met Adrien, just yesterday. She remembered the way he'd shown almost no interest in the photograph of his own indiscretion when she'd swiveled her computer monitor toward him. "He just ... doesn't seem to ever react the way I expect him to," Alexa said, realizing how lame it sounded as a reason to mistrust somebody. But, she said nothing more. It was all she had. That and her instinct.

Ezra considered this, his jaw still working, arms still crossed. Finally, he nodded his head and said, "I understand. But don't forget, grief can cause people to act irrationally. Same when they panic."

Alexa nodded. Pointed to herself. "Like deciding at age twelve to basically become a vagrant until your early thirties."

Ezra held up his hands, gesturing at the space around them. "Or quitting a top-secret government agency, relocating to a town most of America has forgotten, and becoming an innkeeper."

Alexa grinned. "Hey, I think we've done alright. Irrational or not. We're here, aren't we?"

Ezra nodded. "We are. And I'm glad for that."

From the lobby, Herb laughed and shouted, "Well, damn, you clever dog!"

Ezra shook his head, smiled. "That man is one of the most unintentionally entertaining people I've ever met."

"Barlow loves him," Alexa said.

"Everybody loves him. At least the ones that give him a chance." Ezra looked at the door for a beat, fondness in his eyes, and then he turned back to Alexa. "The email situation, is that what's throwing this whole thing off for you? Because it is for me."

"That's what I wanted to ask you about, really. Adrien says the email with the pictures came from his own email account, but of course he swears he didn't send it. He's also convinced that Michelle didn't know the password to his account. He actually accused me of hacking the bank, which is ridiculous."

"Maybe he knows you're friends with Black-Ops Batman."

Alexa didn't laugh. "What are your serious thoughts?

Because the way I see it, either Adrien is lying and he sent the pictures himself, or somebody really did hack his account. If Adrien sent them, he's playing a game that I don't understand at all. And if somebody hacked his account, it means they also had access to the pictures of Adrien and Kate. Which means they either got the files from Michelle VanFleet, or they've hacked the Shiffy PI office and stole them from me."

"Or Adrien took them from Michelle and gave them to whoever sent the pictures," Ezra said. "Which, again, means he's playing a game we haven't quite figured out yet." He looked up to the ceiling, thinking, rubbing the side of his face as his jaw clenched. "Okay, nobody hacked Shiffy PI, trust me. I'd have noticed. I have network monitoring tools and audit logs set up for everything, and the firewall we have set up ... let's just say your operation is probably more secure than most Fortune 500 companies."

Alexa nodded. "I have no doubt."

"Now, with Adrien's email account, there's a bunch of possibilities. The first is that somebody did have knowledge of his password, whether he thinks so or not. Especially if he's reusing his bank email password for other sites or services on the web. If said site or service had a data breach, and Adrien's account info was stolen, they'd have a good chance at accessing other accounts of his if they tried hard enough. But..."

"Yes? I knew there was going to be a but."

"Places like banks, they take security seriously. At minimum, for external email access, they probably require some sort of two-factor authentication. Most common these days is either an SMS text message or a code generated from an authenticator app on the user's smartphone. If the bank was using SMS messages, it's possible Adrien's SIM card could have been spoofed and the hacker was able to intercept the code after they'd entered the password. It's one of the reasons most places are opting for the other option, the authenticator app. That lives *locally* on the user's phone and is much harder to circumvent."

"Okay, so it's possible somebody else sent the email. That's what you're saying, right?"

"Yes, but there's something else. See, you're thinking like most folks when it comes to security measures—you're thinking outside in. But there's also the chance the hack came from *inside* the bank."

"You mean another employee?"

Ezra shook his head. "Not necessarily. It would just have to be somebody who was in the building and had access to the network. Again, I'm only speculating, but a lot of places only require the two-factor authentication for external access. They whitelist the local and internal IP address ranges so employees who are physically located inside the place of business don't have to be bothered with the additional code entries every time they log in to do their job each day."

Alexa thought about this. "Okay, so now there's a chance that the email came from somebody who was physically inside the bank, knew Adrien's password, and had access to the photographs."

"It's a good possibility."

Alexa sighed. "I'm right back to pointing my finger at Adrien again."

"It's always the husband," Ezra said.

"It just doesn't make any sense."

"Life doesn't make sense. Why are you so concerned

about this? This isn't your case. It doesn't affect you. Help me understand what's going on here."

Alexa looked down into her coffee mug. She knew it had grown cold but picked up the mug and gulped the last of it down anyway. It was bitter and slimy. "She sat in my office, Ezra. She sat right across from me the last night anybody saw her alive. What if I missed some signs, some signals? What if Michelle knew her husband was dangerous and was trying to tell me and I was so worried about making it to your house for dinner that I chose to ignore her?"

Ezra shook his head. "That's not you. You would have noticed. You would have skipped dinner. You know it and I know it. You're one of the most intuitive people I've ever met."

"And something about this entire situation feels off to me."

"A woman is missing. Of course something feels off."

Alexa said nothing.

"Look," Ezra said, "the police are on this. They'll look at Adrien, and they'll look hard. You know they will, because he's the most obvious place to start. You did your part, Alexa. You caught the bastard cheating. You weren't responsible for whatever happened after that."

She nodded, but it didn't feel convincing.

"What does Piper think about all of this?" Ezra asked.

Alexa couldn't help but smile. "She said the same thing you did. That I need to let this go. Focus on my other jobs."

Ezra glanced at his watch. "Speaking of which…"

Alexa stood. "Yeah, I need to hit the road. Thanks for taking Barlow for the night."

"My pleasure. Maybe we'll play chess after dinner."

Alexa laughed, gave Ezra a hug, which seemed to surprise

him at first, but then he wrapped his arms around her and gave her a quick squeeze back. He hadn't asked for specifics about where she was headed when she'd told him she was making a trip for work. It was one of the many things she loved about him: he didn't ask questions...

Unless she wanted him to.

Which made her guilt about keeping her Abatelli secrets from him all the more painful.

Back in the lobby, Barlow was curled up on his dog bed behind the counter, and Herb, a few whisps of his remaining hair standing up like a breeze had blown through, was leaned over the counter, resetting the chess board.

"Who won?" Ezra asked.

"I did," Herb said. "But the little bugger is getting better."

Alexa told Barlow and Herb goodbye and exited the lobby, cranking her Oldsmobile to a rumbling start and then pulling out onto the road. As she merged onto the highway, she pushed thoughts of Adrien and Michelle VanFleet away and replaced them with the gruesome images of Victoria Jameson's murdered body. The quarters that had been placed over the girl's corpse's eyes teased her with their twinkle. Alexa cursed them and drove on.

CHAPTER 19

With the evening rush hour traffic around East River clogging up the highway, it took Alexa nearly two hours to reach the subdivision where Collette and Troy Jameson had their home. Where Francis Abatelli had his base of operations at the Xpedited Xchange facility to the northeast of East River, the Jamesons' slice of the American Dream was nestled twenty miles south. Theirs was one of a handful of sprawling homes with looming yet decorative gates protecting professionally manicured landscaping and winding driveways. The houses themselves were all shrouded by an abundance of high-reaching trees and immense shrubbery, set well off the road and separated from the rest of the world by the expanse of lawn and the blanket of shadows. The common word one might use to describe the aesthetic would be *privacy*.

To Alexa, the homes looked as though they all held secrets locked away inside, dangerous truths cloaked behind money and the shield of social status.

But Alexa did tend to sway toward the cynical.

The sun had just dipped below the horizon, the gray hue of dusk seeping up from the ground to fill the air like a fine mist, when Alexa pulled up to the gate of the Jameson residence. The nose of the Oldsmobile bumped the wrought-iron rails with a screech and a clang as Alexa tried to fit the car onto the strip of asphalt outside the gate in order to roll down her window and reach the call button on the intercom box mounted on a matching pedestal.

"*Shit.* Hope nobody saw that," she said under her breath and then groaned as she caught sight of the security cameras mounted on the top left corner of the entrance gate. There was another small red light indicating a camera on the intercom box, and Alexa forced on a smile as she unfastened her seat belt and leaned out of the car to hit the call button.

Nobody spoke to her through the speaker, but after fifteen seconds or so, the gate began to open with barely a whisper of noise. Alexa waved to the red dot on the intercom box and drove forward, switching on her headlights as she drove beneath the tree cover that shaded the driveway, trying to limit the amount of vehicular damage she'd cause today to only the gate.

Alexa parked behind a three-car garage the size of most homes she'd ever been inside and killed the headlights and then the engine. She pushed open her door, whose hinges let off a cry that echoed through the trees like a prehistoric bird's. When the sound faded, Alexa was left in such a tranquil silence it felt like the home and those who lived here were part of a whole other world.

It reminded her of the first time she'd arrived at Ezra's farmhouse, the desire for seclusion palpable.

Warm exterior lights clicked on—accent lights hidden in

the bushes along the front of the home, lampposts guiding one's way along the sidewalk that led to the front door. Even though Alexa was sure the lights were merely on a timer, she suddenly felt exposed, as if a great spotlight had been cast upon her, its eye questioning and skeptical. She hurried along the sidewalk, the home's stone exterior towering above her, her reflection appearing small and unimportant in the darkened windows.

She reached the stoop and hesitated for a second as she reached a finger out for the bell. *It's only a job*, she told herself as she finally pressed the button, an elegant melody of bells chiming from behind the ornate wooden door. For a reason she could not pinpoint, Alexa found herself more afraid of stepping across the threshold of this home than she had the moment she'd stepped into Francis Abatelli's office.

Maybe it was just the atmosphere. The long day.

Maybe it was the fact that Victoria Jameson's body had been found right here, somewhere inside the imposing fence line.

The image of Michelle VanFleet's corpse buried beneath leaves and twigs and dirt flashed again through Alexa's mind. Those eyes still staring, still pleading.

The sound of a substantial lock disengaging was quickly followed by the heavy door being pulled open, a blast of warm air and the aroma of cinnamon escaping and hitting Alexa in the face.

Collette Jameson was tall, with dark brown hair and a nose that came to a severe point. Where her brother Francis was extremely overweight, Collette was broad but toned. She appeared powerful. In more ways than one.

Dressed in jeans and a cream sweater and boots, she had

at least five inches on Alexa, and from across the threshold, she loomed over her the same way the stone walls had. Her eyes narrowed to slits and her lips pursed as she looked Alexa up and down. "You're a woman," she said, her voice soft but not quite pleasant.

Alexa nodded. "Last time I checked."

"Franny didn't mention that."

Franny?

"Is it relevant?" Alexa asked.

"Details are always relevant. If you disagree, I'd have to assume you aren't very good at your job."

Alexa liked this woman, despite her detached coldness.

"Your brother's the one who hired me."

Collette nodded. "And he is very good at his job." She stepped back from the door and motioned Alexa inside. "Come on in."

Stepping inside felt like being swallowed by an issue of *Architecture Digest.* The home's interior was cavernous yet cozy, exposed wooden beams and rustic furniture, tasteful art on the walls, gas logs burning in a living room larger than Alexa's entire apartment. Everything was neat and tidy, not a single throw pillow out of place or a speck of dust to be found. It almost looked staged, as if for a photo shoot. If Alexa had stuck her tongue out, she would have tasted money.

Alexa knew from the files that she'd received on Victoria's life, as well as some of her own research, that Troy Jameson's father had owned a couple of high-end car dealerships which he'd passed on to his son. One in East River, and another larger—and more profitable—one outside of Richmond a couple hours away. Alexa knew there was the prospect of big money in the luxury car market, but as she followed Collette down a wide hallway toward the bright lights of a kitchen, she was growing more confident that there was dirty money in these walls.

To further accentuate the display of wealth, when the women entered the kitchen, a housekeeper appeared at their side, as if conjuring herself from a hidden cupboard, and asked if they'd like coffee or tea. The woman looked to be in her sixties, with long gray hair she wore pulled back and piercing jade eyes that didn't quite match the pleasantness of her smile. Alexa wondered how many secrets this woman had locked away inside her, how many conversations she'd overheard over the years that were surely kept quiet with a hefty paycheck and favors granted on occasion. Loyalty is more often purchased than earned.

Collette looked to Alexa, said, "Or something stronger, if you'd prefer. Or do you not drink on the job?"

Alexa grinned and shook her head. "I'd love a coffee, please."

Collette looked disappointed, or maybe that was just her normal look. She nodded to the housekeeper. "Coffee for both of us. Thank you, Jane."

Instead of taking a seat at the kitchen table, which sat six and was decorated with full place settings for each seat, as if Thanksgiving dinner was to be served at any moment, Collette stepped around the table and flipped the lock on a set of French doors. "Do you mind if we talk out on the patio? I could use some air. I've been cooped up inside this house ever since Victoria..."

"Of course," Alexa said.

The patio was an intricate mosaic pattern of stone and

brick, with an overhang comprised of wooden beams that matched those inside the home. A gas firepit burned with ferocity in the center, surrounded by Adirondack chairs. Collette chose the chair that faced directly back to the home. Alexa found herself torn between sitting in the chair across from Collette, which would put her back to the doors, or sitting next to the woman, which would make it difficult to see her face, try to gauge her emotions as they talked. She went against her instinct and chose the chair across from Collette, crossing her fingers that this wasn't all some sort of twisted and elaborate scheme to get rid of her and that when Jane delivered their coffee she wasn't going to also deliver a hypodermic needle into Alexa's neck.

The heat from the firepit did well at banishing the chill of the night air, and the flames cast dancing flickers of light across Collette's face. The two women stared at each other across the flames, and Alexa was about to ask how Collette was holding up, knowing what a ridiculous question it would be considering the woman had just lost her only daughter, when Collette broke the silence first.

"I need to say something before we get started," she said.

Alexa nodded. "Okay, sure."

"I don't think I have to tell you how tragic this has all been. How devastating. To lose her, well ... I don't have to say it."

Alexa shook her head. "No, you don't."

"Franny filled you in on why we're keeping the police out of this for now, I'm sure."

"He did."

"And you're completely okay with this?"

Alexa swallowed. "I'm only doing a job I was hired to do."

Then, perhaps to add some element of solidarity, she added, "Plus, I fucking hate the police."

Collette chuckled, the first real sign of emotion she'd displayed since Alexa had arrived. "Don't we all." Then her face quickly iced over again. "Well, what I need to explain to you is this: no matter how angry Franny is, no matter how terrible the things are he wants to do to the person who killed my girl, you need to believe me when I tell you that those things are nothing compared to what I will do. Whoever did this to her, they're going to die at my hands." Collette paused here, leaned forward, inches from the flames, her face a glowing orange mask of subdued rage. "Same goes for anybody who gets in our way. Do you understand?"

Alexa held the woman's gaze for several seconds. Finally, she nodded. "I do."

Collette leaned back again. "Good. Very good. That said, I will be completely honest with you, as long as you are completely honest with me. If I don't believe something you're telling me, or if you can't repay my honesty with the candor and discretion it deserves, we're done. Finished. Franny may have hired you, but this is my call. Got it?"

Alexa nodded. "Yes."

The French doors opened behind Alexa, and Jane came out with a serving tray with two mugs of steaming coffee that looked more the size of beer steins, as well as cream and sugar. After the woman took their coffee, Jane returned inside.

"Now," Collette said, cupping her mug in both her hands but not yet taking a sip. "Why did my brother hire you?"

Alexa gambled that her own coffee wasn't poisoned and took a sip. It was remarkably flavorful, as if she'd never really experienced coffee until right at that moment. Again, the taste of money. Collette's question could have been answered several ways, but Alexa could certainly read the room, so she went with the cold hard truth. She suspected Collette Jameson might already know the answer, and this might be a test.

"We had a bit of a misunderstanding a few months ago," Alexa said. "Three of your brother's goons ended up dead. I'm still here. He's made some assumptions based on that information."

"You killed them." It wasn't a question.

Alexa took another sip. "I'm still here. They aren't. I suppose Francis believes me capable ... of a lot of things."

Collette nodded, apparently accepting this answer. "It's a shame more men don't recognize what women are capable of."

Alexa nodded. "Who needs 'em? But, speaking of which, is your husband going to be joining us?"

"He's gone."

A breeze blew across the yard, slanting the flames, filling the air with the sound of tree branches rustling from out in the yard. "Gone, like at work?" Alexa asked.

Collette shook her head. "No. Gone, like he got spooked and tucked tail and ran off like a little pup." She waved a hand through the air like it was unimportant. "He'll be back."

The way she said it, Alexa thought it sounded like the woman was trying to convince herself. "I don't understand. Spooked by what? Victoria's murder?"

"More like ... what happened *after*."

Alexa thought about this for a moment, took another sip of coffee. Collette stared at her, as if wanting to see if she could piece it together. "He didn't know, did he? He didn't know about who your family really were?"

Collette grinned, and the way the fire flickered across her features gave Alexa a chill. "Did I ever tell him? No. Did he suspect, did he hear rumors? Absolutely. But you see, it's easy to not really care about a thing when it doesn't directly impact your life. At least, in a negative way. The positive, though..." She waved a hand through the air again. "The house, the cars, the vacations, the country club, those things can help wash away any bad taste that might otherwise be left in your mouth. He knew my family had money, and after a while he stopped caring where it really came from. Franny has always taken care of us, in lots of ways. The same way our papa used to take care of my mama and us kids." She looked away, off to the side of the yard. Raised her mug to her lips but then set it back down on her knee without taking a sip. "I've seen my share of violence in my life. I once saw Papa smash a man's face in with a cinderblock because the guy questioned whether he'd been underpaid. I was eleven, I think. Maybe twelve. Papa wiped his hands off on his shirt and looked at me and said, 'We may be a lot of things, but dishonest isn't one of them. Remember that.'"

Alexa looked around the patio, checking to see if any cinderblocks were lying around. It was a gruesome story, but she knew how much childhood trauma could shape an adult. She had to empathize.

Collette continued. "Anyway, Troy had pretty much put the truth in a box and locked it away. If he thought there were risks involved in being married to me, he must have thought they were worth taking. My family has always been kind to him, and we do love each other. Truly. We're just very ... different. But maybe that's why we work so well."

Alexa nodded. "Sure."

"But when Victoria was killed, it obviously shook our entire foundation. I could feel it, you know? I could feel something between us get severed the moment we saw her body, and the reality settled in. And then when Franny and his—what did you call them, goons?—showed up and said to keep to police out of it and I agreed, Troy started to lose it. He got erratic, started blaming us—me, my family. Said we were all criminals, that his little girl's blood was on all our hands.

"When they loaded Victoria into the van to take her away, Troy broke down. He started screaming, and then he actually grabbed Franny by the shoulders and told him that if we weren't going to call the police then he would, and that Franny couldn't stop him."

"Oh, Jesus," Alexa said, now wondering how permanent the word *gone* had been when Collette had used it earlier.

"Franny didn't even flinch. He took Troy's hands off his shoulders, looked at me and then looked back to Troy and said, 'You're smart, Troy. So you know that would be a mistake.'

"I've heard my brother use that voice before," Collette said, "and I know what it means. Troy must have realized it too because he backed down after that. But he was still broken. He didn't talk to me at all after the van pulled away and Franny and his crew left. Neither of us slept that night. I've never cried so hard in my life, and I doubt I ever will again. My body still aches from all the sobbing. The next morning, Troy packed a bag and said he needed to get away, that it was all too overwhelming for him. I wanted to call him a coward, call him weak. Ask him how he could leave me now. But I realized I was being selfish. I'd grown up hardened, he'd grown up pampered. Our brains were processing it all so differently. If that's what he needed in order to grieve, I wouldn't stand in his way."

Alexa waited to see if there was more, but when Collette lifted her mug and took a sip, something in her eyes told Alexa that was all she was going to learn about Troy Jameson for the time being. The next question she had was important, but also sensitive. Collette had asked for honesty and candor, so Alexa pushed on. "What about Victoria? Did she know the truth about your family?"

Collette sighed and looked down into the flames. "Do you have children?" she asked, not looking up.

"No."

Collette nodded. Narrowed her eyes, as if examining something only she could see in the fire. "You want to give them the world. From the moment they're born, you commit yourself to protecting them, no matter the cost. You know you'll use your dying breath to fight and keep them safe." She looked up, locked eyes with Alexa again. "It doesn't take long to realize the only way to truly do that is to lie to them. Because these days, the truth ... it's the fucking worst."

"So ... that's a no?"

Collette leaned back and crossed her legs, setting the coffee mug on the arm of the chair and then wrapping her arms around herself as if she'd caught a chill. "I told myself I was going to tell her when she turned eighteen. I figured I'd raise her and give her the absolute best life I could. Show her how much I loved her, and how I'd do anything on earth for her if she only asked. Then, when she became an adult, I'd tell her the truth. However she reacted, I knew I'd have to deal with the consequences. But I hoped she'd understand why I had kept it from her, and one day when she was—" Collette stopped and looked away, amber-tinted tears sparkling in her eyes. She swallowed down the rising emotion and continued. "One day when she was older and had children of her own, I knew she would understand why I'd kept it from her."

Alexa gave the woman a moment, crossed her own legs, mimicking Collette's body language. "But you never told her?"

Collette smirked, and her soft laugh was eaten by the ambient noise of the fire. "I was afraid. Her eighteenth birthday came and went and every time I was alone in the house with her and thought it was going to be the time, I just … couldn't do it. I think for the first time in my life I was truly terrified. I was scared that once she learned the truth, my baby girl would hate me. And I wasn't sure that was something I could come back from."

Collette was quiet again, lost in her own thoughts, but then she cleared her throat and said, "But that doesn't answer your question."

"It doesn't?"

"You asked if Victoria knew about my family. My not telling her doesn't mean she didn't know the truth, or at least have her own suspicions."

Alexa said nothing.

"Victoria was *smart*. Did Franny tell you that?"

Alexa shook her head. "He didn't tell me anything about her except that she was his niece and that she was dead.

Sorry." Alexa didn't mention the digital info dump she'd received, but that hadn't been the question.

Collette rolled her eyes. "All business, Franny is. Big surprise. Well, she was top of her class in high school and had just finished her first semester at UVA with a 4.2 GPA. Did you know you could even have a GPA higher than a 4.0? I didn't."

Talk about school reminded Alexa of a question she'd thought of when she'd been going over the files she'd received. "Wait," Alexa said, holding up a hand. "I wanted to ask about that. If she was attending UVA, why was she here and not at school? Aren't they midsemester right now?"

"She attended virtually. Victoria still lived here with us."

Ah. God bless technology.

"And that was her choice?" Alexa asked. "She wasn't itching to get out of the house like a lot of fresh high school graduates?"

Collette pointed behind Alexa to the French doors. "Have you seen our house? Victoria's room was basically her own apartment."

And God bless money.

"Plus, we didn't smother her," Collette said. "Once she got her driver's license, she was basically free to come and go as she pleased."

"But I bet you tracked her, didn't you? One of those apps on the phone?"

No hesitation. "You would do the same thing."

"I hope I never have to find out."

If Collette found this answer offensive or odd, she chose not to press the matter further. "Regardless, Victoria was smart.

Extremely capable and resourceful. She was the type of person who, when they wanted to know something, they'd find out. If there was a question, they wouldn't rest until they found the answer or found somebody could help give it to them."

Alexa saw where this was going. "You think she got curious and started digging around your family's past? Maybe learned the truth on her own?"

Collette nodded.

"Recently?"

"Maybe a couple months ago? All I know is I started getting a feeling something had changed with her. With us."

"What sort of feeling?"

Collette took a deep breath, blew it out. "A mother's intuition. And fuck you if you think that's not a real thing."

Alexa was not a person to tell somebody she didn't believe in trusting one's instinct, no matter the circumstances. "I completely think it's a real thing," she said. "The Universe is a strange and powerful beast. More people should listen when it speaks."

A good friend had taught her that.

Her next question was so obvious it almost didn't need to be asked. "And do you think, if Victoria did find out something about your family, it could have somehow..."

"Killed her?"

Alexa shrugged.

Collette shook her head. "God ... I hope not. I can't think of anything worse than that being the reason. But I'm not naive enough to think it's not a possibility. I don't know how, or why, but like you said ... the Universe is a strange and powerful beast."

Another breeze danced through, whispering secret messages among the rafters of the overhang.

"I don't know why she had to die," Collette said. "And if I knew who killed her, you wouldn't be here right now. But I'll tell you what I do know. Whoever took my daughter's life ... it wasn't a stranger. It was somebody Victoria knew."

Alexa felt her heart pump hard in her chest. "How can you know that?"

Instead of answering, Collette Jameson stood from her chair and picked up her coffee mug. Then she walked over and took Alexa's as well. "Come on," she said. "Let me take these inside and grab a flashlight, then I'll show you where we found Victoria's body."

CHAPTER 20

"Did you ever sneak out of the house as a teenager?" Collette asked Alexa.

The two women walked side by side through the backyard. They'd passed a swimming pool complete with a covered cabana and a water slide and a gazebo the size of a carnival carousel and were now on a brick path that weaved through an extensive garden, shrubs and plants growing up all around them. In the darkness, the whole thing gave Alexa the uneasy feeling of being lost in a hedge maze, even though she could easily see over the top of all the greenery. Stone statues of angels grinned at her, appearing more like sneering gargoyles in the shadowed recesses of the pathway. Alexa zipped her jacket, but it did no good to fight off the chill growing inside her as she marched toward where Victoria Jameson's body had been found.

She might as well have been walking through a graveyard.

"I left home at age twelve and never went back," Alexa answered. "So I guess you could say I snuck out for good."

From the corner of her eye, Alexa saw Collette give her a

sideways glance, a slight shift of her head, the flashlight beam guiding their way making the tiniest deviation in its trajectory. But the woman did not ask more questions.

"Victoria did," she said. "Even though we didn't smother her, she did have a curfew and wasn't always allowed to do what she wanted, especially on a school night. It wasn't that we didn't trust her, mind you. The rules were more to instill a sense of guidance and structure. To show her responsibilities and the consequences of failing them."

"And to make sure she understood that she was still a child and you and your husband were the ones in charge," Alexa said.

Collette considered this. "Yes. I guess that's the blunt way of putting it. She was smart, and with the smart ones it's even more difficult to teach them that they don't know everything about life once they decide they can start thinking for themselves.

"So, yes, in high school she did sneak out from time to time."

Collette suddenly veered off the path to the left, walking between two low bushes and then heading across the grass and mulch. Alexa followed, seeing the dark black image of the fence coming into view ahead, highlighted by the flashlight beam.

Then she saw the gate. Bigger than the one at the front of the property, with a green push button mounted to its left to open it from the inside.

Collette walked up to the gate and stopped, pointed through the railing toward what Alexa could see looked like an access road comprised of mostly dirt and gravel. "For the construction and landscaping trucks," Collette said. "Blackmill Road is a half mile that way." She nodded the way the road disappeared into the night. "That's where they turn off. When we moved here, Blackmill was just a county road leading out of town. Last few years it's been so built up with shops and restaurants, traffic has gotten bad, and we get a lot more accidental visitors who turn off onto our road." She sighed and shook her head. "Franny once offered to put a guard shack at the entrance, but I told him that was ridiculous. I wasn't going to make some poor soul sit in a stuffy box all hours of the day with absolutely nothing to do except make sure nobody unexpected stumbled upon our back gate. So we put up a bunch of private property signs and left it at that. But now..."

But now the guard shack seems like a brilliant idea. Damn hindsight, Alexa thought. She looked through the fencing and saw another call box on a pedestal, also just like the front of the property. At the sight of it, she looked up and saw the security camera mounted atop the corner of the gate. "How could she sneak out here with the cameras?"

In the glow of the flashlight, Alexa saw Collette give a small grin, a sad fondness settling in. "All the cameras are activated by motion sensors. They only start recording when something triggers them—otherwise, we have to be watching the feed live to see what's happening. Victoria knew this, and knew exactly how to walk out of the house to avoid the backyard cameras and get to this point."

"Okay," Alexa said, "Sure. But what about once she *got* here? How do you get out of the gate without triggering the cameras?"

Collette sighed. "An oversight, really. The system wasn't designed to keep a teenage girl *inside* the fence." She pointed to the pedestal with the intercom box again. "See how far back from the gate it is? That's because of the size of the trucks. The camera's field of view is limited to basically be able to monitor everything driving through the gate, but it doesn't look straight down, and it can't see the call box at all with the way it's set off the road. In theory, the camera on the call box would record anybody in front of it when they arrived. So, in a normal situation, we were covered."

Alexa thought this all through. "So if the gate opened, Victoria could basically step out and hug the fence until she knew she had gotten out of the camera's field of view, and then she could head up the road?"

"Yes."

"But what about getting back in? You said the camera on the gate can't see the call box, but wouldn't the box record her when she got back?"

Collette nodded, smiled again, and then winced. Her amusement at remembering her daughter's resourcefulness sinking a dagger of pain in her heart. "The only thing I've been able to figure is she went behind the intercom, crouched low, and then reached up from beneath it. She would be able to hit the keypad to punch in the code without the camera seeing a thing."

Alexa would never meet Victoria Jameson, but she had to imagine she and the girl would have gotten along just fine. Hell, maybe she could have hired her. Smart *and* clever seemed to be a rare breed these days.

"Anybody who came to pick her up or drop her off would just need to park back far enough not to trigger the cameras, and I'm sure Victoria factored in plenty margin of error. Hell, she might have walked all the way from Blackmill Road for all I know."

"How did you ever find out she was sneaking out?" Alexa asked.

"Again, mother's intuition."

Alexa said nothing.

"Plus," Collette said with a smirk, "the security system logs every time the gate opens and closes. All I had to do was check them to verify my suspicions."

"And the night Victoria was killed, did you check the logs?"

Collette nodded. "One seventeen in the morning the gate opened and closed. Twenty-four minutes later it opened and closed again. And that's it."

"And this is where she was found?" Alexa asked, taking a step back, as if she suddenly realized she were standing on a grave.

Collette breathed in deep. "Yes. Right inside the gate. She was..." The woman appeared to be working hard to fight away the tears that wanted to accompany the words she didn't want to say.

"I saw the pictures," Alexa said.

The two women stood silent for a moment, the memory and the tragedy of Victoria Jameson's life cut short floating around them as the breeze skirted through the trees.

Eventually, Alexa said, "So the only way she ends up here is if somebody opened the gate and put her here."

"Or," Collette said, "Victoria opened the gate to let them in."

Alexa took another look at the camera mounted on the gate, then through the railings to the intercom box. *A lot of good you two did*, she thought. Then something else occurred to her. "Wait a second ... Victoria was nineteen. Not a kid in high school anymore. I'm assuming there was no more curfew now that she was an adult, so why was she out here at all? Why sneak out?"

Collette shook her head, the dim light reaching her face from the flashlight revealing a pained look. "She hadn't been out here in a long time." She blew out a deep breath. "So whatever caused her to sneak out here that night, it must have been something she didn't think her father and I would approve of."

"Boyfriend?" It was Alexa's first thought. The most obvious.

Collette nodded. "Maybe. Probably. It's just..."

"What?"

"Victoria's had boyfriends before, and she's always brought them to the house. Like I said before, we didn't smother her. We let her have her privacy. I just ... I don't know what sort of guy she could be seeing that would make her think she couldn't tell us about it."

Alexa had a quick, despairing thought. "Do you think it could have been a guy from a ... uh, rival organization?" It sounded almost comical to say it out loud, like she was in some cheap gangster movie on late-night television. "It didn't seem like Francis's first theory, but he wasn't ready to rule it out entirely. You're obviously aware of that." Alexa thought some more. "You said you had sensed something changed about Victoria recently ... your intuition, that maybe she found out about your family. What if it was this guy who told her? What if they started dating and then he found out who she really was and ... things snowballed?"

"And then he killed her?" Collette asked. "Why?"

Because the world is a fucked-up place, Alexa thought. "Maybe that was the plan all along," she said. "Maybe..."

"Maybe she was targeted," Collette finished for her. "In the cruelest way imaginable."

How many women had ended up exactly like Victoria Jameson, hunting for love only to end up another of evil's prey?

A stronger breeze gusted through the fence and was then replaced with silence as Collette stared off into the darkness. There didn't seem to be anything left to learn out at the gate, so Alexa asked, "Can I see her room?"

Collette Jameson did not answer, but she turned and headed back to the garden path, back to the home. Alexa took that as a yes and followed her, feeling the eyes of the angel statues on her back the entire way.

CHAPTER 21

Collette Jameson had been spot-on with her reasoning as to why Victoria wouldn't be quite so eager to fly the coop; the girl's bedroom *was* nearly the size of Alexa's studio apartment and was equally furnished. A king-sized sleigh bed was pushed into one corner, adorned with comfy flannel bedding, and an expensive-looking wooden desk was on the wall across from it, either an antique or meant to appear like one. A laptop computer sat atop the desk, along with various notebooks and planners, all organized into neat stacks—presumably for schoolwork. On the opposite side of the room were a cushy love seat and a wooden coffee table in front of a television mounted on the wall that Alexa guessed was at least seventy inches. A PlayStation gaming console was the only piece of electronics on the shelf below.

"Gamer?" Alexa asked.

Collette nodded. "Always has been." A pause. "*Had* been."

Like the rest of the Jamesons' home, Victoria's room was well ordered and clean, and Alexa had to wonder how much of that was the result of Victoria being one of the tidiest teenagers in existence and how much was Jane's meticulous housekeeping. On the surface, it was just a young woman's bedroom. But when you looked more closely, spied the nuanced details of life—the cell phone charging cord draped over the corner of a nightstand, never to give another charge; the PlayStation controller tossed casually onto the coffee table, never to be played with again; the bottles of perfume and lotion lined up in a neat row atop the dresser, never to be worn again—that was when the room stopped being a normal bedroom and became what it would forever be remembered as to all who lived here: A museum, a freeze-frame of how tragically, and wholly unexpectedly, a life can end.

Alexa walked across the smooth wooden planking of the floor and pushed open a door that led to the bathroom, flipped on the lights. She was greeted by the expected over-the-top luxury befitting the rest of the home, and the sweet aroma of shampoos and conditioners and body wash. She glanced down to the sink and scanned the countertop, and found herself unable to look away from the toothbrush sitting alone in its cup. She wondered when Victoria had used it last. The morning of her final day alive, or had she used it again later that night, before she'd gone to meet whoever had been waiting on the other side of the backyard gate?

Alexa fought away a chill at the bleak idea of brushing your teeth and having no idea it would be the last time you'd ever do so. How trivial some things were, when you really examined them.

She switched off the bathroom light and closed the door,

turned and found Collette sitting on the love seat, holding the PlayStation controller in one hand and absentmindedly circling the top of one of the thumbsticks with her index finger. Alexa could see the change taking place in the woman. Collette Jameson was tough as nails and smart, that was for sure, but spending an evening digging up her daughter's tragic death—a wound no doubt still fresh and raw—was beginning to take its toll on her.

Alexa wondered if the woman had been in this room at all since Victoria had been killed.

She decided to make things quick. She made a fast lap around the room, opening and closing dresser and night-stand drawers and casting a cursory glance over them all. She found nothing but what you'd expect. At the desk, she opened the top left drawer and found two USB flash drives attached to key rings. She scooped them up and laid them out next to the laptop. The rest of the desk drawers were mostly full of cables and file folders, and Victoria's high school yearbook from her senior year. Alexa pulled the yearbook out and set it on the desk along with the flash drives. She eyed the stacks of notebooks and planners and, even though the odds were that everything in them was going to be schoolwork, she decided to take them too. She created one large stack of them and then closed the laptop and unplugged it, coiling the charging cord and setting it atop the stack of notebooks. She tossed the thumb drives into her jacket pocket.

She cleared her throat, and Collette slowly turned toward her, setting the game controller back on the coffee table. "I'm going to take all this, if that's alright. I'll bring it all back."

Collette nodded. Said, "I don't know her password."

"Oh, it's okay. I, uh, have a computer guy."

A computer guy who has no idea I'm working for the mob. This'll be fun.

"What about her cell phone?" Alexa asked.

"I couldn't find it," Collette said, and then she looked away, fast, staring at the wall. She swallowed and took a deep breath that wavered as she blew it out. "So I tracked it. It must have been in her pocket when Franny took her away. It's still with her."

"Oh," Alexa said again, hating how dumb she sounded. "That's ... fine. I'm sure they're taking care of it." She made a mental note to call Joey and see if she could get that phone.

"I've thought about calling it," Collette said. She was looking at Alexa now with eyes that said she knew she was about to say something crazy but hoped the person listening would tell her she wasn't, even if that meant lying. "I just want to hear her voice again."

Collette put her face into her hands. She was silent, but her shoulders rose and fell in a gentle rhythm. Alexa walked slowly to the love seat and laid a hand on the woman's shoulder. "You do whatever it is you need to do. Always," she said. "And fuck anyone who tells you otherwise."

CHAPTER 22

Alexa went through the drive-through of a burger joint and was overcome with a twinge of guilt as soon as the speaker box asked for her order, so she stared longingly at the picture of a double cheeseburger with bacon on the menu board and forced herself to order a grilled chicken sandwich instead. She still got fries, though. Baby steps. She pulled into a parking space directly beneath the glow from one of the light poles and pulled the sandwich from the bag and unwrapped it. Snapped a picture of it with her phone and sent the image to Piper. A few seconds later, Piper responded: **Proud of you! How was the secret work thing?**

Alexa took a bite of the sandwich and chewed. It was pretty good but could have used some more mayo. And some more beef. She wiped her mouth with a napkin and typed: **Full disclosure, I still got the fries. Work was**

She stopped and thought. What could she say? On one hand, it'd had been a good trip, an informative conversation to help gather details where there had previously been almost zero. But on the other, it had been a very sad and emotionally distressing visit with a woman who had just had her daughter murdered.

A woman who was the sister of a prominent mob boss. Let's not forget that part.

Alexa typed: **Work was productive.**

Vague. Sufficient. She hoped.

Piper replied: **Good! And thank you for not lying about the fries! Baby steps.**

Alexa grinned, but it was short-lived. She might not have lied about eating french fries alone in a mostly empty fast-food restaurant parking lot, but she was lying about much worse.

Alexa continued to eat and when her phone buzzed she was certain it was going to be Piper, probably finished with her own work for the evening and wanting to chat before climbing into bed. Alexa would have normally welcomed hearing her girlfriend's voice, eager to fall into their increasingly comfortable rhythm of conversation. But her mind wasn't in the right gear, still shifted into thoughts of Victoria Jameson, still haunted by the images of that frozen-in-time bedroom.

She looked down at her phone and saw the screen was still dark, but the buzzing continued.

Shit.

She pulled the burner phone from her pocket and answered.

"How was your visit with Collette?" Joey asked. "How's she holding up?" In the semidarkness of her car, alone in the night, his casual tone grew almost melodic, soothing. It invited you in and asked you to stay awhile. Alexa understood why Francis Abatelli sent this guy out to talk to people. If you weren't careful, he could be completely disarming.

"You're not paying me to determine how she's holding up," Alexa said. "I don't know the woman." She pushed all emotion away from the center of her mind, shifted gears again until she landed on detached. "It was productive," she said, using the same phrase she'd given Piper. "It was good to hear Collette's opinion on everything, and helpful to see the murder scene. I also got Victoria's laptop and some note-books from her bedroom."

"What do you think you'll find on the laptop?" Joey asked. "A calendar invite from her killer?"

"Hey, fuck you. I might. Did Collette tell Francis she thought Victoria had a boyfriend she was keeping secret from them?"

"No." Joey paused, and the slight hiccup in his usual quick retort was enough to tell Alexa that he knew Francis would find this information as interesting as she had. "Francis ... hasn't spoken to Collette since the day we went to collect Victoria's body. He's detaching himself from anything and anyone that might elicit an emotional response. Honestly, I think it's the only thing keeping the big boss together. A shrink would probably say it's incredibly unhealthy, but..." A heavy sigh carried across the connection. "He loved his niece dearly."

Alexa nodded in the car. "Which is why I'm going to chase every lead I can find on this. One, because that girl deserves justice, and two..."

"Two?"

"Well ... that's between Francis and me."

"Fair enough."

"Which brings me to a couple questions."

"Okay."

"Victoria's cell phone. Collette says it went with the girl's body when you all came to take it away. Do you all have it?"

"Probably," Joey said. "I'll have Francis ask his people. I might be the only one he's letting talk to you, but he's the only one allowed to talk to the ... let's just call them the Lab."

Alexa didn't want to touch whatever that meant, but her imagination had already run wild, conjuring up images of what might be *Breaking Bad: Morgue Edition*.

"If they have it, I'd like it, please."

"Like I said, I'll ask," Joey said.

"Next, the quarters." The image caused a chill to creep up her spine, tingle the back of her neck.

"You know what they mean?"

"Other than this sick bastard is probably thinking he's making some sort of twisted art when he kills, or that the coins on the eyes are honoring his victim somehow, like some sort of old ritual, no, not a clue."

"So what about them?"

"Fingerprints. Has the, uh, Lab checked the quarters for prints?"

"They have. And surprisingly they found some partials that were clear enough to pull. Ran a check against every criminal database in the country. Zero hits."

Alexa was about to ask how they could possibly do such a thing but then remembered Ezra and his basement command center and figured anything is possible these days with the right keyboard strokes and enough brainpower.

"Can you send them to me?"

"The quarters?"

Alexa sighed. "No, Joey. I don't need your loose change. Can you send the fingerprint files to me?"

"Oh, right. Sorry. Yes. I'll ask Francis. I'm sure they'll be in your email by morning."

"Thanks. I know they're federal currency and have probably passed through a million people's hands, but—"

"But you're going to chase down every lead you can on this," Joey finished for her. "Good. That's exactly why Francis hired you."

Alexa knew the truth: Francis had hired her because he felt a debt was owed. Plus, he knew she could keep secrets.

Silence filled the car for several seconds. Alexa wanted to end the call, wanted to eat her fries in peace. But she pushed on, one last pressing question. "Collette told me that she never told Victoria the truth about who her family was. Did you know that?"

"Wow. She really opened up to you. Collette is usually very private. Like, won't tell you what she had for breakfast if you asked private."

It wasn't an answer. Alexa waited. Popped a fry into her mouth and sucked off the salt.

"Yes," Joey finally said. "Francis knew. In fact, he took great pains to make sure it stayed that way."

"Why? Seems like a hard secret to keep, given the circumstances."

"Not really. Collette isn't much involved in anything day-to-day. Husband has a reputable enough business to assume that between that and the Abatellis' *legitimate businesses* the wealth was all on the up-and-up. Plus, how often does a teenager go digging into her family's bank accounts?

"And as to why, Francis loves his sister, just like he loved his niece. He respects Collette, and there's definitely a bond between the two. Growing up the way they did ... well, if there was a secret she wanted to keep from *her* daughter, he figured he had no right to stand in her way."

"You seem to know a lot about how Francis thinks," Alexa said.

"He's like a brother," Joey blurted quickly, and Alexa could hear the ice slip into his voice. "He trusts me."

Alexa nodded. "That's why he attached you to me."

Joey didn't respond, so Alexa asked one last question. "Joey, if big brother Francis asked you to kill me, would you do it?"

The silence that said more than any words would have was all Alexa needed to hear. "Thanks, Joey. Don't forget, the prints."

She ended the call.

THE NEXT MORNING, as Alexa was taking the elevator down to the lobby of the hotel where she'd stayed the night, knowing the Abatelli pockets were deep enough to reimburse her suite upgrade, her phone buzzed with an incoming message. It was from Clara: **Colin wanted me to let you know they found blood in the back of Michelle VanFleet's SUV. But also to tell you that you don't know that.**

Alexa's stomach dropped along with the elevator. *The hell I don't.*

She didn't even stop for coffee on the way to back to Silent Falls. Pressed the Oldsmobile's accelerator to the floorboard and kept it there.

CHAPTER 23

The Alexa Shifflett who had existed less than six months ago might have been so overtaken with rage and adrenaline she'd have driven her car straight through the front entrance of the Silent Falls Sheriff's Office, demanding answers. Strike first, ask questions and deal with the consequences later.

But, one of the greatest and most often-debated marvels of the human condition is that people *can* change, and the Alexa Shifflett that drove her Oldsmobile past the sign marking the Silent Falls city limits was a version of herself who for the first time in over twenty years felt as though she might actually have something to lose. She knew that deep down she was still as feisty and as willing to kick someone's ass when needed, still willing to ask all the tough questions and still not really giving a shit what anyone thought about her, but now she also understood the value of patience, of a cooler head prevailing where she would have previously chosen words and fists full of fire.

Alexa slowed the Oldsmobile as she entered town. She

couldn't go storming into the sheriff's office mostly because this wasn't her case, and Sheriff Byrd sure as shit wasn't going to let anyone talk to her, but also because she knew she couldn't betray Colin like that. The kid, for a reason Alexa wasn't sure she fully understood, unless he was still trying to play nice and apologize for accusing her of murder, was keeping her in the loop. Which meant he trusted her. It was a relationship Alexa didn't want to ruin. Partly because she felt it could continue to prove beneficial to her business over time, to have a local cop she could trust who might slip her some intel now and again, but mostly because of Clara. Colin was an extension of his sister, and Alexa genuinely cared for the girl and valued their friendship. Hurting Colin's career would be a huge black spot there, and as the saying goes, blood is thicker than water.

Though Alexa would argue that the phrase was grossly oversimplified.

So no, she wouldn't go to the sheriff's office. But...

She stuck her Bluetooth earpiece in and risked scrolling through her recent calls until she found Colin's number. It rang four times, and just when Alexa figured he was going to ignore her call, he answered on the fifth ring.

"Clara, I'm sort of busy right now, can this wait?"

"Hi, friend. This isn't Clara."

"Well, what time do you have to go to work?"

Alexa's mind blanked for a split second before she realized the kid was smarter than she wanted to give him credit for. He must have been around people, presumably other cops, who would cast suspicious glances at him and likely go play tattletale if they knew who he was really talking to. But still ... he'd answered.

Alexa heard Colin sigh. "Okay, fine," he said, and then to somebody else, his voice softer as he must have pulled the phone away and covered the microphone, "I'll be right back, guys."

Another voice said something unintelligible, and Colin said, "If you think you have a chance, ask her out yourself, asshole. I'm not your wingman."

Spunky, Alexa thought. *Like his sister.* The more she saw the real Colin Wanamaker begin to show himself, the more she was starting to like him.

She heard footsteps on tile and then the sound of a door opening and closing.

"Okay," Colin said, "Make it quick."

"Is that what your girlfriends say to you?"

Colin groaned. "I see why you and Clara get on so well. But if you're going to waste my time—"

"Sorry. *Sorry*," Alexa said. "That was uncalled for. But you kinda set it up for me. Anyway, thanks for the tip on the blood. Tell me everything. Fast."

"Not much to tell. Our team went over Mrs. VanFleet's vehicle and pulled what they could. Hair, fibers, prints, and then they found the dried blood in the back cargo area. It wasn't a lot, like maybe somebody had cleaned up most of it, or maybe just a bit had smeared across the edge of the trunk liner, but blood is blood. We sent the sample to the state lab we use—oh, and we're bringing Mr. VanFleet in to get some samples to test against what we've found. I mean, it was his vehicle too, so obviously we need to be able to eliminate traces of him."

"Eliminate? What the fuck, Colin?"

"What? He co-owned the car. Of course his DNA is going

to be all over it. We can't arrest a guy for murder because we found his hair or his fingerprints in his own car."

"Or his blood?"

"What if he cut himself loading his kids' soccer gear into the back?"

"But you *are* thinking Michelle's been murdered?"

"What?" Colin fumbled his words. "I didn't—"

"You said you can't arrest the guy for murder because..."

"I was only making a point."

"Uh-huh. He's fishy, Colin. I'm telling you. He knows something he's not telling us."

"Us?"

"Don't act like I'm just going to let this go. By the way, did you know he got fired from the bank yesterday?"

Colin was silent. Alexa smiled. She'd toss him a bone, repayment for the one he'd tossed her. "Yep," she said and then quickly told him the story of Adrien showing up at her office yesterday accusing her of emailing the photos of him and Kate Williams.

"Did you do it?" Colin asked. His tone wasn't accusatory, more genuinely curious, and something about the way he said the words meant a great deal to Alexa, as if, even if she'd said yes, Colin Wanamaker would have simply ingested the information and the turned the other cheek.

"I can see why you'd think so, but no, I didn't. But I do have another question."

"Quick, please. I really do need to get back inside."

"Did you find any of the photographs I gave Michelle VanFleet in the SUV?"

"No."

"You're sure."

"Positive. We documented every single item in that car, and everything in her purse. No nude photos, trust me. That would be the talk of the office. Hell, they'd probably be emailed to everyone on *our* contact list."

"Sounds like a real tight ship you guys run there," Alexa said, the disgust only partially hidden in her voice.

Colin didn't attempt any defense other than "We're not *all* assholes."

"I know, Colin. I know." This was a confession six-month-prior Alexa would have never made. "Okay, thank you. Keep me posted, please. And for the love of God, try to beat a confession out of Adrien, would you?"

"I'll pretend I didn't hear that."

He hung up.

ALEXA STOPPED by her building to take a quick shower and change, and on the way out her apartment door she grabbed the envelope with the photographs of Victoria Jameson's murdered body. She didn't need to see them anymore, but it was time to show them to somebody else.

On her frantic drive from the hotel back to Silent Falls, as her mind had whirled and twirled with endless possibilities of what the blood in the back of Michelle VanFleet's SUV might mean, her thoughts were also intertwined with possible scenarios of what exactly had happened to Victoria Jameson. Alexa knew she was supposed to compartmentalize, to separate everything into nice and neat silos in her brain, but the more she tried to force everything apart, the more both cases seemed to want to coexist in some chaotic scatterplot of fact and theory. It was as though each case had her by an arm, pulling from each side at the same time, resulting in Alexa being stuck in the same spot no matter how hard she tried to shift herself to one side or the other.

She needed help. Needed to off-load some of the burden —of both the work and her own guilt. She couldn't lie to Ezra anymore. She would show him the pictures of Victoria Jameson and then tell him the truth of who the girl was and why she had the photographs at all.

As she shut her apartment door behind her, her phone buzzed. Alexa glanced at it and saw the notification that she had a new email. It was from the same secure messaging service that somebody in the Abatelli camp had used last time, when they'd sent her the files on Victoria.

The fingerprints, Alexa thought and hurried down the stairs and unlocked her office. She downloaded the files and saw that the file format was something she'd never seen before and that her computer could not open. Which was fine. She moved the files to the Shiffy PI secure private cloud folder. Something else for Ezra.

She grabbed a large Americano with an extra shot of espresso at the café and then pushed out the backdoor into the noonday sun, feeling the hint of warmer temperatures on the way as she climbed back behind the wheel of the Oldsmobile and drove to the Silent Falls Inn.

She tried to ignore the fact that in a matter of minutes she might lose the best friend she'd ever had.

CHAPTER 24

Alexa had Victoria Jameson's laptop computer under one arm and the envelope with the photos of the girl's murdered body gripped tightly in her hand, not wanting to risk a surprise gust of wind catching it and airmailing it across town for a stranger to find, when she pulled open the door of the Silent Falls Inn.

She heard the jingle of the tag on Barlow's collar before she saw him trot around from behind the counter and then scurry to her with his tail a blur. Ezra had been standing at the counter, typing something into the computer, and he smiled and said, "Somebody has missed their mommy."

After returning Barlow's greeting, Alexa stood and said, "Oh please, we both know he's starting to like you more. Male bonding and all that nonsense."

"Hey," Ezra said, holding up his large hands in surrender, "let's not argue. Co-parenting is tough, but we'll make it work."

Alexa walked to the counter and set the laptop down in front of Ezra. Barlow made his way back behind the counter and curled up in his bed, apparently having earned his next nap.

"What's this?" Ezra asked, pointing to the laptop.

Alexa set the envelope atop the laptop's lid and patted the stack. "I need your help."

"Are you willing to renegotiate my fee? Remember, I'm grossly underpaid."

Alexa only stared at him, and Ezra instantly picked up on what he saw in her eyes. His face turned to stone and he asked, "Should I call Herb?"

She nodded.

Ezra picked up the desk phone and made the call, and a minute later Alexa saw Herb through the lobby's glass door, stepping out from his room and making his way across the parking lot in his jeans and black t-shirt that looked like it had been through a thousand wash cycles. Some of his few remaining wisps of hair waved in the breeze like stray blades of grass missed by the mower.

When he stepped into the lobby and saw Alexa at the counter, his eyes did a quick dance back and forth between her and Ezra and he rolled his eyes. "Time for another top-secret private meeting, I see. Never mind this is when I watch my programs."

Ezra grinned and nodded for Alexa to follow him to the kitchen. "Thanks, Herb."

Herb waved them off. "Yeah, yeah. Just let me know if I need to shoot another bad guy and save your ass again."

"Jesus, Herb," Ezra said, using a hand to gesture for the guy to lower his voice.

"What?" Herb said, looking around in disbelief. "Who's going to say anything? The dog?"

Barlow grunted, as if letting them know he couldn't care less about whatever they were talking about.

Herb shrugged. "See?"

Alexa laughed, Ezra sighed, and the two of them stepped into the kitchen and closed the door.

They took their usual seats across from each other at the table against the wall, and Alexa set the laptop and envelope between them. Ezra leaned back and sat straight up in his chair, crossed his arms. Waited.

Shit, I can't do this. Alexa felt the panic begin to rise inside her. Now that she was actually here, seated directly across from the person who had so unassumingly and selflessly given her so much, she wasn't sure she could say the words, tell him that she'd gone behind his back and started working with a literal enemy.

Thankfully, Ezra broke her paralysis. He gave one quick nod toward the laptop and envelope and asked, "Does this have to do with what's happening with the VanFleets? Is that Adrien's laptop?"

Alexa shook her head. "No. This is ... something else."

Ezra waited. Alexa felt her throat constrict, the words trapped.

"Okay," Ezra said, giving her an odd look. "So who does the computer belong to, and why did you bring it to me?"

Alexa forced herself to take a deep breath. With a hand that she was surprised to see was trembling, she reached for the envelope. Before she could touch it, Ezra reached out and took her hand. Fast, but gentle.

"Alexa, what is going on?" His voice was concerned, but she could also hear the anger rising. And she knew it wasn't anger directed at her but preparing to be launched at whoever was the cause of her current predicament.

Shit. You're such a fucking idiot, Shiffy.

She'd tell him. She would. She'd fight through and tell him the truth. He deserved the truth from her, more than anybody else she knew. But she'd show him first. Show him what she was dealing with and then rip off the Band-Aid and brace for the sting.

Alexa eased her hand out of Ezra's and picked up the envelope, slid out the photographs and laid them flat on the table, turning them so they were oriented toward him. "The laptop belongs to her. I met with her mother at her house last night. I saw where the body was found and got the computer from the girl's bedroom. I need you to hack into it so I can check out the contents. Her mother didn't know the password."

Ezra leaned forward a tiny bit, never uncrossing his arms, and surveyed the photos, giving each one a single long stare. His face betrayed zero emotion. He might as well have been looking at the blank tabletop. When he was through, he leaned back again and said, "So this is the job your big client has you on? The one with the NDA and everything? I don't understand. Do they have you working in conjunction with the police?"

Alexa felt herself sinking, the water rushing in to drown her. "The police don't know about this. Not yet."

Ezra grew quiet, and Alexa used all her willpower to keep eye contact with him, watching as the muscles in his jaw worked as he thought. A regular person might have asked the question of why the police wouldn't have been brought in to track down a murderer, but not Ezra. His past allowed him to formulate answers to such questions with ease. Who wouldn't want the police involved in their business? Simple. Bad people. Dangerous people who would rather settle the score on their own. So, Ezra didn't ask why. Instead, he asked, "Who is she?"

Alexa stepped up to the cliff's edge and prepared to jump. "Her name was Victoria Jameson." She swallowed, took a final breath, and leapt. "She's Francis Abatelli's niece, and he's asked me to find out who killed her."

Ezra did not react at all. A few seconds that felt like endless hours ticked by, the heat pouring from the ducts in the ceiling suddenly sounding very loud and the smell of the morning's leftover coffee in the pot on the counter becoming incredibly pungent. Alexa felt as though all her senses were all at once hyperaware, adrenaline surging as her heart beat too fast and her entire being braced for some sort of impact.

But the impact did not come.

Ezra only cleared his throat and said, "Tell me everything. Please."

So she did.

ALEXA HAD BUILT up the moment so much in her head that when she finally found herself expunging all the bottled-up truth, she was shocked to find the whole thing finished so quickly, and with so little fanfare.

She told Ezra everything, starting with the day she'd been forced into the back of that black SUV a handful of months ago for her first meeting with Francis Abatelli, moving on to her visit from Joey at the Shiffy PI office, the drive and meeting with Francis and his goons at Xpedited Xchange, and ending with her trip the previous evening to meet with Collette Jameson. She gave Ezra the condensed version of her conversation with the woman but kept any further theorizing to herself.

There. In just a couple short minutes, the weight of what she'd assumed to be a potentially catastrophic secret had lifted from her shoulders and she found she could suddenly breathe again.

Ezra listened without a word of interjection, like he always did. Soaking in the details and running them through his internal processor, probably already spotting things she'd missed or ignored.

But right then, Alexa didn't care about his theories on Victoria Jameson's murders. She only cared about whether the next words out of his mouth would be the last words he ever spoke to her, their friendship severed. And then, her brain poured more fuel on her fire of despair; she realized there was no way she could ever explain to Barlow why they didn't go visit Ezra's farmhouse or the inn anymore. Why he couldn't see his buddy.

"You're lucky they didn't kill you," Ezra said. "That day when you got into the SUV, there was probably a fifty-fifty chance they were going to drive you off and chop you up and—"

"I know. I'm sorry, I just—"

"And that's completely my fault."

Alexa blanked. "Wait, what?"

"What we did to his men ... the three we killed. That was my plan."

Alexa shook her head. "We both knew there was a chance they'd suspect us."

Ezra didn't say anything.

"I made the choice," Alexa said. "I pulled you into it."

Ezra stayed quiet, and she watched as he clenched and unclenched his jaw. His eyes stared ahead, over her shoulder, unfocused, mind working. Alexa shuddered at what terrible things he might be thinking, images of her chained to a bench in some warehouse while one of Francis's goons drilled holes in her knees.

"Well," he finally said, taking in a deep breath and shaking his head, as if literally clearing his mind. "I'd say this probably the best outcome we could hope for."

Alexa looked around the kitchen, trying to decide if what she was seeing and hearing was real. "Are you serious?" she asked.

Ezra nodded. "Absolutely. Keep your friends close and your enemies closer. Ever heard that?"

"Yeah, but—"

"Like I said, there was probably a fifty-fifty shot of Francis killing you that day. The odds were in your favor. Turns out the assholes we took out were already on his shit list, so ... they didn't kill you, and instead it looks like they've decided to trust you."

"They thought I might be useful to them. The moment I'm not..."

"They have no reason to kill you now. What do they think you're going to do, take down their entire operation? If the state police and the FBI and who knows how many other agencies have never been able to successfully topple the Abatelli empire, why would they think you can?"

Alexa said nothing, raised her eyebrows.

Ezra shook his head. "No. They have no idea who I am. Trust me. They might have their contacts and their resources, but my real identity is so far erased I couldn't even dig up my own past if I wanted to. If one day my own memory fails me, my previous life will have never existed at all.

"Plus, I've got better things to do than try to take down a crime syndicate."

Alexa eyed him. "Like what?"

Ezra shrugged. "Run this place, read books, play video games, throw the tennis ball with Barlow. Honestly, anything at all."

"But..."

"What happened in December with us and the Abatellis was personal. They went after you, they assaulted Clara, and we made sure the bad men paid the price. For those sins and probably several others." He paused, looked down at the table again, scanning the pictures. "There's always bad guys out there, doing bad things. If one of them gets in my way, or somebody needs my help, I'll take care of it. But I'm not in the business of saving the whole world. I'm just a guy running an inn in a sleepy little town and trying to do the right thing."

"So..." Alexa couldn't help but let a tiny grin twitch across her lips. "You're not mad at me. You don't hate me?"

"I could never hate you, but yes, I'm pissed as hell. I'm pissed as hell that you thought you had to keep this from me." He sighed and shook his head again. "I understand what you must have been thinking but, listen to me, that mindset of being a lone wolf, of trusting nobody, of keeping secrets bottled up to the point you explode ... that's still your past working against you. I know, because I've dealt with the exact same thing. You know what helped?"

Alexa shook her head.

"You," Ezra said. "And Barlow, and Herb, and this place." He held up his hands. "This town. Past experiences can shape who you've become, but don't let them keep the present and the future from shaping who you can be."

Alexa stayed quiet, knowing if she tried to speak, her voice would crack as the tears pricked at her eyes. Ezra looked away, giving her a moment, and when she got her emotions under control, she said, "So, you'll help me with the laptop?"

Ezra laughed, and Alexa joined in, the air seeming to fill the room again, the world once again spinning. "Yes," Ezra said. "I'll see what I can do. If a bunch of mob goons want to kill each other, let 'em go nuts. But ... a young woman? This person needs to be caught."

"What do you think about the quarters?"

Ezra touched one of the photos for the first time, picking it up and bringing it closer. "First guess, Victoria Jameson wasn't this guy's first victim. This looks like an MO, something he's done before. Like a calling card of sorts."

Alexa nodded. "Serial killer?"

Ezra considered this. "Serial killer takes out a family member of a mob boss? Risky ... or dumb. Hit man would fit better."

"What's the difference?"

"One gets paid to be dumb. Do you think the killer knew who she was? Who her uncle was? Or was it a coincidence? From what you've told me about what you saw and what the

186 MICHAEL ROBERTSON, JR.

mother told you, Victoria knew the person well before the night she died."

Alexa nodded. "It would definitely seem that way. And they were close enough that she was risking sneaking out to see them or sneak them onto her family's property."

Ezra thought some more. Rubbed the top of his head. "The person she knew, the one she was going to meet, might not have been the one to kill her. It could have been some sort of setup, a bait and switch. Call it whatever you want. There's nothing to say there wasn't more than one person involved."

Again, Alexa cursed the camera mounted atop the Jamesons' back gate. Then she said, "I've got something else for you."

"I can't wait."

"Check our cloud folder—I put some prints Abatelli's guys were able to lift from the quarters. They told me they ran them through all the criminal databases, but ... I guess I figured you might have better luck."

Ezra, true to form, didn't bother asking about who Abatelli's "guys" were, or how they were able to do what they did. He just nodded and said, "Got it."

Alexa's phone buzzed in her pocket, and she pulled it free and checked the screen. It was a number she didn't recognize, but with everything going on, she knew better than to risk not answering it.

"Hello?"

"This is Jane. From last night," a woman's voice said, barely above a whisper.

It took Alexa's brain only a second to place the name and

the voice. "Thank you for the coffee," she said. "It was excellent."

"Miss Collette does not know I'm calling."

"What can I do for you, Jane?"

There was the sound of something muffling the microphone, and the woman's voice dropped even lower. "I have to show you something. There's a little motel outside East River on the north side. It's halfway. Can you meet there?"

Alexa knew exactly what motel Jane was talking about. It was the same one Adrien VanFleet had used to have his affair. It wasn't exactly halfway, but it was close. "I know it," Alexa said. "What time?"

"I'm off in one hour."

Alexa checked her watch. "I'll be there."

She ended the call.

"Who was that?" Ezra asked.

"The Jamesons' housekeeper. She said she needs to show me something."

"About Victoria?"

"What else would it be?"

"Why is she telling you and not Victoria's mother?"

"I have no idea. But I'll find out soon enough."

Ezra nodded. "I know I don't have to say this, but be careful."

Alexa waved him off. "She's half my size and twice my age."

Ezra tapped the photos on the table. "Remember, it might not be her who shows up."

CHAPTER 25

Alexa arrived early, backing the Oldsmobile into the same parking spot at the rear of the motel's small lot as she had on her trips to spy on Adrien VanFleet. She imagined the woman behind the desk in the lobby probably had her nose buried in another magazine, or maybe was watching YouTube on her phone, and might have given a cursory glance out the window at best when the sound of Alexa's aging engine had passed by.

The sun was out today, bright and happy, but even its cheery disposition didn't do much to change the feeling one got when they set their eyes upon the motel's neglected facade. This was a place a person came only out of absolute necessity or desperation or both. Lives lived by the unseen, or people who wished to temporarily visit that world and transact their business before returning to reality.

Alexa had stayed in plenty of places like this over all her years on the move. Out of necessity or desperation or both. She had been mostly unseen, forgotten, unless she found cause to be otherwise. She scanned the parking lot, took inventory of the two other beat-up sedans parked in front of rooms, both license plates from out of state, and realized she probably had more in common with the people hiding behind these motel room doors with their peeling paint and faded room numbers than she did with anyone else in her current life.

Ezra's words returned to her. *Past experiences can shape who you've become, but don't let them keep the present and the future from shaping who you can be.*

With a sudden and unsettling wave of self-doubt building tall and preparing to crash down on her, Alexa reached out and clung onto her friend's words and held them tight, hugging them to her chest and trying to focus on all the good she had found in Silent Falls, remembered just how far she'd come, how happy she'd been these last few months as a life that had seemed so far out of reach for so long had become obtainable, if she'd only buckle up and enjoy the ride.

A car slowed on the road and turned into the parking lot. A blue BMW sedan. Not brand-new, but new enough to still turn some heads. It looked out of place, much the same way Adrien VanFleet's Lexus SUV had when it had been parked outside of room 7. Alexa rolled her eyes and figured if she pulled out her cell phone and snapped a few pictures of the BMW and whoever was about to climb out of it, she could maybe get a head start on another case of infidelity.

But these thoughts vanished when the BMW drove along the length of the motel and then headed straight for Alexa's Oldsmobile, parking next to it on the left.

Jane was behind the driver's seat, and she gave a curt nod to Alexa after the car was shut off. She turned and looked over her shoulder, as if checking for anyone who might be watching.

No need, Alexa thought. *Nobody here sees anything ever. Well ... unless you slide a hundred across the front desk.*

Jane got out of the car and stayed hunched down as she quickly popped open Alexa's passenger door and jumped in. She was quite quick for a woman her age.

Alexa took stock of the woman in one sweeping gaze. She was dressed very much the same as last night, blue jeans and a white blouse and black sneakers with thick rubber soles. Her hair was pulled back, and in the daylight the color more closely resembled a metallic silver than gray.

Like shiny new quarters...

The real reason for Alexa's scan of the woman's body was to look for the bulge of any sort of weapon. The hilt of a knife or the butt of a pistol. The cuffs of the woman's pants were too tight for an ankle holster, and her blouse was tucked in, so for the moment, Alexa figured she was safe.

She hadn't really expected any trouble from Jane, but Ezra had a point about being careful, remaining vigilant. The moment you let your guard down...

"Thank you for meeting me," Jane said. She looked straight ahead out the windshield when she spoke.

"Nice car you've got there," Alexa said. "The Jamesons must pay you well. Or maybe you invested in crypto. I hear that's getting big these days."

Jane kept her eyes facing forward, but she nodded. "The car was a gift from Miss Collette and Mr. Troy for my twenty years of service to them. They're very generous."

Alexa smiled. "I'm sure."

"They take care of me."

"Again, I'm sure."

So much being said here remained unspoken. The BMW was likely one of several keys used to lock the vault doors of Jane's memory.

"I've failed them," Jane said, "and Victoria died because of it."

Alexa felt her heart rate kick up, and she had to take a deep breath to keep herself from getting too excited at the prospect of this whole thing with the Abatellis being finished right here, right now, all because of the words of a longtime housekeeper.

"What do you mean?" Alexa asked as patiently as she could.

"I think I know who killed Victoria."

Alexa's patience vanished. She spun in her seat and sat up on one knee. "Who? Why haven't you said anything to anyone?"

Jane remained stoic, her gaze holding straight ahead still, out the windshield. "It's too late. I should have told them earlier, before Victoria was killed. It might have stopped it. But now..." She closed her eyes. "If they find out I knew this thing and said nothing..." The woman cleared her throat and took a deep breath of her own, and for the first time she turned and looked directly into Alexa's eyes. "They are dangerous people. You know that."

Alexa's heart was still beating fast, but now there was a new knot forming in her gut. "You think they'll kill you?"

Jane nodded. "Or worse. The Abatellis will stop at nothing to settle a score, to recoup a debt owed."

Alexa said nothing. Didn't have to.

"I'm trusting you with my life," Jane said. "What I show you, you can never tell them where you got the information."

"You know Collette's brother is the one who's hired me, right? Why would you trust me?"

Jane's eyes found Alexa's again, and this time they were imploring, as if searching for something lost, and then they suddenly hardened with a found resolve and the woman nodded her head once. "You're not like them," she said. "You're a good person, I can tell. I've seen lots of bad people over my years. You're not one of them. You'll do what you need to do, but I trust you."

Alexa would have been touched, if it wasn't for the fact that she was basically drooling in anticipation of what Jane had to say about Victoria's killer.

The woman reached down to her side, and for a fleeting instant Alexa had a nightmarish vision of Jane pulling a gun and shooting her between the eyes. Instead, the woman retrieved her cell phone, an older iPhone with a cracked screen. Instead of bringing the screen to life, she clutched the phone in both hands. Nodded to herself and said, "Two days before Victoria's body was found, Miss Collette had me run to a little bakery she likes, to pick up an order of croissants she had placed. The bakery is very good, but its location ... not so much. The area of town where shops pull down metal gates over their storefronts when they close up in the evening. I don't even park my car close on the street. I use the garage six blocks south and walk. And only in the daylight."

Alexa knew she should let the woman speak, but with the growing potential of this case being blown wide open looming just out of reach, her emotions took over. "Jane, what the hell do croissants have to do with who killed Victoria? Get to the point, please."

Jane was undeterred. She looked at Alexa and cocked her head ever so slightly. "Details are always relevant. Isn't that what you and Miss Collette agreed on last evening?"

Damn. She does hear everything. "Sorry," Alexa said. "Go ahead."

"The point is, I was in an area of town that Victoria would never be in. Or, at least she would never expect us to expect her to be in. She would also never expect to see any of us there—her mother or father, nor me."

"But you saw her?"

Jane nodded. "I was standing inside the bakery, and they were busy, so I was just inside the door, off to the side by the big glass storefront, waiting my turn in line. I happened to glance out to the sidewalk because I saw a couple of people walking by, and I was genuinely startled to see Victoria. I waved to her, and the motion must have caught her eye through the glass, because her head jerked my way, and instead of the eventual friendly recognition I would expect from her, her face quickly turned ... afraid."

Alexa was confused. "She was afraid of you?"

"No. It was a look of somebody who was afraid they'd just been caught."

Ah. The pieces were clicking into place. "Collette said she suspected Victoria had a boyfriend she was keeping a secret from everyone. You caught them, didn't you? You caught her with her secret guy and now we all think he's the one who killed her."

Jane shook her head.

"No?" Alexa asked. "You don't think the boyfriend killed her?"

Jane looked down at her phone and unlocked it. She tapped the screen and brought up her photos. Found the one she wanted and made it full-screen. She held it up for Alexa to see.

"The person with her wasn't a man," Jane said.

Alexa leaned in closer and examined the image. It was taken from inside the bakery, and a glare on the big glass display window streaked half the image, blurring details. It was also slightly out of focus. Alexa understood why. This photo was taken in haste, a quick fumbling of the phone in a hurried attempt to capture a moment that carried a palpable importance, even if the person taking the photograph had no idea why.

Instinct. Always trust it.

In the center of the frame, the clear image of two young women side by side on the sidewalk, their backs to the camera, heading away. One had auburn hair, so that had to be Victoria. The other woman, dressed in black slacks and a puffy coat, sensible heels on her feet, had blond hair spilling over the collar of her coat.

"Whoever that is," Jane said, "Victoria was clearly upset that I had seen the two of them together. I've known that girl since the day she was born, and I'd never seen worry on her face like that. I should have asked her about it, but I didn't. I should have said something to Miss Collette, but I didn't." Jane paused and turned to look out the windshield again. "Two days later, Victoria was dead."

Alexa fell back into her seat, disappointment settling over her. A picture of the back of a blond woman. It wasn't a complete dead-end lead, but it was close. Like trying to put together a puzzle without the picture on the box.

"I need you to send me that picture," Alexa said, wondering what exactly she was even going to do with it. Even the best of Ezra's software couldn't create somebody's face just by looking at the back of their head.

But then she got another idea.

"And I need the address of that bakery."

CHAPTER 26

Jane hadn't been exaggerating about the state of things in the area of town where the Buttercup Bakery held shop. On the outer limits of downtown East River, the bakery was one of four units squeezed into a two-story brick building with a crumbling facade and skeletal frames over doors that had long ago lost their awning skin. Buildings nearly identical to this one were across the street and the next block up as well, four corners of disrepair, relics of an age long ago prosperous. The bus station had been maybe a quarter mile before the bakery, and the sidewalks were dotted mostly with the homeless and those drifting by, perched on corners, sitting down and leaning against buildings. Some held signs asking for help, some didn't. The ones that didn't had enough experience to know either that the signs would do no good or that their own appearance was the only sign they really needed.

Alexa parked on the street right outside the bakery. Street parking was ample here, and she could guess why. Across the street from the bakery three young men, two white, one black, dressed in jeans and baggy sweatshirts and with beanies on their heads, didn't shy away from eyeing her and the Oldsmobile as Alexa climbed out. One of the white guys was smoking a cigarette, and as Alexa stared at him he took a long drag and then made a show of blowing the smoke into the air, little white clouds rising toward the sky.

"Fuck you lookin' at, bitch?" he asked.

Alexa sighed. The world lacked creativity these days. She ignored him and turned to face the bakery. The owners had done a good job trying to make the place look appealing and welcoming despite its surroundings. The inside lights were warm and bright, and the big glass windows were clean and sparkling, the silhouette of a steaming coffee mug and a muffin painted on each beneath an elegant cursive font spelling out the bakery's name. A handful of people were in line or seated at a couple of the small tables clustered inside, brave souls who would not be deterred by the neighborhood in their pursuit of a hot beverage and fresh pastry. The two women Alexa saw working behind the counter wore smiles and seemed to possess an energy otherwise foreign to the rest of the world outside the bakery's walls. The aroma of ground coffee beans and baked goods could almost make you forget what a shitty part of town this was.

Good coffee had lots of superpowers, in Alexa's opinion.

She looked above the door frame and along the tops of the windows, searching inside and out for what she was looking for. Was disappointed but not surprised not to see a security camera. She was certain the bakery had cameras on the inside, any self-respecting business in this part of town would, but the owners might not be of the type of mind that would think they'd need to monitor the street in front of their shop. It was an oversight, in Alexa's experience, but hey, she didn't own the place.

She pulled out her cell phone and pulled up the picture of Victoria Jameson and her mystery friend that Jane had sent her. Made sure she had her bearings straight to see which way the girls had been walking. After making sure she had the right direction, Alexa walked up the sidewalk back in the direction of the bus station.

The unit directly adjacent to the Buttercup Bakery was vacant, white posterboard occupying the windows advertising that the space was for lease. The once-black lettering was so badly faded it barely registered as gray. The place had been empty for quite some time, and Alexa didn't imagine anything aside from a hefty city-funded gentrification initiative would ever tempt new tenants.

The next unit down was exactly the type of place she'd hoped for. A payday advancement and check-cashing business with metal wiring installed over the windows and not one but two security cameras mounted right inside, pointing out and down toward the sidewalk.

Alexa pushed through the door and was greeted with the scent of weed and body odor. A long counter separated the space in half, and a young white guy who looked like he could have easily joined the three men outside on the sidewalk and completed the four horsemen of thugs was leaned back in a metal folding chair with his sneakers up on the counter. His ball cap had a wide, flat brim and was the same neon color of school zone traffic signs. He also wore a baggy sweatshirt, and pinned below the brand logo on his left chest was a name tag that identified him as just "T."

"Is that your whole name or did the rest of the letters fall off?" Alexa asked, stepping up to the counter.

The guy leaned the chair back down and stood. He was about Alexa's height, but the look in his eyes told her the guy thought he was a lot bigger. "Everyone calls me T."

"Okay, T, I need your help."

"How much you need?" T asked, pulling the keyboard from the computer on the counter toward him.

Alexa shook her head. She pulled out her PI license and held it up. "I need to see your security footage. It won't take long."

T squinted at the license and then took a small step back, sizing her up. "Boss won't like that."

"I don't care. Plus, he doesn't have to know. I'm not a cop. I couldn't give a shit what else you guys are doing here. I just need a peek at the footage." Alexa was only speculating that other less-than-legal transactions might take place here, but it seemed like it was the correct guess.

T shook his head and said with too much bravado, "I don't have a clue what you're talking about."

Alexa reached into her pocket to pull out some cash, and T stepped back fast, his entire body poised to spring away. "Whoa," Alexa said, slowly pulling out her hand. "It's just money. How much will make you forget about your boss for a few minutes?"

T's eyes were glued to the cash, and Alexa could see him trying and apparently failing to work something out in his head. Then the guy's gaze shifted from the money to her torso, and she felt the bile in the back of her throat begin to rise when T gave her a grin that could only have one meaning.

"Show me your tits and I'll show you the footage."

Alexa swallowed down the bile. Forced herself to breathe normally. "Are you joking?"

T shook his head. "Cash I got," he said. "But don't get a lot of hunnies in here. Especially none as fine as you. I mean, you a little older than my usual, but I ain't that picky."

"I'm going to ask again. Are you joking?"

"Look, I got something you need, and you got something I want. Supply and demand, babe."

"What? That's not what that..." Alexa looked over T's shoulder, saw the door that must lead back to the office or some sort of storage area. She sighed dramatically, nodded to the door. "Is the security camera server back there?"

T nodded. "Yep. Stores thirty days' worth," he said, like he was sweetening the deal.

Alexa somehow managed a bashful grin, as if what was about to happen might actually be fun, or exciting. She looked over her shoulder, back toward the street, then walked to the door and engaged both the deadbolts. T didn't question anything, just stared with a dumb look on his face while she returned to the counter and pointed to the door behind him. "Fine. But I'll only do it back there. I don't want anyone else to see."

T looked downright giddy, shocked that he was actually pulling this off. He used a key from his pocket to unlock the partition at the end of the counter and swung it back so Alexa could step across, then he used the same key to unlock the door that led to the back room.

"Come on in," he said, making the mistake of being neither a gentleman nor a very smart criminal and choosing to enter the room first, ahead of her.

He had taken half a step across the threshold before Alexa shot a hand out and grabbed his left wrist, twisting his arm backward and pistoning his hand up damn near to between his shoulder blades. T let out a squeal that sounded like a pig getting slaughtered, and farted. "Hey! What the—"

The end of that sentence was replaced with another squeal and a grunt as Alexa used her other hand to grab a fistful of his hair and slam him facefirst into the cheap wooden desk on their left. She did it again for good measure, and any and all resistance she'd felt coiled up inside T's body disappeared and he went almost fully limp, his legs like Jell-O.

Oh, what the hell..., Alexa thought, *He deserves this.* She slammed his face into the desk one more time, and this time his legs did fail him and Alexa let go of his wrist and let him fall to the floor. She grabbed his hair and spun him around, propping him up against the wall. His nose was bleeding and his bottom lip was split, and his eyes were rolling around unfocused, as if discovering some big and mesmerizing space for the first time, unable to figure out where to look first to begin to take it all in.

She snapped her fingers in front of his face three times, and the third time his eyes focused on her—and when they did, they filled with fear. "Please...," he said.

"Fuck your please," Alexa spat. "Listen to me, because this is your only chance. The people I work for, the ones who sent me here, they care less about your life than even I do. The difference is, if I was going to kill you, I'd just do it fast, get it over with. Probably shoot you in the head. Quick and easy. But these people ... *my boss* ... they don't like getting fucked around with. When they ask for something, they get it. And if

I tell them that all I asked you to do was show me some security footage, and even offered to pay you for your trouble, and you not only flat-out refused but *also* sexually assaulted me..."

T tried to squirm. "Hey, I didn't—"

Alexa slapped him across the face. Blood from his split lip peppered the wall, tiny pinpricks of crimson. "They'll do much worse than just kill you, trust me. I've seen it with my own eyes. I mean, just last winter they cut a guy to pieces, left his head in the middle of a ball field and scattered the rest of him around the infield. You might have read about it, assuming you stopped jerking off long enough to do anything else online but look at porn, you sick fuck."

Alexa stood up, stared down at the guy. He slumped further down the wall, but she was pleased to see he was nodding his head. "Okay," he said. "Okay, sure, no problem. Just don't hit me anymore."

What a pathetic wannabe.

"Wise decision, T. I don't suspect you've got the brightest of futures ahead of you, but at least you're smart enough to realize alive is better than dead."

T pushed himself from the ground, and when he seemed confident he wasn't going to fall over, he wiped his bloody nose with the front of his sweatshirt and said, "I like my head where it is."

Alexa couldn't help but laugh.

But five minutes later, she wasn't laughing at all.

She stood behind T as he sat in front of a computer terminal that had been crammed into the corner of the back room, wedged between stacks of cardboard boxes that, if Alexa had to guess, weren't full of flyers for the newspaper or forms for customers to fill out. Ethernet cables snaked down from the drop ceiling and fed into the back of the terminal T was working on. Alexa counted ten cables in all and figured that meant ten cameras. For a place this small, that seemed like a hell of a lot of cameras. Shit, maybe the cardboard boxes were full of cash, or gold bars.

No, if they were, there'd be somebody a lot smarter and a lot better at protecting himself than the little scrub in front of her.

Alexa used the time stamp from the metadata of the photo Jane had sent her—God bless smartphones—to give T the right time window to look through. As she peered over top his blinding bright ball cap, Alexa had to admit that despite the guy's numerous shortcomings, he knew exactly how to work the camera software. He clicked the mouse and typed a few keystrokes and then hit the play button and leaned back, letting her get a better look over his shoulder.

Within seconds, Victoria Jameson and her friend came into view and walked past the storefront. Their steps looked hurried, and Alexa knew at once that Jane hadn't been mistaken when she'd said Victoria had looked afraid when she'd noticed the housekeeper inside the bakery. The two girls were moving with purpose, and just before they disappeared out of view, Victoria Jameson gave a quick glance over her shoulder, perhaps to see if Jane was going to come out and try to catch up with her.

Alexa's heart and brain started an unsettling tango of confusion and excitement, causing the room to do a quick spin. She closed her eyes and took a deep breath. Said, "Play it again."

T didn't argue. Click. Type. Play.

"Pause it. There."

He did.

Alexa leaned closer, just to be sure, though she didn't really need to. The cameras were high-definition and the day had been sunny, the light perfect.

Alexa had seen the blond woman walking beside Victoria Jameson before. Had, in fact, seen the woman in pictures Alexa herself had taken. Though, in most of those pictures, the woman had been naked.

The blond woman was Kate Williams, Adrien VanFleet's bank teller mistress.

CHAPTER 27

That unshakable sense of connection between Michelle VanFleet's disappearance and Victoria Jameson's murder had finally gained some validation, and Alexa allowed herself a tiny moment of triumph in the fact that her instinct had refused to fully separate the two cases, despite her having no real understanding or possible explanation for why.

But the moment was fleeting, because right on the tail of that excitement came an entirely new and overwhelming sense of confusion that loomed high overhead like a tsunami wave, towering toward the sky and hiding all reason in its shadow, blocking her view of logic.

But they are *connected,* she thought, staring at the wave, unafraid. *It's my job to figure out why.* Gaining helpful new information always reignited the drive inside her, propelled her into action. Nuggets of intel like the discovery that Victoria Jameson had met with Kate Williams was like gulping down multiple espresso shots, her mind reinvigorated with energy, gearing up to assemble the puzzle now that more of the pieces had been laid out on the table.

"Can you save that clip and export it for me?" Alexa asked T.

The guy nodded so fast his hat bobbled on his head, and he took it off and tossed it onto the desk before he took control of the keyboard and mouse again and did as asked. Alexa could see there was real fear in him now, her previous words obviously hitting home. Which likely meant one thing: T knew exactly who the Abatellis were, and he was smart enough not to want to cross them.

"Done," T said. "You want me to email it to you?"

Alexa gave the guy her work email address and then confirmed receipt of the file with her phone. "Thanks," she said before turning to leave.

"Hey!" T called, just as she reached the store's front door. "I helped, right? I did what you asked. You aren't going to fucking send anybody after me, right? I'm ... I'm sorry about before, you know, about..."

"About asking to see my tits," Alexa finished for him. "What, too chickenshit to say it now that you got your ass beat?"

T started to mumble some response but she held up a hand and cut him off. "What's your real name?" she asked.

The guy's face turned pale, like somebody had flicked a switch and powered him down. The dried crust of blood beneath his nostrils looked like rust. "It's an easy question, T." She took a step forward. Which was all it took.

"Timothy," T blurted. "Tim."

Once again, Alexa couldn't help but laugh. "I see why you

go by T. I bet it's real difficult to live that thug life with a name like Timmy. Hard to get respect, right?"

Timothy aka Tim aka T said nothing.

"Well, Timothy," Alexa said, "how about this? You forget you ever saw me today and we're all square. I won't send the big scary monsters after you, and you can go about your days pretending to be a gangsta ... or whatever the hell you think you're playing at."

She turned and unlocked the door and walked out, hearing a faint "Thank you" squeeze through the doorway before it closed.

She headed for her car and then stopped short.

The three guys from across the street earlier were leaning against the side of it, their sneakers propped up on the sidewalk, their hands stuffed into the pockets of their pants. In unison, like a pack of dogs picking up a scent, they turned their heads to look at her. The white guy who'd been so kind with his question earlier smiled when she locked eyes with him, and he pushed himself away from the car and stepped onto the sidewalk, facing her and staring her down like they were two gunslingers from the west about to have a duel.

"I don't have time for this," Alexa said, already calculating her moves, anticipating how each of the other two guys would react once she chopped the first guy in the throat and then smashed his testicles up to his gut before he could even register the first blow. Would they come after her together, or one at a time? Would they even try to fight, or was the first guy the ringleader, the only one with any real bravado, and the other two would simply run away, unsure what to do without their boss calling the shots?

"You have time for whatever the fuck I say you have time for," the first guy said, taking a step forward. He stood tall and tried to puff out his chest, and with one hand he reached into the front pouch of his baggy sweatshirt. It was meant to be intimidating, Alexa figured, but she didn't so much as flinch. He had no weapon in that pouch—she knew because she would have noticed the weight pulling the fabric down. Definitely not a gun. Maybe, at best, a small knife. But even then, the guy wouldn't use it. He wouldn't stab her right here in broad daylight with customers in the Buttercup Bakery. He'd try to scare her, that was all. Which would only result in the guy ending up face-down on the sidewalk gasping for breath and clutching his sack.

"Cash and keys, bitch. Right fucking now," the guy said, taking another step forward.

Here we go, Alexa thought. *Time to embarrass another thug.*

"Yo!" a voice called from behind Alexa, stopping the flow of the moment.

The guy on the sidewalk's eyes flicked up and to her right, over her shoulder. Alexa kept her gaze straight ahead, but she recognized the voice.

"The fuck you want, T?"

"Leave her alone," T said. "She's connected."

"Bullshit," the guy replied, only the slightest hint of his earlier enthusiasm gone.

Alexa heard T laugh behind her. "Fine, don't believe me. Your fucking funeral."

The guy on the sidewalk stared over Alexa's shoulder for another few seconds before looking back at her, and Alexa could see the change in his eyes. Finally, he turned to his two companions and said, "Come on. Let's get the fuck outta here."

He strolled down the block, his dutiful followers right on his heels, and then all three of them disappeared around the block. Only when they were out of sight did Alexa allow herself to turn around. T was standing half out of the door of his shop. He'd managed to wipe most of the blood off his face. "All square?" he said.

Alexa nodded. "All square."

T slipped back inside and Alexa hurried to the Oldsmobile, thankful for his assistance. She hadn't been lying to the guy on the sidewalk—she really didn't have time for any more stupid today.

SHE WANTED to make the call right away, but she'd had enough of the particular area of East River where the Buttercup Bakery had thankfully decided to set up shop. She'd gotten what she'd come for but had had to assault one guy and nearly fight off a threesome in the process. Why push her luck?

She drove back the way she'd come, passing the bus station and watching as, the further she drove, the more elegant and modern the storefronts became and the taller the buildings reached for the sky. Returning to a world where, for most people, the things that happened near the Buttercup Bakery were more statistics than reality.

It was late afternoon when she passed the bank where Adrien VanFleet used to work. The bank where he'd met Kate Williams and had started sleeping with her and had gotten Alexa involved in this whole mess to begin with. Alexa stopped at the stoplight at the intersection and pulled out her phone to look at the metadata for the photo that Jane had sent her again. The time stamp was twelve forty p.m.

Lunch hour, Alexa thought, looking at Kate Williams's professional attire: the heels and the slacks. She did the math on how long it had taken her to drive from the bakery to this stoplight and figured that on foot Kate Williams could have easily made the round trip from bank to bakery and back within an hour's lunch break.

She went far enough away, and to a sketchy enough part of town she didn't think anybody would see them. Nobody that mattered, anyway. But not far enough away that she'd have to take time off from work, or visit after hours.

The horn from the car behind Alexa honked twice. The light had turned green. Alexa waved apologetically—hey, she could admit when she was in the wrong—and drove on, finding a parking space on the street a couple blocks up. She parked and then pulled up her email on her phone. She forwarded the video file that T had sent her to Ezra and was just about to call him when her phone began to ring.

It was Ezra.

She answered the call. "Good timing. You're not going to believe what I found out. Check your email," Alexa said, watching as a man in a suit and tie stepped out of an office building ahead of her. He looked tired and sad, his suit wrinkled and his hair sticking up in the back. As he surveyed the street while he waited at the crosswalk, Alexa couldn't help but think the guy looked more like he was waiting to jump in front of a bus than for his opportunity to cross safely.

Corporate America. No, thank you.

Ezra hadn't said a word, but Alexa heard his keyboard

strokes and mouse clicks as he pulled up the video to watch. "So, it was a girl that Victoria met that day?" he finally said.

"Yep?"

"And it sounds like you already know who she is, based on the unhealthy enthusiasm I'm sensing in your voice."

"So do you," Alexa said. "Well ... you haven't seen her, but I've told you about her."

The line was silent.

"You're no fun," Alexa said. "The other girl in that video is Kate Williams. The woman that Adrien VanFleet was having his affair with."

The line remained silent. For a long time. Alexa felt herself grow cold as the weight of that silence grew. "Ezra?"

He cleared his throat. "You're absolutely positive the girl in that video is the woman Adrien VanFleet was sleeping with?"

"Ezra, I've seen every inch of her naked body in high-resolution photographs. It's her."

"Well, then, that makes things interesting."

Something in his voice. The temperature in the Oldsmobile continued to drop. "Why? What did you find? Something on the laptop?"

"No," he said. "I'm still working on the laptop. It was the fingerprints from the quarters."

"You got a hit."

"I did."

"See, I knew you'd find something the Abatelli guys missed."

"I'm not sure that was the case, actually. It was more a matter of timing."

"What do you mean?"

"The prints from the quarters matched a brand-new entry in the system, just added today."

Alexa leaned back against the headrest. Today seemed to be the day that kept on giving. "Holy shit," she said. "You're right, that is good timing. Where did you find it?"

"Right here," Ezra said.

"What? Here where?"

"Silent Falls."

Now it was Alexa's turn to stay silent.

"They must have brought him in to get some samples to compare to what they found in Michelle's car."

Alexa's phone call earlier with Colin Wanamaker came rushing back to her.

"Wait, are you saying—"

"Yes," Ezra said. "The prints on the quarters found with Victoria Jameson's body belong to Adrien VanFleet."

CHAPTER 28

Alexa fumed with anger.

She was going ninety down the highway, headed back to Silent Falls, her vision tinted with red and her mind blinded with a kaleidoscope of images of all the things she was going to do to Adrien VanFleet the moment she saw him.

"Alexa?"

In her rage-driven reaction, pulling the Oldsmobile wildly from the parking space on the street and running at least one red light as she found the highway entrance ramp, she'd forgotten she'd been on the call with Ezra. The phone was still pressed to her ear.

"I'm here."

"Don't."

"Don't *what*?"

"You went completely silent, and I can hear that poor engine of yours screaming. You're upset."

"Damn right I am. He—"

"Don't!"

Ezra rarely raised his voice. This might have been only the second time she'd ever heard him speak in anything but his usual laid-back tone. Even when he would get serious, his volume rarely rose or fell; his words would evolve into something different, growing an extra bite, gaining a heavier weight when he spoke them so that they'd hit you in the chest and make you pay attention, the way a subwoofer from the trunk of the car next to you at a stoplight might rattle your teeth when the beat dropped.

He had her attention now. This was what she loved about him. He could tell when she was headed off the rails, about to fall off the wagon of caution and good sense, and slow her down, force her to think things through and consider the big picture, evaluate the consequences.

"Don't go to see him," Ezra said.

Alexa eased off the accelerator and slowed the Oldsmobile down to a reasonable sixty-five. Counted to ten to slow her heart and catch her breath. "If those are his prints on the quarters, that means he probably killed Victoria," she said. "And if he killed Victoria, there's a damn good chance that means he also killed his wife. Think about it, Ezra. Something about both of these women's cases has felt off to me from the beginning, and I've told you from day one that Adrien VanFleet is bad news. He's been lying to me, Ezra. He's been lying to everybody. He needs to pay. He needs to be *stopped.*"

Ezra didn't say a word. He was letting her think.

Alexa sighed and hit the steering wheel with her palm. "*Fuck.* I can't even go to the police with this because, for starters, I can't tell them about the quarters or anything about Victoria Jameson without completely destroying my deal with the Abatellis. And, as crazy as it sounds, I kinda trust those wackjobs to take care of things way better than the fucking Silent Falls Sheriff's Department. Plus, if the Abatellis find out it was me who led the police to Adrien before they got their shot at him—and *who else* would it have possibly been but me?—they'll probably decide to just kill me as some sort of consolation prize. Punishment for going behind their backs.

"And speaking of the sheriff's office, how would I even explain the evidence I have? I can't exactly tell them that I had a friend of mine with top-secret government connections tap into their systems. I don't see that going over too well with Sheriff Byrd, do you?"

Ezra still said nothing.

Alexa hit the steering wheel again. Harder this time. "I knew it, Ezra. I knew it from the moment that slick shit came into my office."

She was out of breath again and her heart was beating too fast. Piper would tell her she needed to add more cardio to her weekly routine.

Despite everything, at the thought of Piper's fitness lecture, Alexa laughed. Because really, what else could she do?

"Are you finished ranting?" Ezra asked, his voice back to normal. Calm, collected, knowing.

"Yes."

"Good. I didn't say to *never* go see Adrien VanFleet. Just don't go yet. Come to the farmhouse first. We'll go later tonight. If this guy really has killed two women, and maybe more, I'd like to join you. We'll have a chat with your ex-banker buddy."

Alexa smiled. "Perfect."

AT NINE P.M. Alexa and Ezra left Barlow guarding the farmhouse and climbed into Ezra's truck.

"They'll hear your car coming before we reach the city limits," Ezra said. "Plus, it looks like a houseboat ... it doesn't exactly blend in. Even in the dark."

Alexa didn't bother telling him that the Oldsmobile had in fact served as her house for more nights than she cared to remember. When you'd been homeless since you were twelve years old, a car big enough to stretch out in at bedtime was a luxury.

"We look like we're about to commit a crime," Alexa said as Ezra pulled onto the road. She was wearing clothes that he'd lent her—black sweatpants and sweatshirt, both about three sizes too big, the cuffs and sleeves of each bunched up around her ankles and wrists. In her lap were a pair of dark gloves and a black balaclava.

Ezra wore similar. Only his pants were made of a light-weight tactical material, and the sleeves of the black jacket he wore had Velcro straps that secured them around the wrist, cinching the fabric tight. "We are," he said. "Potentially."

"Potentially?"

"Sure. *Potentially* breaking and entering, trespassing ... assault."

"Assault. Really?"

Ezra shrugged. "We might not like his answers. Or ... he may attempt to withhold them. At first."

"But again. Potentially."

Ezra took his eyes off the road and looked over to her. "Right. Who's to say he doesn't invite us in for coffee? He's a slick shit, right? Your words."

They made the drive in silence. Alexa had pulled the VanFleets' address from the paperwork Michelle had filled out for her billing information, and Ezra didn't bother punching it into the truck's GPS. He hadn't been in Silent Falls too much longer than Alexa had, in the grand scheme of things, but he apparently had a complete map of the town in his head. He never seemed to forget anything.

The neighborhood was quiet. Most of the upscale homes had their interior lights down low or completely off. The ambience of evening relaxation and bedtime. Ezra killed the truck's headlights and drove slowly along the street, eyeing the house numbers and slowing even more as they approached the VanFleets' driveway. Ezra eased the truck in and parked with the truck's front end no more than two inches from the garage door. Alexa looked out the passenger window and took in the home, an elegant brick two-story that failed to impress her after she'd visited the Jamesons' mansion. Funny how fast your perspective of what wealthy means can change. Being a banker had paid Adrien well, but not as well as being blood relatives with the mob.

Ezra reached across the center console and opened the glove box. The blackness of the pistol looked cold and menacing. He gripped it with a deft hand and set it in his lap. Alexa shut the glove box. Asked, "Will you really shoot him?"

Ezra pulled on his balaclava. "If he really did kill his wife and the Jameson girl, would you care if I did?"

Was she a terrible person for already knowing the answer was no? That she wouldn't care one bit if Ezra ended Adrien

VanFleet's life, stopping the man from hurting any other women, making him atone for his previous sins?

She didn't think so.

She didn't answer, and Ezra must have taken her silence as answer enough. "You ready?" he asked. "Remember the plan?"

Alexa nodded. "Yes."

"Good. Stick to it. Remember, he knows your voice. If he recognizes you and we walk out of here without killing him tonight, you're going to have Sheriff Byrd up your ass so fast tomorrow you'll be in a jail cell before your morning coffee."

"I got it," Alexa said, frustrated and impatient. "Go!"

Ezra grabbed the door handle and looked back to her one last time before he pushed the door open. "Five minutes," he said. "If I haven't done it by then, drive away. Go back to the farmhouse and wait for me."

Alexa knew Ezra was good at what he did, and on the entire drive over she'd had the utmost confidence that the guy could pull off any plan or mission he'd ever been given while hardly breaking a sweat. It was odd, when you really thought about it, how many people like him might be walking around among normal civilians every day—people who could incapacitate you with two fingers while hacking your entire digital life with the other hand. People unafraid of the law and consequences because they had been behind the curtain and seen how the machine really worked. People with contacts more powerful than even seemed possible.

She'd had all these thoughts, and all the confidence in the world in Ezra right up until now. But now, the split second before things got started, she couldn't help but feel the rumble of nervousness in her stomach as the plan became a real course of action. Things always had the potential to go wrong, and as Ezra's eyes looked at her through the holes cut out in the black fabric of his mask, Alexa was all at once over-whelmed with how much she cared for the man.

"Be careful," was what she managed to say.

Ezra nodded. "Roger that." And then he jumped out of the truck, grabbing the small black bag from under his seat. He moved like a cat in the night around the side of the house, disappearing into the backyard.

Alexa climbed over into the driver's seat and counted the five minutes out loud, her voice sounding hollow and small in the empty truck cabin.

CHAPTER 29

At five minutes and two seconds, the VanFleets' garage door came to life and yawned open, revealing Adrien's Lexus SUV and an empty parking spot next to it where, in a better, less cruel world, his wife's vehicle would have been. A shadow moved in the back corner of the garage, and Alexa squinted her eyes to barely make out Ezra's tall dark shape waving her in. She pushed the button to start the truck and crawled it into the parking spot next to Adrien's Lexus. The garage door was already closing as she shut the truck off and stepped out, pulling on her gloves and balaclava.

"You were two seconds late," she whispered as she reached Ezra, who was standing by the entry door into the house.

"Sorry," he said. "I dropped one of the zip ties."

As he opened the door and they stepped inside the house, Alexa found herself hoping that a dropped zip tie would be their biggest obstacle of the night.

They passed through a mudroom off the garage and entered the kitchen, where one of the chairs from the dining table had been pulled out and placed in the center of the space between the table and the kitchen island. Adrien was seated in the chair. He was facing them, but he couldn't see them because a strip of duct tape was over his eye. Another strip covered his mouth. His hands and ankles were zip-tied to the chair's legs and backing. He was wearing what looked like the same sweatpants as the first day he'd come to visit the Shiffy PI office, and a t-shirt that Alexa recognized from the pictures she'd seen of the guy on Facebook—the YMCA logo and the name of his children's soccer team in red letters on the front.

It was a pathetic image, but it also felt off. Adrien seemed completely calm, wasn't breathing hard, wasn't panicking, wasn't struggling to free himself.

He's cold on the inside, Alexa thought. *A stone-cold psychopath.*

Or maybe..., the other voice inside her thought, *maybe you're looking at a guy who's lost his wife and has given up on everything else. Including himself.*

Alexa turned to Ezra, her eyes peeking out from the holes in her mask and finding his. He read her mind. "He didn't put up any fight at all," Ezra said. "I said I wanted to talk about his wife and he complied with the whole thing."

Adrien tried to speak, a muffled garble of trapped words.

Ezra ignored him. He nodded toward the hallway and said, "Go on. If we find her body, it'll make things a lot quicker. It'll give us all the answers we need."

Adrien tried again, and this time the noise was louder and

his head jerked as he spoke the words nobody but him could understand.

"He didn't like that," Ezra said.

Alexa shook her head. *Fucker.* She wanted to kick the guy in the face. Hoped the chair would topple over and his head would split open against the tile.

"Go." Ezra said.

She went.

The full sweep of the house didn't take long, but Alexa made certain she was thorough. She checked every room—every closet, under every bed, every storage space, every shower stall and bathtub. She opened the large armoire in what appeared to be a guest bedroom and for some reason was sure that when she did she'd find Michelle VanFleet's broken corpse folded inside like a child's stuffed animal that had been hastily shoved into the first place out of sight the kid could find when told to clean up their room.

The armoire smelled musty and held only clothes.

She found the pull-down steps leading up to the attic and climbed them with creaks and groans from the wood, using the flashlight on her phone to survey the space. It turned out to be more of a crawlspace than an attic and contained only Christmas decorations and mousetraps.

She made her way back downstairs and went back to the garage, checking what now occurred to her to be the most obvious place a person might attempt to hide a dead body at their home, aside from burying it in the backyard. The chest-style freezer was full of nothing but frozen meat and ice cream.

Alexa returned to the kitchen, where Ezra was standing

exactly where she'd left him, his arms crossed, the barrel of the pistol hanging limp from his hand and pointed at the oven. He turned to her as she came up beside him. She shook her head.

He nodded. "Remember," Ezra said and pointed to her lips.

Alexa gave him a thumbs-up. Pulled out her phone and opened the note app. Typed: **Ready.**

Ezra cleared his throat and took a step forward. He slid another chair from the kitchen table and placed it in front of Adrien. The man jerked at the noise but quickly settled back down. Ezra sat across from the guy, set the pistol casually in his lap. "I'm going to take the tape off your mouth now," he said. "If you scream, I'll kill you. I can't make that any simpler or clearer. Nod if you understand."

Adrien nodded. Just once. Still calm.

Ezra peeled off the tape, fast and efficient. Adrien didn't make a sound. Alexa stepped to the table and stood behind Ezra.

"There's two of you," Adrien said.

"The banker can count," Ezra said. "I mean, ex-banker. Also, another rule. If you speak without being told to, I will hurt you. Badly. Nod if you understand."

Adrien nodded.

"Please repeat the first rule to me," Ezra said.

"If I scream, you'll kill me."

"Good. Now, do you think you'll scream if I hurt you?"

Adrien didn't answer.

"I think you will," Ezra said. "So, you can work out that equation for yourself. Bottom line is, break a rule and I'll kill you. I've got questions that I'm going to ask, and you're going to answer them. Quickly and honestly. If you hesitate or if I think you're lying, what do you think will happen? You may answer the question."

"You'll kill me."

"Close. I'll hurt you. And then you'll scream. And then I'll kill you. Rules are rules.

"If you answer the questions, and I deem your answers to be satisfactory, I'll leave and you get to live. But I gotta tell you, I don't like your odds. Because we think you've done some very bad things, and if that's the case ... well, I'll kill you. Because you deserve it."

Alexa watched this conversation unfold with complete awe. The Ezra seated across from Adrien VanFleet was not the Ezra she knew. She'd seen a glimpse of his skills that day behind the abandoned factory with the Abatelli goons, and of course she knew and understood his past. He'd been open and forthcoming about it, but to see him working like this, adopting an entirely new persona that was more akin to a robot than anything human, was unsettling.

She was glad he was on her side.

And she was glad she possessed the memories of the warm, kind, easy-going friend that he really was to help melt away the glacial chill that he seemed to be filling the room with.

Ezra turned to her, almost as if sensing she was having these thoughts about him. She nodded once, and Ezra's hardened gaze again settled on Adrien.

"We'll start with an easy one," he said. "Just to make sure you understand the rules. Is that okay with you?"

Adrien didn't speak, but he nodded.

"Good. Now, were you having an affair with Kate Williams?"

"No," Adrien said.

Alexa's inside flashed hot with anger, but also fear. The fear was because she was unexpectedly knocked off guard by the idea that Ezra would kill this guy before they'd managed to pull the slightest bit of information from him. Rules were rules, right?

But no, Ezra was smarter than that. He'd realize what a waste this entire effort had been if he shot Adrien VanFleet through the head right now. He'd give the guy another chance, right?

Right?

"Well," Ezra said, "I guess you're even dumber than I thought you were. Or maybe—"

"No," Adrien said, shaking his head.

"Or maybe you're just a guy who knows that telling the truth is going to get him killed anyway, and he'd rather take his secrets to the grave. Is that the case, Adrien? Because, if that's the way you're thinking, I'm going to have to amend the rules. Maybe I'll allow some screaming after all."

"No!" Adrien shouted, the first real emotion he'd showed. "I mean, yes. No. I don't know. I was sleeping with Kate Williams, yes. Hell, the whole town probably knows that by now, all thanks to those pictures that fucking bitch investigator took. *Illegally*, I might add."

Alexa grinned beneath her mask. She'd been called a bitch a lot today. And the last thing Adrien VanFleet needed to worry about right now was the legality of how she'd obtained those photographs.

"But it wasn't an affair," Adrien said. "I wasn't cheating on my wife. Michelle knew all about Kate. Hell, she encouraged it!"

Alexa's earth stopped spinning on its axis, the kitchen, the house, Silent Falls, everything coming to an abrupt and shocking halt. She'd come into this house with such preloaded expectations of how things would go, had already worked out all the possible conversation paths Adrien VanFleet might go down in an attempt to prove his innocence in the murders of two women, or eventually provide in detail the motivations of said murders, condemning himself to their punishment.

There was hard evidence that Adrien and Kate Williams were connected, and also evidence that Kate and Victoria Jameson knew each other and had been seen together two days before Victoria's death. This information, plus Adrien's prints on the quarters, had added up to a high probability that Adrien had been involved in the killing of Francis Abatelli's niece.

There were lots of questions that still needed to be answered, however. Most importantly, where in the hell was Michelle VanFleet and what had Adrien done to her? The answers to these questions and more were exactly what Alexa and Ezra had come to find out.

What neither of them had expected was for Adrien VanFleet to throw such a wrench into the gears of their interrogation on the very first question that he would leave them both completely speechless as they struggled to understand the implications. It was a question that up until a few seconds ago had been derived from a cemented fact, one that had instantly cast Adrien VanFleet into a less-than-favorable light from the moment Alexa had first learned his name from Michelle VanFleet's lips. Now, the cement had been chipped apart, allowing the exploration of entirely new and unexpected perspectives.

"Explain," Ezra said, sending the world back into motion. "Why would your wife encourage you to sleep with another woman?"

Adrien VanFleet cocked his head to the side, and if his eyes had been visible, Alexa imagined he would be looking at Ezra with a look of fresh curiosity. Finally, he said, "I will answer your question, but may I please ask one of my own first?" His voice had grown softer, sadder, and it struck something inside Alexa, setting off warning bells that this entire plan had been a mistake. That she'd somehow missed something terribly important and now everything was collapsing around her.

"Go ahead," Ezra said. And Alexa knew it was only because he was as confused as she was.

"When you first broke in, you said you wanted to talk about Michelle. I ... I thought you were going to ask for money. I thought you were going to tell me how to get her back. I don't know what my relationship with Kate has to do with any of this, but ... can you just tell me one thing? Can you at least let me know if Michelle is alive? Just tell me she's okay and you haven't hurt her. At least give me that reassurance before you ... before you kill me."

Ezra turned his head and looked over his shoulder to Alexa, and she could see in his eyes that he realized their mistake, too. Something was off, they'd missed something, and now it seemed that Adrien VanFleet might have answers to questions they hadn't even known they needed to ask.

Alexa typed onto the note on her phone and held it up for Ezra to see: **What do you think?**

Ezra read the message and shrugged. "I've asked a lot of questions to a lot of people."

"I'm sure," Adrien said.

"Shut up. I'm not talking to you."

Adrien's mouth closed with a *pop*.

"I don't understand it," Ezra continued, "But, I believe him. This whole thing is screwier than we thought."

Alexa closed her eyes and sighed. Nodded for Ezra to go on.

"I have no idea where your wife is," he said. "I can't tell you if she's dead or alive. We thought you killed her, or had her locked away somewhere. We came here to find out why. We also came to determine your involvement in the murder of a young woman named Victoria Jameson."

Alexa understood why Ezra had tossed on the last bit about Victoria so casually. He wanted to catch Adrien off guard, gauge his reaction.

The reaction was abject shock. "*What?* I have no idea who that is! I haven't killed anybody! And Michelle..." He settled down, his chin drooping to his chest, defeat settling over him. "Why would you think I would want to hurt her? I'm doing everything I can to *find* her."

Ezra didn't allow the man time to wallow in his sorrow. "I answered your question. Now it's your turn. Explain your situation with Kate Williams."

Adrien lifted his head and nodded, recomposing himself. "It's like I said. I was sleeping with her, but it wasn't behind Michelle's back. Michelle and I have always had an open marriage. I know that sorta thing is taboo here in our conservative little town, but it's just the reality of things, and a lot more common than most folks around here probably think. But what can I say? Michelle and I love each other unconditionally, but in terms of the physical, we've agreed we can enjoy other people as well."

Alexa watched as Ezra considered this. "Has your marriage always been this way?" he asked. "Or is this just a convenient story you're concocting because you think it's going to get you off the hook for something? You know, since Michelle isn't here to validate your claims."

Adrien nodded. "Just about from the beginning," Adrien said. "We met in college and dated off and on, but always seemed to end up back with each other. It's like we were magnetic. But we both had, uh, difficulty avoiding temptation. You know what I mean? We were mature enough to soon realize we didn't have to choose. We could have our love and our pleasure, without any compromise.

"Anyway, with Kate ... I don't know what more to add. She started working at the bank a few months ago, and she was definitely very flirty with me. At first I thought that might be the way she was with everyone, but eventually I realized she seemed to be coming onto me. Which was surprising, given the age difference, you know? After that, one thing led to another.

"We used a motel for privacy, but not to keep secrets from anybody. Well, at least I didn't. I know Kate was a little worried about getting caught because she didn't want to lose her job, but otherwise..." He shook his head.

Ezra asked, "Did your wife ever meet Kate?"

"Yes. Once. She came over for dinner one weekend when

the kids were sleeping over at friends' houses. And well ... we had a good time."

"Meaning?" Ezra asked.

"We had a threesome. Just the one time."

There was a beat of silence then. Alexa was thinking of how incorrectly she'd judged who the VanFleets really were, and everybody in the room seemed to have arrived at the same question, going right back to where, for Alexa, the entire thing had started. Adrien kept them from having to ask it, seeming to already know what was coming next. "I have absolutely no idea why Michelle hired that woman to spy on me and Kate under the ruse of my having an affair," he said. "It's what has me the most torn up about all of this. Not only that something terrible has happened to her, but that before it did she might have been going behind my back with something, trying to set me up. I just can't for the life of me understand why. We've always been so honest with each other. But..."

"But what?" Ezra said.

Adrien went quiet for several long seconds, shaking his head, as if trying to convince himself of something. But when Ezra shifted in his chair, the noise caused the man to spill his thoughts. "The strangest thing of all to me is that Michelle was the one who tried to set me up like I was having some sort of affair, when in reality I was starting to get the feeling that she was seeing somebody else. Which I know is ridiculous, because she'd never do that to me and the kids, but the last few weeks, something felt ... different."

"I thought you had an open marriage," Ezra said.

Adrien nodded. "We did. But we were always honest with each other and always asked permission before we'd ever get physical with another person. Like I said, we don't keep secrets from each other."

Alexa now understood why Adrien VanFleet had reacted the way he had that day in her office when she'd shown him the picture of himself and Kate Williams at the motel. He'd been just as dumbfounded as she and Ezra were now.

Ezra shifted gears. "Have you spoken to Kate Williams since the day you two were terminated by the bank?"

Adrien shook his head, the dull gray of the duct tape over his eyes briefly catching the kitchen's recessed lighting and flashing a pop of silver. "No. And not for a few days before that. She'd been sick, so I figured she'd wasn't in the mood to talk. After we got let go, I tried calling a bunch. Goes straight to voice mail. She's ignoring me. I guess I don't blame her— she probably thinks I've ruined her life."

Nobody spoke for almost a full minute then. The only sound that could be heard over the hum of the refrigerator was Adrien VanFleet's heavy breathing. Ezra had turned and was looking at her, both of them, it seemed, having come to the same conclusion: Adrien VanFleet was not a killer. As much as Alexa hated to admit it, the guy seemed to have been an innocent pawn in some bigger picture that had yet to reveal itself. But actually, it was even worse ... for him. He'd said it himself. It seemed like he'd been getting set up for something.

With Michelle VanFleet missing, there was only one other person linking the VanFleet and Jameson case together who she would have to track down. Somebody who, if Adrien VanFleet hadn't put those quarters over Victoria Jameson's eyes, would have had the ability to swipe some spare change that the man had touched. Maybe from the cupholder in his car ... or from a bedside nightstand in a motel room.

Alexa typed out the message on her phone and showed it to Ezra: **Where does Kate Williams live?**

Ezra asked the question.

Adrien stiffened, and fresh panic laced his voice. "You're not going to hurt her, are you?" he asked. "Please don't. She's young, she ... she hasn't done anything wrong."

Ezra shook his head. "I think you're wrong about that," he said. "Now answer the question. Or have you forgotten the rules?"

Adrien jerked against his bindings, the first attempt at a fight he'd shown since they'd arrived. But it was short-lived. Just a quick, useless tug against resolute plastic that cut into his skin. Then his body went slack again and the wave of defeat crashed over him and he sighed. "Please don't hurt her. She's a sweet girl."

But survival instinct is a funny thing. Adrien told them where Kate lived. He'd been there once, he said, for a lunchtime quickie.

Alexa could tell that Ezra was ready to leave, and she didn't blame him. Adrien VanFleet had exhausted his worth to them for now. Ezra stood and nodded for Alexa to head back to the garage. She nodded and turned to go, but at the last second before she started to walk, something on the refrigerator caught her eye.

A magnet was affixed to the top left corner. A white rectangular calendar showing in tiny print all twelve months of the year. It was the logo at the top of the magnet that had stopped her. Two overlapping Xs. Xpedited Xchange.

A sinking feeling hit so hard and fast she nearly doubled

over, but it was pushed away by the spur of adrenaline that came along with realizing one of the missing puzzle pieces might have just revealed itself.

She rushed around the counter and pulled the magnet from the fridge, bringing it back to Ezra. She pointed to the logo and then typed out on her phone: **Why do they have this?**

Ezra looked at her like she'd gone crazy for a second but then turned and asked, "Xpedited Xchange. What does that mean to you?"

Adrien answered as if it was the most insignificant question in the world, irrelevant to anything that concerned him in the slightest. "That's where Michelle works," he said. "And I manage their account at the bank. Well ... I used to manage their account."

Blood rushed in Alexa's ears, ocean waves crashing. She typed: **I thought Michelle worked from home? Something with travel?**

Ezra hadn't fully picked up the thread, Alexa realized, because she'd never told him the name of the place she'd gone to meet with Francis. So, he read the questions out loud exactly as she'd typed them.

"She does work from home," Adrien said. "They let her start working remote once we started having kids. She's been there a long time, so they trusted her, were willing to make the concession to keep her on. She's one of their logistics supervisors. Coordinates shipments and stuff like that."

Adrien's words were spinning through Alexa's head like a tornado, but one phrase finally came into focus when the dust settled. *So they trusted her...*

Her fingers were a blur over her phone's keyboard. She showed Ezra her new message: **Did it pay well?**

Ezra asked the question, and Adrien VanFleet actually laughed. "Oh yeah. She made more than I did. Xpedited Xchange is very generous to their top employees."

I bet they are, Alexa thought.

CHAPTER 30

Ezra told Adrien not to move and then cut the zip ties securing the guy's left hand and ankle, freeing them from the chair.

"Count to a thousand," Ezra said. "Slowly. Then you can take the tape off your eyes and figure out how to get out of the rest. One word of this to the police, and I'll come back. There won't be any rules this time. Just game over."

Adrien sat completely still but nodded his head. "Thank you," he said. Then, "Will you find her? Will you find my wife?"

Ezra didn't answer, and neither did Alexa, but she did find herself feeling for the first time a small amount of pity for the man still half-secured to the chair in front of her. His wife had stabbed him in the back and set in motion the events that had led to his eventual humiliation and firing from his job, and this very moment, being held prisoner and interrogated inside his own home, yet in his voice Alexa could tell the man still had concern for Michelle, still loved her. He wanted to know she was safe. Wanted her home.

Alexa didn't think the woman was ever coming home
again. Her initial suspicion that Adrien had done something
terrible to his wife might have been wrong, but it was clear
that Michelle had gotten mixed up in something bad, and if
she had somehow crossed her employers the same way she'd
crossed her husband ... well, Alexa had seen how much
mercy the Abatellis were willing to show to those who
stepped out of line.

"Start counting," Ezra said.

He and Alexa were closing the mudroom door just as
Adrien reached the count of six.

In the truck, once they were safely out of the VanFleet's
neighborhood, Ezra switched on the truck's headlights and
pulled off his gloves and balaclava. Alexa did the same with
hers.

"Well, that was interesting," Ezra said.

"I'll say. You were fucking terrifying. I mean, your whole
voice changed and ... my God, for a minute there I was afraid
you might shoot *me* if I said something without being asked."
Alexa grinned in the dark of the truck's cabin, but when she
looked at Ezra his face was a blank wall, hard and cold.

"That's not what I meant," he said.

"Right. Sorry. Yeah, that didn't go like I expected. I had the
guy pegged for a slimebag from the beginning, and now it
looks like Michelle is somehow the one doing the shady shit."
She filled Ezra in on the Xpedited Xchange/Abatelli angle,
and her theory that Michelle must have been on more than
just the regular payroll. "Think about it," she said. "Logistics,
scheduling shipments ... she was part of their underground
operation. Had to be. You heard the way Adrien talked about
how they treated her, how they paid her."

Ezra nodded. "And I bet she was the one that managed to get Adrien somehow in charge of Xpedited Xchange's account at the bank. He was probably handling money funneled in from all sorts of illegal activity and didn't have a clue. Jesus, she was setting her husband up as a potential scapegoat and probably getting an extra end-of-the-year bonus for it."

"Yep. But what happened?" Alexa asked. "Why pretend to accuse him of having an affair and then get him fired?"

"I don't think it had anything to do with her husband at all," Ezra said. "Think about everything we just heard. Think about the picture and video you got today. There's only one real connection here. The one person connected to all of them: Adrien, Michelle, and Victoria."

"Kate Williams," Alexa said. "Our mystery girl herself."

"You can wait to go talk to her tomorrow," Ezra said.

"Why wait? Why don't we go give her the same treatment we gave Adrien? She's the one who's got to have the answers, right?"

Ezra shook his head. "If for some reason she's really the person behind all this, she's already long gone."

Alexa thought more about Adrien's story. "She wasn't sick at all, was she?"

"Nope. My guess is she skipped town the moment everything all went down."

"I still need to go try. Maybe I'll get lucky and when I show up I'll find Michelle VanFleet tied up in a closet or something."

Ezra slowed the truck and turned onto the back road that would lead to his farmhouse. "Or dead," he said. "You might find a corpse."

"You're real optimistic at night, you know that?"

"I know one thing," Ezra said.

"What's that?"

In the light from the dash Alexa saw him grin. "You always seem to step in the Abatellis' bullshit without even trying. Maybe next time you try and find some different bad guys, huh?"

He turned and winked at her.

"You know," she said, "if you weren't Black-Ops Batman I'd punch you."

Back at the farmhouse, Barlow groggily greeted them as they entered the front door, looking as though the deed was more out of duty than desire, sleepy-eyed after being awakened. Alexa said she was going to take a shower and headed up the stairs. Ezra called out to her when she was halfway up.

"Hey," he said, something pressing in his voice.

"Hmm?" She turned and leaned against the banister, looking down on the top of his head, the first time she'd ever felt bigger than him. But it was only an illusion, in so many ways.

"Have you told Piper about any of this?" he asked.

"Oh shit! I was supposed to call her." Alexa pulled her cell phone from her pocket and checked the time. It was too late; Piper would already be asleep. She sighed and slid the phone back into her pocket. "She knows about the VanFleets, but nothing about the Abatellis. I told her the same as you at first, that it was a big client with a big NDA I had to sign."

Ezra nodded but then looked away, and Alexa could tell he was hesitating, torn between whether he should say what he wanted to.

"Ezra," she said. "We're beyond the candy coating, especially after this morning. What is it?"

He looked at her with those friendly eyes that had greeted her on her very first night in Silent Falls, the friendly eyes that could never quite hide the deep intelligence he possessed. "Do you care about her?" he asked.

"Yes."

"Love her?"

Only the briefest hesitation here. The realization fast-formed, but the courage to say the words out loud required a few more seconds of processing. "I do."

Ezra nodded, as if he had already known this answer. "Does she love you back?"

"I hope so."

"Then you need to tell her. Trust me. I've been down this road. I'm not saying that if Cheyenne had known the truth about my job, things would have been any different the night she had her accident, but..." He paused. Swallowed. "At least I wouldn't have to spend the rest of my life knowing that the woman I loved more than anything died without knowing exactly who I really was. She died in love with a lie, and I can't think of anything more cruel than that."

The stairs creaked beneath Alexa's weight. The sound of Barlow leaping onto the sofa and grunting in satisfaction as he snuggled up into his corner reached them.

"What if I tell her the truth and she hates me?"

Ezra shook his head. "What she'll hate more is waking up one day to learn you've disappeared, and never having any idea what could have possibly happened to you."

Alexa sighed again. Knew he was right. "You could tell her ... if that happened."

Ezra shook his head. "I love you too," he said. "I think you know that by now. And I'll do anything within my means to help you. But in life, Alexa, we all have our own crosses to bear. One of yours was trying to make yourself capable of loving again, and you can't do that without accepting all the responsibilities that come along with it. Otherwise..."—he shrugged, then nearly winced—"you're still just that little girl who's been floating through life all these years, pretending to be whoever you need to in the moment."

AFTER THE MOTEL rendezvous with Jane, the visit to the Buttercup Bakery and subsequent less-than-peaceful negotiation with T at the payday loan business, several hours in a car, and the late-evening home invasion, Alexa was thankful for the hot shower. But while it warmed and relaxed her body, it did little to slow her thoughts, calm her mind.

She tried to focus on the cases, on the facts and the data and the evidence, working to discard earlier theories that now seemed no longer possible and conjure up new and more likely scenarios based on all she'd learned in the span of roughly twelve hours.

Just like that. Half a day and the entire landscape of what Alexa had thought she'd known had shifted.

Kate Williams had bridged the fault line in Alexa's brain between Michelle VanFleet's disappearance and Victoria Jameson's murder. Two separate landmasses now becoming one new continent in desperate need of exploration.

But the expedition would have to wait, because as Alexa closed her eyes and let the water cascade down her body, she wasn't seeing corpses with quarters over their eyes or the life-less faces of missing women staring out at her from where they'd been buried in the dirt and leaves. Instead, she saw Piper from the previous morning, sticking her head out from the shower, her naked body behind the fogged glass shower stall like a Siren's song pulling Alexa forward. The steam and the heat from Piper's shower had been the perfect accompaniment to how Alexa felt in that moment, seeing Piper's mischievous grin, Alexa understanding that what she was feeling on the inside stretched well beyond the boundaries of simple attraction and infatuation that can easily blind the early days of relationships.

She loved her. Loved all of her. Even the parts of her that might annoy Alexa in the moment somehow grew charming later. She didn't want this feeling to end, wanted it to grow, to be nurtured and given the attention and respect it deserved so it would never leave her.

Alexa shut off the water. Ezra was right.

She would tell Piper everything...

When the moment was right.

In the guest bedroom dresser she kept some clothes to sleep in, t-shirts and sweatpants and a baggy sweatshirt for when the weather was colder. In those early days when she was getting her apartment and the Shiffy PI office in order, she'd slept here more than the apartment—partly for convenience and partly because of the company. In those beginning stages of acclimating to the idea of putting down roots in a town for the first time since she'd been twelve, it felt important to remain close to a source of happiness and comfort. Ezra was that source, her first true friend with whom she shared a deep connection born of loss and tragedy in their past, and a new secret in the present. They were the support system that neither one of them had expected.

Alexa knew then that being alone could be dangerous, because when the lights went down and things grew quiet, that was when the demons would creep in and the doubts would start and the anxiety would build. In those moments, it was a blessing to have somebody to reach out and hold on to.

Plus, Barlow loved the big backyard.

She tossed on some sweatpants and the sweatshirt and padded barefoot out into the hall. From the top of the stairs she could see the lights in the kitchen casting shadows to the end of the downstairs hallway. Ezra must have still been awake, so she made her way down the stairs and to the kitchen and stopped when she saw that the door that led to Ezra's basement was open. The lights were off, but she could hear typing.

"Ezra?" she called from the top of the stairs.

"You're going to want to see this," he called back, as if he'd been doing nothing but waiting for her.

Alexa glanced to the clock on the microwave and saw that it was a couple minutes until midnight. "Will I have to use my brain?" she called, already heading down the steps. "Because if so, I'm making coffee first."

He didn't answer, but when Alexa rounded the corner she found him seated at the desk at the back of the room, the glow of his large computer monitors silhouetting his head and shoulders.

"Can I turn on the lights?" she asked. "Or would you prefer I trip on the coffee table and break my face open?"

"Sure. Sorry, I hadn't planned on being down here long."

Alexa hit the switch by the stairs and the overhead lighting burst to life. She used the dimmer switch to abate some of the harshness, giving the space a warm glow, the way she and Ezra both preferred when they watched movies down here on his enormous television.

She walked around the sofa and settled into the desk chair next to Ezra's. A chair that hadn't been there the first few times Alexa had been in the basement but had arrived a few weeks after. An addition Ezra had made that spoke volumes.

Alexa had long ago forgotten the importance of feeling at home.

Both the screens were filled with what looked like scanned copies of reports, official-looking forms with answers typed onto blank lines, signatures and dates at the bottoms.

She didn't bother reading them. "Too many words for too late in the day, Ezra. What am I looking at?"

Ezra spun in his chair to face her. "The quarters," he said, "on Victoria Jameson's body. You know how we were talking this morning about how it looked like some sort of calling card, an MO for somebody who'd done this sort of thing before?"

"Yeah," Alexa said, glancing again to the forms, getting a new and hopeful sense of what Ezra was about to say next.

"I told my guy about it. Asked him if anything like that had popped up on any radars. Multiple murders with this sort of detail, especially within a certain geographical radius, might be enough to bring in federal support, like the FBI."

Ezra had lots of "guys." Connections from his past that Alexa didn't bother asking for more details about. All she

knew—and all she *needed* to know, really—was that the information they could find and provide to Ezra was both aston-
ishing and accurate. The way things were going, Alexa
figured she'd probably need to figure in a Christmas bonus
for Ezra's "guy" in the Shiffy PI budget.

The server and networking equipment in the metal rack
next to the desk hummed quietly, the nearly silent gatekeeper
and gateway to the world of information that Ezra had the
ability to plug into.

"I'm guessing since you called me all the way down here
at midnight," Alexa said, "he found something?"

Ezra nodded. "Three cases, all within a hundred miles of
each other. All three victims were young women, all three
found with quarters over their eyes. The murders took place
over the span of just four months. That's fast. Means there'll
likely be more bodies found."

Alexa felt the tingle of excitement begin to wake her up.
Her blood started pumping harder and she pulled her legs up
under her in the chair. "Holy shit. Where was this?"

"South Carolina," Ezra said.

The tingle became a chill. "Close enough," Alexa said.

"Close enough, indeed. Especially if you think the water's
getting hot and you need to find a new pond. One where
nobody's expecting you."

Alexa could see it. "So you get in a car and you drive. But
one state away doesn't feel far enough, so you keep going."
She paused, letting the new scenario play out in her mind.
Then she shook her head. "But then what? He happens to
end up in our neck of the woods, and his next victim just
happens to be a mob boss's niece? We're back to some strong
coincidences, now."

Ezra nodded. "True. But it's not impossible."

"And what about Kate Williams? How does she factor into Victoria Jameson's murder now? Our new killer is an additional variable that completely changes the equation."

Ezra didn't say anything. Crossed his arms and stared at her, waiting.

"Oh for God's sake, just tell me. I'm too tired for your smart-ass games."

"You're assuming our newly discovered serial killer is a man," he said.

The words slapped Alexa across the face. *Oh shit.*

Ezra saw the recognition hit her. Nodded. "Bingo," he said. "What if Kate Williams is our killer?"

CHAPTER 31

E zra had offered her a gun before she left. Something small and compact she could wear on her ankle. Alexa had declined, opting instead for a small tactical knife that she'd slid into her pocket right before she'd rubbed Barlow behind the ear and headed down the farmhouse steps to her car.

"Are you sure you don't want me to come with you?" Ezra called from the porch.

Alexa waved him off. "She doesn't know who I am or why I'm coming. I can handle myself." Which was mostly true. Over the years Alexa had managed to attend several self-defense seminars and even a few martial arts classes. She'd also kicked enough men's asses to know that a twenty-something-year-old girl wouldn't pose much of a threat.

Unless Kate Williams answered the door with a gun in her hand.

But Alexa found the odds of that happening to be slim. Especially in broad daylight.

"Plus," Alexa added, "the two of us showing up on her

doorstep together will look way more suspicious than just me by myself."

"Hey, we could pretend to be Jehovah's Witness. What's so suspicious about that?"

"Listen, this might not be the Deep South Bible Belt, but it's close enough for that plan to only increase our odds of getting shot at."

They looked at each other for a beat, the morning sun stretching into the sky and the trees rustling in a warm breeze that tempted Alexa to simply toss the whole idea away and share another cup of coffee with Ezra on the porch.

"Be careful," Ezra finally said. "Any signs of trouble, get out of there and call ... somebody. Me, the police, your Abatelli boyfriend, I don't care. Nothing about this is worth losing your life over."

"I will," she said and found that she meant it. "And please, we both know that if I was ready for a boyfriend it would be you."

Ezra smiled. Alexa smiled back.

"She probably won't be there anyway," Ezra said before turning and heading back inside.

"Only one way to find out." Alexa climbed into the Oldsmobile and cranked the engine, trying to decide if Kate Williams actually being home would be a good thing or a bad thing.

Again ... *Only one way to find out.*

According to Adrien VanFleet, the home Kate Williams had been renting was a single-story tract house in the middle of a cul-de-sac in a lower-income neighborhood to the south of East River. As Alexa drove the streets, she couldn't help but notice how close Kate Williams lived to the uber-upscale neighborhood where the Jameson family had their mansion. As the crow flies, Alexa would bet the homes were less than two miles apart. Two miles and at least five times the average household income.

She found the turnoff from the main road and drove slowly down the street, waving to a woman jogging at a steady pace—*Piper's type of gal*, she thought—and scanning the houses and yards, getting a sense of déjà vu. These small homes with their postage stamp yards, some tidy, some a mess, the palpable sense of being surrounded by people who are simply doing their best to go through the day, reminded Alexa of the very neighborhood where she'd found Barlow. The dog's original owner had been killed while working his waiter job at the local diner, and Alexa had gone to save Barlow from being forgotten.

Little did she know how much the dog would help save her in the end.

She reached the cul-de-sac and instantly recognized Kate's white Toyota Camry parked beneath a carport that was detached from the side of the house. It was backed in, facing the road. The badly cracked asphalt driveway led straight to the carport, and as Alexa drove forward to park in front of Kate's Camry, she noticed the mailbox. An ancient metal thing badly rusted and dented, but apparently it still did the job, because it was stuffed to the gills, the front flap barely held closed with a strained rubber band that the mail carrier must have kindly added to keep the box from falling open and having the contents scattered in the wind.

Alexa parked in the driveway and got out. She walked back down to the mailbox and pulled the rubber band free and slid out the first envelope she touched. It was addressed to Occupant, so she stuffed it back inside. The next envelope she pulled free caused a flush of excitement, another piece of some bigger picture revealing itself. The envelope was the electric bill, and it was addressed to Samantha K. Williams.

Shit ... Katherine is her middle name.

It was no wonder Alexa found so little about the girl on social media. She pulled out her cell phone and snapped a picture of the front of the envelope and sent it to Ezra, along with the message: **Full name. See what you can find.**

His response was instant: **Is she there?**

Alexa looked at the stuffed mailbox and then up to the quiet house. Typed: **Car is. About to knock.**

Be careful, Alexa could hear Ezra's voice in her head. It repeated itself as she made her up the driveway.

A cluster of plain gray paving stones mostly overgrown with weeds created a short walkway spanning the six or seven feet between the carport and the home's side door. Alexa knocked three times. She waited a full minute before knocking again, this time with as much force as she could muster, the door shaking violently but the locks holding.

"Miss Williams?" Alexa called, already knowing the woman wasn't inside but needing to make as many attempts as possible to determine this. "Miss Williams!" she called again, nearly screaming. "Do you have time to talk about our Lord and savior?"

Movement caught her eye to the right, and Alexa turned to see the jogger she'd passed on her drive in returning to one of the other two houses in the cul-de-sac. She waited until the woman was back inside before she tried the doorknob. It was locked, of course.

Alexa looked over to the jogger's house once more before she casually strolled around to the backyard.

The backyard was flat and empty. No grill, no patio furniture, no decorative potted plants or flowers. The yard was a square of dull and splotchy grass, but it did back up to a thin outcropping of trees, which was nice, Alexa figured, as it probably provided more privacy than most of the other homes' backyards. Alexa stepped onto the barren back patio and opened the glass storm door, which swung on hinges desperately in need of some lube. The back door had a small rectangular window right above Alexa's eye level, and when she stood on her tiptoes she could just make out the home's living room: couch, TV on a cheap stand, nothing on the walls. She tried the knob, found this one locked as well. She pounded on the door. "Miss Williams? I've called the police, they should be here any minute!"

She popped up on her toes again and peered through the glass rectangle. Saw nothing. Not the slightest hint of movement.

Time for phase two, Alexa thought.

She took two steps back and prepared to throw all her weight into a kick, thinking it would be enough to break the flimsy door in, but at the last second was hit with another possibility.

Spare key. Single woman living alone ... she's got to have one somewhere.

Alexa spent the next five minutes checking the entire exterior of the home, working her way clockwise back to the front and eventually returning to the side door next to the carport, hoping to find a fake rock or a fake pile of dog shit, or even something as obvious as a key under a doormat or above the door frame.

She found nothing.

But as she moved past Kate's Camry, fully intending to head back to the back patio door and smash it in, the sun glinted off the car's chrome trim, catching her eye, and she realized there was still one place she hadn't checked. She tugged on the driver's door handle, fully expecting it to be locked, just like the house, and was surprised and relieved to find that it opened.

The smell that rolled out hit her like a punch, causing Alexa to stagger a few steps backward, covering her nose. She choked and gagged and kept moving away until her back slammed against the side of the house.

Her phone buzzed in her pocket, and because she was already so rattled, she actually yipped in surprise. She ripped the phone from her pocket and saw that it was Ezra calling. She turned her head to suck in a deep breath of fresh air and then answered.

"Samantha Kate Williams is no bank teller," Ezra said. "At least, not really. She's a journalist, Alexa. Works for a big media outlet in South Carolina."

South Carolina.

Two states away. Better than only one, if you think the water's getting hot.

Oh shit.

"Alexa? Are you there? If you're in trouble, say 'I'm fine, we'll talk later.'"

Alexa swallowed and cleared her throat. "I'm okay, Ezra. Seriously. Kate, or Samantha, or whoever, she's not here. But," she turned back to the car, eyed the trunk, knowing that what was inside had to be the source of the smell—"I think I'm about to find Michelle VanFleet."

"That doesn't sound good," Ezra said.

Alexa sucked in a deep breath and held it, approaching the rear of the Camry. She kept the phone to her ear with one hand and used the other to open the trunk.

The woman inside was dead, Alexa's nightmare vision of lifeless eyes staring back at her finally coming true. The single bullet hole in her forehead left no room for questions. A period at the end of a statement.

But the body Alexa looked down upon was not Michelle VanFleet.

It was Kate Williams.

Movement at the start of the driveway pulled her out of her thoughts, and Alexa stepped back and looked up over the roof of the car, her stomach sinking so fast she finally did turn and puke.

An East River Police Department cruiser had just parked by the overflowing mailbox, the officer already out of his car and heading her way, hand resting casually on the butt of his pistol.

CHAPTER 32

Alexa had acted fast. At the sight of the East River police officer making his way toward her up the driveway, she somehow managed not to panic—which, in retrospect, was the biggest sign of personal growth she'd seen in herself since arriving in Silent Falls.

Instead of turning and running for the trees, instead of sprinting toward the cop with the intent to launch a flying knee into his groin in order to gain herself enough time to hop in her car and burn rubber out of the neighborhood, and instead of hurling a slew of profane names at him and his kind, Alexa knew that in the moment her best option was to stand her ground, not to flee and garner any more suspicion upon herself than was already apparent in the cop's movements, his cautious gait hiding behind a ruse of causal curiosity.

She needed to act like she fucking belonged here and was just as shocked at what she had found as he would be as soon as he rounded the side of the car and saw Samantha Katherine Williams's corpse stuffed into the trunk.

So, in a split second she pressed the button to end her call with Ezra and quickly dialed 911, putting the phone to her ear and, before the emergency services operator had even answered, she started speaking loudly and quickly. "Hi, my name is Alexa Shifflett and I'm a private investigator and I need to report a homicide."

A woman's voice had answered midway through this, and as she started to ask, "Ma'am, did you say homicide?", Alexa acted like she was now seeing the police officer for the first time and started waving for him to hurry, saying into the phone, "Oh thank God, there's already an officer here. Thank you so much!"

She hung up before the woman could respond, but she'd done what she'd needed to. If the approaching cop wanted to check out her story, she would have the call log to prove it, and so would the 911 operator.

The officer, who looked to be about her age, with buzzed hair and a small scar over his left eyebrow, had reached the front of the Camry and, having apparently caught the end of her conversation with the 911 operator, cocked his head and asked, "Is everything alright, ma'am? We got a call about a suspicious person walking around this property. Did I hear you say something about homicide?"

Alexa did not fail to notice that he never took his hand off his pistol as he spoke. She also knew exactly who had placed the phone call to the cops—the fucking jogger. *Maybe she's not Piper's type of gal after all. Nosy bitch.*

She kept her anger buried and kept up her act that she was thankful help had arrived, and that they could solve this problem together. She stepped a few more feet back from the car and said, calmly, confidently, "I did, Officer. I'm a PI from Silent Falls. I was trying to track down Kate Williams for a case I'm working on and, well"—she pointed to the opened trunk— "I found her. But it looks like somebody else found her first."

As she said the words, a breeze blew across her back, and it must have carried the rotting scent from the car toward the cop because he quickly covered his mouth and nose with his free hand. When all the pieces clicked together in his head, he stepped to the rear of the Camry and, eyeing what was inside, instantly changed his entire tone, shifting into a different gear.

"Ma'am, don't move!" he yelled. "Please, keep your hands where I can see them!"

Oh, for fuck's sake...

Alexa did as he asked. "My ID and investigator license are in my front left pocket, may I show them to you?"

The man spoke hurriedly into the radio clipped to his shoulder, and when the response came, Alexa didn't hear a word of it, because everything was becoming a blur, sounds and sights warping into slow motion. She could see it in the officer's eyes. He wasn't going to listen to a word she said. He'd switched into autopilot.

When he patted her down, she thought she'd puke again, her repressed childhood memories trying to squeeze through the crack in the wall, but somehow she kept them at bay. When he pulled her ID from her pocket, she nearly punched him. He found the knife in her other pocket and tossed it into the grass like it was on fire. He took the cell phone from her hand and found the burner phone in her jacket, and she refrained from telling him what a terrible mistake he was making, that he was going to feel real embarrassed soon enough.

Because with a miraculous sense of self-awareness, for one of the few times in Alexa's life, she understood that her best course of action was to do absolutely nothing at all.

A bit of this resolve did waver when he cuffed her, and a bit more when he—gently, to his credit—put her in the back of his cruiser. She watched out the window as he examined her investigator's license and ID, relaying the information into his radio. He got a response, nodded, and then looked at her watching him. He turned around to finish the conversation.

He didn't come back to the car. Instead, he went back to the Camry, and Alexa watched as he spoke into his radio again and then stood silently for a long time, staring into the trunk as though if he wished it hard enough, the body inside might suddenly spring to life, say this was all a misunderstanding, and he could go about his normal day of coffee and cruising.

Alexa leaned her head back, closed her eyes.

You did nothing wrong. You did nothing wrong. You did nothing wrong.

It was true. Aside from trespassing on private property, she had not committed a crime here, and no matter what the cop thought or might try to spin, there was absolutely no evidence to show that Alexa had killed Kate Williams. For starters, there was no gun on her when the officer had searched her. Even if a team did manage to find the weapon that had killed Kate, here or anywhere else on the earth, any prints that might be found on it would not be Alexa's.

But the longer she sat, the longer the silence inside the

confines of the cop car seemed to beat down on her, the more her anxiety began to rise. She could feel it, starting deep down in her gut, spinning to life, ready to fully wake and reach her heart. Doubts would begin to creep in, thoughts of crooked cops and conspiracy theories and planted evidence and the desire to have a quickly shut case more than a lingering cold one being cause for swift accusations and arrests.

She tried to push these thoughts away, push away the idea that when the rest of the world looked at her they saw the word *trouble* written across her forehead. It was ridiculous. She'd been doing so well. She had a business and an apartment and a girlfriend and a dog and a best friend and a ... a fucking life!

The back door of the cruiser was ripped open, and Alexa's eyes flew open with it. She jumped in her seat, pulling her legs up and ready to piston them out to kick her attacker.

"Get out," the cop said, standing back from the door.

She knew she had no choice. She got out.

The officer stepped toward her and Alexa's entire body tensed, and she knew then that in the next three seconds, all that she'd been working so hard to achieve would be gone, all her progress wiped clean. Her anger brewed and boiled, and she knew that if the cop touched her, she'd unleash all the ferocity she had in her, a compulsion she knew was wrong but could not prohibit.

Then she saw what the cop was holding out as he approached her. The key to the cuffs. She stood and watched as he unlocked them and then tucked them back into their sleeve on his belt. She didn't know what to say, what to do. On one hand, she was surprised that her story and credentials had checked out so quickly and had been enough for him to simply release her. On the other, it seemed too good to be true.

Which, it was.

"You've got some good friends," he said. "Sorry for the trouble. But now, with all due respect, get the fuck out of here."

He handed her back all of her stuff and Alexa did as asked. She got the fuck out of there.

She had just reached the end of the neighborhood, and when the burner phone buzzed in her jacket pocket, the cop's words finally sank in and she understood. She idled at the stop sign that guarded the intersection of the neighborhood and the main road, and pulled the phone free, answering it.

"How many donuts do you guys send the East River Police Department each month?" she asked. "Or is it a daily thing?"

Joey wasn't in the mood for jokes, apparently. He didn't raise his voice, but Alexa had talked to the guy enough to recognize when he was serious. "How did you know to look for Samantha Williams's body?" he asked.

A car pulled up behind her, and Alexa rolled down the window and motioned for the person to go around. When the car, a black Honda Accord, pulled up beside her, Alexa saw that the driver was the jogger from earlier, the one who had ratted her out. They locked eyes through their windows, and Alexa gave the woman the finger, keeping it there until the Accord drove away in a hurry.

"I'll answer your question if you answer mine," Alexa said. "How do you even know who Samantha Williams is, and why did somebody put a bullet in her brain?"

Joey didn't answer her question. Instead he said, "Feel like meeting for coffee?"

"Sure," Alexa said. "But we're doing it on my turf. These last couple days have gotten me real sick of East River."

She hung up. Joey would know where to find her.

CHAPTER 33

As soon as Alexa had ended the call with Joey, she tossed the burner phone into the passenger seat and then popped in her Bluetooth earpiece. She drove out of the neighborhood and called Ezra. He answered on the first ring.

"Are you okay? What happened?"

"I'm okay," she said, and for a split second she was surprised to feel an uprising of tears, a lump in her throat swelling to the point that she knew if she tried to speak right then, no sound would come at all. She'd been tough in the moment, had somehow managed to keep her emotions at bay. All those years of anger and resentment and absolute hatred of police that had so often spurred her to lash out and usually end up hurting somebody—or herself—she'd strong-armed back, locking the feelings away so she could stay present and focused.

She was proud of herself, but now the reality hit like an aftershock, and she needed a moment.

"Alexa?"

She swallowed, blinked away the tears that blurred her vision. "I'm okay," she said again. "I'm headed back to town to meet with my Abatelli boyfriend. He knows more than he's been telling me." Then she told Ezra what had happened, talking fast, her mind already working to think three steps ahead as she replayed the story for him, piecing together new scenarios. She was almost certain she knew who had killed Kate Williams and would bet good money it was the same person who had killed Victoria Jameson.

She just didn't quite understand why.

But that was exactly what she hoped to learn from Joey. He knew Kate Williams was dead—had known her real first name too—which could only mean one of two things: he knew who had killed her ... or he had done it himself.

Ezra had listened to her story without a single word of interjection, as usual. When she stopped talking, he allowed a few seconds of silence, making sure she was finished, and then he completely changed gears. It was another thing she loved about him: he didn't bother going over it all again, explaining theories and working through it all with her. He knew she was smart enough to figure things out on her own. If he thought she was missing something, or if she asked for help, that was when he'd speak up.

"You know," he said, "the boyfriend joke's not as funny when you say it. Anyway, I got into the laptop," he said. "Password cracked this morning right after you left. I was going through it when you sent me the picture of the envelope with Kate's full name."

Alexa sat up straighter in the seat, gripped the wheel. "Please tell me you found a file named 'Here's a picture of my killer.'"

"No. But I definitely found motive."

"Meaning?"

"Victoria Jameson's mother was right about something changing with her daughter ... and partially right about her having a secret boyfriend."

"The 'boyfriend' was Kate Williams, right? The picture and video I found probably prove that."

"Yeah, and what I've got solidifies it. Victoria's got an encrypted folder on her laptop full of audio and video recordings of her mother speaking to somebody on the phone. I didn't listen to much, but it was obvious she was trying to catch her mom in the act of something. There's also a video file of her mom and a large man who she calls 'Franny' several times, seated at a ridiculous dining table. I can only assume that's Francis Abatelli."

"Handsome, right?" Alexa said.

"He looks like the result of breeding a pit bull with a holiday ham."

"Anything else in the folder?"

"Oh yeah. Lots of PDF documents. Scanned images of bank records. Checking and savings accounts, investment portfolios, and the last two years' tax returns for JAG Inc. Any idea what that is?"

Alexa thought for a second, and it hit her fast. "Jameson Automotive Group Incorporated. Or something like that, probably. It's Collette's husband's business. Car dealerships. Inherited it from his father."

"Okay. Well, that's in here, too."

"She was trying to stockpile evidence," Alexa said.

"I don't think the Abatelli family is dumb enough to be able to have their entire enterprise felled by a few bank records. That's why they hire people like Adrien VanFleet and others ... to manage the clean money so well the dirty money slides right by security without a second glance."

"We know that, sure. But you know who might not know that? A young and ignorant reporter trying to blow the doors open on something big, make her whole career before she turned twenty-five. And ... God, and the young and ignorant informant she thinks will give her the dynamite."

"Yeah, about that," Ezra said. "When I launched the Messages app on Victoria's MacBook, I found a handful of texts from a number that didn't have a contact name saved to it. The last few messages came in the night she was killed."

"Let me guess," Alexa said. "They were to arrange the time to meet."

"Yes. Victoria was hesitant at first. Said it could wait till the next day at the usual place. But the other person was insistent. Said it was an emergency. That there might not be another chance. Victoria eventually agreed. Told them where to go and how to avoid the cameras at the gate."

Alexa already knew what the answer was going to be when she asked, "Did you look up the phone number?"

"I did. No name, just a business."

"The media outlet where Kate Williams worked."

"Why do you even need me?"

"Moral support. And a free babysitter for Barlow."

Alexa had been so occupied with the phone call, she'd missed the turnoff for the highway and had ended up on the outskirts of downtown East River, not too far from the Buttercup Bakery and the bus station. A traffic light turned red, and Alexa stopped the Oldsmobile behind a Ford pickup truck. Traffic coming into the city was heavier than she would have expected that morning, and when she glanced in the rearview she saw a long line of cars begin to form behind her.

Ezra said, "So we know Kate Williams was using Victoria Jameson as a source to try to expose the girl's corrupt family business. Something must have happened, something bad, and the last time they met, Victoria gets killed."

"And today I find Kate Williams shot through the head."

"It's hard to piece the rest together without knowing how long Kate's been dead. It could have happened the same night, or it could have happened this morning."

"You didn't smell what I smelled, Ezra. It definitely wasn't this morning. It had been a while."

Ezra was quiet for a moment, and Alexa knew he was working something out. But finally he sighed and said, "We're thinking Michelle VanFleet, right? I mean, she's the last link to all this. She's either the one who killed both women, or she's a third victim and we haven't found her yet. Which means the killer's still out there."

"And we still don't know why. Also, the quarters, remember? Kate Williams worked at a media company that must have covered the killer in South Carolina, so she's the one you'd want to point the finger at for Victoria's death..."

Ezra chuckled, the sound full of resignation. "We're spinning wheels here, going in circles."

"I know."

A beat, then: "You know, if I were Victoria Jameson," Ezra said, "I would have let the person I was meeting that night get caught on camera. That footage could have been used as insurance, or for blackmail, or *something* to try and protect or exonerate her later. I mean, she was part of the family—I feel like ol' Franny would have been a lot quicker to forgive his niece than a non-blood relative, right? I mean, he might be pissed, sure. Might cut her out of the will or whatever, but he wouldn't *kill* her, right?"

The light turned green and the truck in front of Alexa drove off, clearing her field of view. She moved her foot to step on the accelerator but then stopped, easing back on the brake. She stared through the windshield at the traffic light above. The car behind her blared its horn, but Alexa didn't budge. She looked at the camera mounted on the pole between the lights as more horns sounded, an angry barrage of impatience. She thought about Collette Jameson saying how busy the road had gotten where access to their maintenance road was.

The car behind her honked again, long and agitated, and for the second time that morning Alexa raised her middle finger up and drove away.

"Ezra," she said. "I need you to call your guy. And he needs to be fast."

"I can't just—"

"Now, Ezra." She didn't raise her voice. She didn't need to. He'd taught her that.

"Okay," he said. "Sure. What am I asking for?"

IT TOOK AN HOUR AND A HALF, but considering that Alexa figured Ezra's "guy" was performing this favor in between actual world-saving antiterrorism jobs, it might as well have been ten minutes, nothing more than a short coffee break. Her phone pinged with the incoming message from Ezra, which contained a link to a new folder in their secure cloud space. She clicked it, found the two video clips, watched them each only once.

She called Ezra.

"Is that him?" he asked.

"Yep. I told you this whole thing felt off from the beginning," Alexa said. "Now I know why."

"Always good to trust your instinct. So now what?"

"Now I'm going to hand-deliver all the answers to Francis Abatelli."

She heard Ezra let out a deep breath. "I'm not going to like this next part, am I?"

"Probably not."

She told him her plan.

"You're right. I don't like it at all," Ezra said.

"But you think it'll work, right?"

"I've heard worse ideas."

"Is that a yes?"

"That's a maybe."

Alexa smiled. "So you'll help?"

"Of course."

CHAPTER 34

By the time Alexa parked her Oldsmobile behind her building and then walked around to the front entrance of the café, it had been almost two and a half hours since she'd spoken to Joey on the phone. He was seated at the small table in the corner by the front window, his back to the wall, able to survey the entire space. In front of him, three cups of coffee sat atop the table, spread out in a triangle. When he met her eyes as she walked across the room to him, she could tell he was pissed.

"Where in the hell have you been?" he asked. "I've been sitting here forever."

It was the first sign that Alexa had been correct. Joey had never shown irritation before. Like Ezra, up until now he'd been masterful at keeping a blank face, never betraying his true thoughts.

"Traffic," Alexa said, pulling out the chair across from him and sitting down. She nodded to the coffee cups. "At least you had good coffee to keep you company."

"I left from East River the same time you must have, and I didn't hit any traffic."

Alexa shrugged, acted as though nothing could possibly matter less. "I guess we took different routes. Oh, and I did stop for a quick bite to eat. Finding dead bodies makes me hungry."

Joey looked to his left, over to where a middle-aged man sat three tables away, headphones on, staring intently at his iPad screen. Other than the man, there were a few people in line at the counter, but the lunch rush was over, and the place was otherwise empty.

"I have questions," Alexa said.

Joey opened his mouth to speak, but Alexa cut him off before a single word could be delivered. "How long have you been sleeping with Michelle VanFleet?"

Joey closed his mouth. Looked at her with eyes that couldn't quite hide his surprise. After a few seconds, he nodded and leaned back in his chair. Reached for the cup of coffee closest to him and picked it up. Took a sip.

"Six months or so," he finally said. "How did you know?"

"I'm good at my job," Alexa said.

"No, seriously. How?"

"Perfume," Alexa said. "The first time I saw you in my office, I smelled it on you. I thought it was just a lingering scent, since Michelle had just left, but then I smelled it faintly again when you let me into Xpedited Xchange to meet Francis. Plus, Adrien VanFleet had his own suspicions that Michelle was going behind his back with somebody. I didn't think much of it then, but now..." She pointed at him. "Now I realize you two have been in this together from the start. I know you know where she is. I think you all are hiding her somewhere."

Joey smiled, almost like he was enjoying the game. "Why would we do something like that?"

"Because she's a valued asset. Her husband told us as much. And she proved her loyalty to you all by killing Kate Williams, the journalist who was stupid enough to think she was going to expose your operation, who also happened to be sleeping with Michelle's husband. I don't know all the details, but I don't think you do either."

Joey eyed her cautiously. "Meaning?"

"Meaning Michelle also killed Victoria Jameson. How angry do you think Francis is going to be when he finds out you've had him harboring the killer he's been having me search for?"

Alexa saw it then, the brief flicker of surprise in Joey's eyes, followed by his entire body relaxing. He picked up the coffee again and drained the rest of it. "You know for certain Michelle killed Victoria?" he asked.

Alexa nodded. "I do."

"How can you prove it?"

She shook her head. "Nope. Not yet. I've told you a lot, but you haven't told me shit. So go on, it's your turn. You want what I've got, all it's going to cost you is the truth. I've done the legwork, and almost got arrested today, so you owe me that much."

"Hey, we got you out of that mess the moment we saw your name go across the system."

"Perhaps I'd be more grateful if I hadn't realized that your secrets were the reason I was there in the first place."

Joey didn't say anything. He scooted away from the table

and crossed his legs. Seemed to be thinking something through.

Alexa rolled her eyes. "Listen, Joe, you've got a choice. If I go to Francis directly and tell him Michelle killed Victoria, he's going to turn her into a pile of blood and bones. Now, something tells me that since you've already gone through all the trouble of keeping her hidden, plus being coy with me all this time, on top of sleeping with the woman for six months, you probably care for her. And since you care for her, you probably don't want to see her chopped up. Just a hunch. So, here's the deal: you tell me what really happened, and I'll give you the evidence I have that Michelle killed Victoria. After all, I'm supposed to go through you for everything, remember? Those were Francis's words. Maybe you can figure something out, work out a deal with your boss to keep Michelle alive. Maybe once I give you what I have, you throw it away, pretend you never saw it and then you and your girlfriend can run off and live happily ever after together. Honestly, I don't give a fuck. It's up to you."

Joey looked out the window, watched as a mother pushing a stroller made her way past, heading toward the clock tower in the center of town. He was weighing his options, searching for all the available escape routes, Alexa figured. When he turned back to her, she could already see the decision on his face.

ON THE DRIVE from East River back to Silent Falls, Alexa had pieced together most of the story in her head, stacking bricks, building the wall of possibility. Joey's account of the situation was the mortar to fill in the cracks, hold the entire thing together.

He spoke with his usual casual flair of indifference, but Alexa could tell something was slightly off, that the entire time he talked, he was resisting an urge to hurry through it all, to get it over with so he could do what he'd really come to do.

Neither Joey nor Michelle had ever learned exactly how Samantha Katherine Williams had decided to home in on the lore of the Abatelli empire, and now they never would. It was easy to assume that, being a journalist, she'd at some point read an article or overheard an editor somewhere along the line make mention of Virginia's great crime syndicate, and something about the story must have sparked the ambitious fires in her. How she had apparently convinced her boss to allow her to relocate two states away and go essentially undercover at the bank in East River was another mystery.

"She must have at least been able to dig up something big on us beforehand," Joey said. "She must have gotten ahold of somebody who snitched, given her enough for her boss to green-light the whole thing, probably thinking a Pulitzer Prize–winning journalist on staff would help subscription sales."

Alexa smiled. "Or she might have, you know, just slept with him."

Joey cocked his head to the side. "Well, yeah, I guess there's that, too."

"It's what she did with Adrien VanFleet, right?"

"I'm getting to that."

Samantha Katherine Williams, in all honesty, must have had a gift for research, or had some very good connections

(Alexa could relate to this part), because she had discovered that the Abatellis did business at East River Bank & Trust, and once she'd gotten her job as a teller, she'd set her sights on the account manager who handled everything—Adrien VanFleet.

"We would have never known what she was up to with Adrien," Joey said, "if she hadn't had gotten a little overzealous and blown her cover, kinda."

"How so?"

"One night, she pretended to be delivering Uber Eats to Xpedited Xchange. The guard who was on duty at the time saw the bag of fast food in her passenger seat, saw a cute girl driving, and let her right in." Joey shook his head. "He doesn't work for us anymore."

Alexa could read between the lines on that one.

"So she drives right up to the loading docks and starts poking around, asking questions about what we're shipping, what's getting delivered, how many trucks we see a day ... she was ballsy as hell, I'll give the woman that," Joey said. "Thankfully, the men working third shift, when she showed up, they knew better than to say anything to anyone they don't know or haven't been specifically given permission to speak to. No matter how cute the person asking the questions is, or how flirty they get. One of them, guy who's been with us long enough to know exactly what is happening, takes out his cell phone and tells her she's trespassing and he's calling the cops. She took off after that. She was ballsy, and a whole lot of ignorant, but she wasn't stupid. Was probably smart enough to know that if anybody was on the other end of the guy's phone call, it wasn't going to be the police. It was going to be a lot worse.

"He reported it immediately and security pulled all the camera footage and we got a real good look at her face. Sent out an email telling all staff about the breach in security and if they had any information on who the woman might be, to come forward immediately."

Alexa nodded. "And Michelle VanFleet came forward."

"She did."

"To you, specifically."

"Correct."

"Because you two were fucking."

Joey sighed. "We've already established that."

"I know, but you're cute when you blush."

Joey stared at her.

"So what?" Alexa continued on. "Michelle tells you she recognizes the girl as her husband's side chick and, since both of you are fairly intelligent, it's pretty obvious at that point that Kate is after more than just Adrien's dick?"

"You're very elegant," Joey said. "When you want to be."

"I'm flattered. Go on."

"You pretty much nailed it," he said. "I told Francis that Michelle and I had a lead on the girl, and he trusted me to take care of things. So Michelle and I did, and we worked out our own plan."

"To kill her."

"No. I mean, not at first. First we wanted to find out who she was and what she knew, and if she was working for somebody else, or *with* somebody else."

"Like a snitch."

"Yes. Somebody with insider information. Somebody who would also need to be taken care of. Honestly"—he leaned in closer—"I would have preferred if we'd been able to just scare her off, make some threats and watch her tuck tail and run. Let her know she's not ready to play with the big boys. But it was evident from the start that wasn't going to work with the girl."

Alexa narrowed her eyes. She knew that was bullshit. Kate Williams hadn't stood a chance once she'd been ID'd. "Michelle VanFleet has no objections to people being 'taken care of'?" she asked.

Joey shook his head. "You don't work for us as long as Michelle has, and get to the position she's in, without understanding our business requires certain techniques and protocols in order to continue to operate at the highest level and outpace any competition."

"You're very elegant," Alexa said. "When you want to be."

Joey ignored her, kept pushing on.

"It was Michelle's idea to play sort of a double agent. She figured since she had actually already met the Williams girl—"

"She did a lot more than just meet her."

Joey sighed. "Since she'd already met the Williams girl, it wouldn't be too hard to convince her that her plan was a legitimate one. Michelle was going to tell her how she'd been ID'd by the cameras and that she knew the girl must be more than just a bank teller. Whatever the Williams girl's motives were, Michelle was going to say that she wanted in. That she'd been trapped working for us for too long and was tired of all the bad stuff she'd seen happen over the years, that she was ready to flip the script on us."

Alexa felt skeptical about this. "Okay, so let me make sure I've got this straight up until this point. Samantha Katherine Williams, a journalist from South Carolina, gets a hard-on to take down the Abatellis. She moves to Virginia, finds one of the—I'm assuming—many banks you guys do business with, and figures the best way to get a chance to gain access to some financial records or get a better understanding of what sort of money you all are moving through East River Bank & Trust is to seduce the account manager—Adrien VanFleet. In addition, one night she gets super ambitious and drives to one of your distribution facilities and starts asking questions, a facility where, perhaps unbeknownst to her, the wife of the banker she's seducing just happens to work and is able to easily identify her. From that point, Michelle comes to you, her lover—don't give me that look, that's what you are, right? —and you tell Francis you'll take care of things, probably looking to score some brownie points, right? Keep the big guy from having to worry about small fish like Kate Williams? So Michelle's grand plan she lays out for you is to basically pretend to be exactly the type of source Kate Williams has been looking for. She tracks her down at lunch one day and offers her services, right? She pretends to drip Kate some information, just little bits of things that are probably easy enough to find out if you look hard enough, and eventually Kate tells Michelle she's got another source on the line too. That the three of them together can be the heroes of the story. So naturally, you and Michelle need to find out exactly who this other source is, and once you do, you can put an end to everything once and for all and get a congratulatory slap on the back from the big man upstairs himself." She stopped for a breath. "Is that about right?"

The man with the iPad a few tables down pushed his chair back and stood, the noise causing Joey to jerk toward it, but he quickly settled back down. Even waved a friendly goodbye to the man as he headed for the door, like they were two old chums who'd run into each other at their favorite watering hole. "Yeah," Joey said, "that's about right. I know it sounds—"

"I don't care how it sounds," Alexa said. "Can I take a guess what happened next?"

Joey held out his hands, palms up. "By all means."

"The rest is pretty easy, though, right? I mean, the dead bodies sort of tell the tale, but my guess is things got a bit out of hand. My guess, Michelle succeeded in getting into Kate's circle of trust, and then she sprang her trap. What did she do, show up at Kate's house one night under the guise of dropping some secret intel, only to abduct her at gunpoint and force her to take her to meet her other source? I've seen the text messages that came from Kate's work phone that she sent to Victoria Jameson the night Victoria was killed. She said it was an emergency and couldn't wait. From what I gather, they'd been meeting in broad daylight up until this point— I've got photos and video of them together walking past the Buttercup Bakery in East River—so why the big rush? What was so important? Victoria's biggest mistake, aside from trying to rat out her entire family to begin with, was agreeing to go out to that gate that night. The messages show she tried to resist at first, tried to push back, but eventually Kate's insistence won her over. Just like Kate Williams, Victoria's youthful ignorance got her killed, and she was so worried about what her parents might think if they found out, she even helped her killer get away by telling them how not to get caught on the camera."

Joey nodded his head. "Michelle had no idea Victoria was the source until she got there." He lowered his voice, giving it a somber tone, as if he was grieving. "If she had ... God, things would have been so different." He swallowed, took a deep breath. "When they got there, Michelle said things started out smooth enough. She showed her cards and let the two of them know that we knew all about what they were up to, threatened the wrath of all evil on the two of them, lined them up beside each other and waved the gun back and forth between them, told them all the terrible things that would happen to them if she made just one single phone call. Said they'd never be safe a single day for the rest of their lives if they didn't forget everything they were doing, stop playing Nancy Drew. She told them there were lucky they were even getting a second chance, that most people don't."

"But it didn't work?" Alexa asked.

"Michelle says she thinks it might have been working for Kate, but Victoria"—he smiled—"Victoria must have had more Abatelli in her than she wanted to admit. She's where it all went wrong. Victoria had slipped a knife out with her, some little tactical thing she probably bought for protection in the city, and when Michelle turned her head for a second, Victoria got brave, lunged at her, knocked the gun out of her hand and sliced her arm. Victoria should have ended it all right there, should have stabbed Michelle to death and saved herself. But"—he shook his head—"most people aren't killers. Especially not smart young women. Instead, they both went after the gun and Victoria got a step ahead of Michelle, so Michelle jumped forward and pushed the girl in the back, hard. Victoria lost her footing in the dark and went down, facefirst."

The photographs of the girl's body flashed through Alexa's mind. "Right into one of the rocks," she said.

Joey nodded. "Knocked her out cold. Michelle panicked, and was angry, and found the knife and leapt on the girl and stabbed her three times in the back before she realized what she was doing. She told me after that she felt like she was in a trance."

"Adrenaline and shock and fear. A deadly cocktail."

"You got that right. Michelle said the Williams girl basically turned into a mumbling statue after that. Froze in place and kept begging Michelle not to hurt her. Michelle, smart as she is, had calmed down a bit and realized she now had even more leverage on Kate Williams to get the girl to leave all things Abatelli alone. Michelle told the girl that if she didn't, Michelle would call her bosses right then and let them know that the nosey journalist had just killed Francis's niece. To her credit, the Williams girl must have realized that Michelle, despite her threats, was going to have a pretty tough sell herself in getting out of the hot water they'd landed in. By now she must have figured out that Michelle's bosses were likely aware of Michelle's game of deception with her, and probably knew she'd gone out that night to eliminate a source. The only thing that the Williams girl had working in her favor was the fact that she'd managed to keep secret that Francis's niece was her source. Whether Michelle had actually killed Victoria or been present and somehow allowed the Williams girl to do the deed, she didn't figure Francis would much care. He'd get vengeance all around."

Alexa was quiet long enough to play the entire thing out in her head, watching the scene unfold like a film noir. "The quarters were Kate's idea," she said, shaking her head. "She'd seen the cases of the killer from her home state and thought that by playing copycat, they'd throw any suspicion off her and Michelle. It was her, what, peace offering? Her saying, 'Hey, I'll help us get out of this if you let me go.'"

Joey shrugged. "I have no idea what the girl was really thinking, but that's as good a guess as any."

Liar.

"And they were driving Michelle's SUV that night, weren't they? They grabbed some quarters from the cup holder and then took off. That's why the prints your guys pulled belong to Adrien VanFleet."

Joey looked away, as if this part bored him. Didn't matter.

Alexa said, "And the blood they found in the back of Michelle's SUV ... before, I thought it might be hers, but now I'm thinking it belongs to Kate Williams."

"It had to be done," Joey said. "Michelle called me and told me what happened and ... well, the Williams girl was a loose end we couldn't risk. She drove straight to Xpedited Xchange and we—"

"Took care of things," Alexa said with some malice.

"I followed Michelle back to the Williams girl's place and we stuck her in the back of that car and she's been there right up until you found her this morning."

"And Michelle called the bank pretending to be Kate calling in sick?"

Joey shook his head. "You don't even have to call these days. Just send a text message."

"God bless technology," Alexa said. "But why leave Kate right there at her home? Why not dispose of the body, hide it somewhere nobody would ever find it?"

Joey gave her a look that told her she should already know the answer to that. "These aren't the type of situations that Abatellis handle with discretion," he said.

Alexa felt sick, and dumb. He was right—she should have known. "You wanted her to be found. Her dead body was a message to send back to her bosses. Letting them know never to come sniffing around your business again. You just didn't expect me to be the one to find her." Alexa rubbed at her temples, like her head hurt from having to process the story. "I need a coffee," she said.

She stared at him long enough for him to get the idea. "Oh," he said, looking only vaguely annoyed. "Please, allow me." He stood and pulled some cash from his wallet, heading toward the counter.

Alexa knew she was testing his patience to the max, but that was the idea. She wanted him frazzled, wanted him on edge. "Americano," she said. "Extra hot."

He looked back to her. "Is that a thing?"

"I never joke about coffee."

She looked out the window while she waited for Joey to return with her drink. When he set it down in front of her and took his seat again, Alexa said, "Okay, I understand everything you just told me, but help me with one more thing."

Joey crossed his arms and checked his watch. "What's that?"

"Why did Michelle get me involved in this in the beginning? Before you came waltzing in with your photos of Victoria's murder scene, Michelle pretended to want me to catch her husband cheating. Why? You already knew exactly who Kate Williams was, and you already seemed to have a plan in place. Why did she drag me into it?"

Joey nodded, must have known Alexa would ask this question eventually. "We needed an insurance policy to get the Williams girl out of the bank, one way or another. The photos would guarantee that."

"You mean, if you hadn't killed her."

"It's good to have options," Joey said, as if they were discussing nothing more serious than paint colors for the living room. "We knew you could get the job done."

"So it was Michelle who sent the email to the entire bank from Adrien's account?"

Joey nodded again.

"How?"

"She had installed a piece of spyware we gave her on his work laptop one night weeks ago when Adrien brought it home with him. It essentially created a backdoor giving somebody remote access, as well as a keystroke logger. Corporate IT departments work so hard at keeping stuff out that they often overlook might already be inside, and they forget to think about their own employees being the bad actors."

Alexa nodded. Ezra had told her a similar version of this same sentiment. "Okay, but Michelle clearly knew that that email would also get her husband fired. His career is ruined now—why would she...?" It hit her, hard and fast. Things finally adding up, settling into a neat and orderly line. *Ohhh, I see.*

Michelle VanFleet wasn't just having a physical relationship with Joey—she was having an emotional one too. They were in love, and...

"You two were going to run away together, weren't you?" Alexa asked.

For a second, Joey looked like he wanted to deny it, to keep his personal life locked away, secretive. Alexa understood that, but she certainly wasn't going to accept it. Not today.

"Joey, come on. We're already through the looking glass."

He picked up his coffee cup, realized it was empty, and then set it back down. Scoffed and then fidgeted in his chair, saying, "Yeah, that was the plan. We'd been trying to figure out a way to do it, for months now, honestly, but it always seemed too big, too scary. We each had lives we'd have to walk away from, each of which would be difficult."

Alexa Shifflett knew firsthand how crazy and unpredictable the world could be, but hearing stories like these, hearing what people would do to each other for their own selfish benefit, never ceased to anger and stun her. "And then your saving grace showed up in the form of Samantha Katherine Williams," Alexa said. "Now I get it. Now I understand why you and Michelle were so adamant about handling things yourselves. She was your ticket out. You thought if you squashed the little gnat flying around the barbecue, Francis might, what, grant you your freedom?"

"Freedom? I'm not a prisoner," Joey said.

"Uh-huh. Sure. Doesn't matter. But that's what you were thinking. Solve a big problem for the boss, get his blessing to fly the coop and take one of his valued employees along with you. And all Michelle Williams had to do was act like she'd been abducted, while—and maybe this part was more accidental than not—pointing some fingers at her husband as the prime suspect in her disappearance, as well as the murder of a crime boss's niece."

Joey said nothing, which told Alexa she had pinned it exactly right.

"You know," Alexa said, "to an outsider, this entire shit

show from top to bottom seems like nothing more than a stinking pile of coincidence. But a good friend of mine had a really interesting perspective on coincidences and I tend to agree with him. You know what it was?"

Joey shook his head.

"They don't exist. The sooner you realize that, the quicker you'll realize everything is happening for a reason, and that'll only get you ahead in life."

Joey stared at her for a long time. She stared back. Eventually, he smirked and said, "What in the hell are you talking about?"

"Nothing. You know, you called Kate Williams ballsy earlier, but I have to say, I think you're the one with the big swinging sack around here. Lying to Francis, acting as though you're just as stunned and devastated by Victoria's murder as he is, going along with pretending to help me track down who killed her. When all the while you've known it was your girlfriend, and in reality, the only reason you wanted to be the point man on this with me, making sure that Francis allowed you to handle all communications, was because you knew that if I ever did find out who killed Victoria, you needed to know first so you could step in and play interference."

"Listen," Joey started, "you don't—"

"I don't fucking care," Alexa spat, then stopped to turn and see if anybody had noticed, had started listening in. Two folks in line had their noses buried in their phones. "I told you already, I'll give you what I have and the rest is up to you. I think you and I both know Francis is a smart, resourceful man. Cunning, you might even say. I think we both know you won't get away with this forever, but you can certainly try. I'm not going to rat you out, because, as much as I hate to say it, I like you, Joey, but if I give you this, you better keep me the fuck out of whatever the rest of your plan is. Because if you don't, I'll be the one to hunt your ass down and"—she made air quotes—"take care of things. And I think by now you know just how damn good I am at finding people who don't want to be found."

Joey sat back and crossed his arms, looked at her like she'd suddenly pulled off a mask and what was underneath confused him. "Who *are* you?" he asked.

Alexa pushed away from the table, picked up her coffee and said, "Somebody who's gotten extremely bored with this conversation. Come on. I'll give you the files and then I want you to get the fuck out of my building and my town."

CHAPTER 35

There's that old saying: Man plans and God laughs. Alexa didn't believe in God, not in the traditional sense you might expect, but her experiences in life had taught her to believe in a higher governing power, a sort of cosmic system of checks and balances, one that she'd only recently settled on calling the Universe. It was as good a name as any. And right now, as she climbed the stairs up from the café, she really hoped that the Universe would hold off on any laughter, at least until she reached the Shiffy PI office door.

She climbed the stairs with Joey coming up behind her. She went slowly, unhurried, hoping beyond hope that her instinct was correct, and whatever harm Joey meant to deal to her, he would wait until they were behind a closed door and not out in an open stairwell. He hadn't been able to hide that brief flash of surprise on his face when Alexa had told him that she had evidence to prove that Michelle VanFleet had killed Victoria, and that alone was enough to give Alexa confidence that he wouldn't kill her until he had it in his possession. He didn't know what it could be, but he probably figured that if Alexa had gotten ahold of it, it might only be a matter of time before somebody else did. He needed to know.

Alexa felt the rush of relief tingle through her body as they reached the Shiffy PI office door, but it was short-lived. In half a second, the stairwell seemed to grow colder, the light from the window shifting from a warm white to a frigid gray. Time seemed to slow, three seconds stretching long past their life. In that moment, Alexa knew ... her instinct, the Universe...

It wasn't laughing.

It was giving her a warning.

With the thumb of one hand she flipped the plastic lid off her coffee, and with the other she reached out for the door-knob just as Joey grabbed her hair, pulling her head back enough to reveal her neck over the collar of her jacket. The pinprick of the knife sent the world back into color, time speeding up again.

"Don't do anything stupid," Joey said.

Alexa was insulted. Joey should have known that she might be a lot of things, but stupid was not one of them. He should have also known the last thing she'd do was go down without a fight.

"Really?" she said. "That's the best line you've got?"

In one fast and fluid motion, she jerked the door handle and pushed forward, ducking down, feeling the scrape of the knife against the side of her neck, up to her ear, the fast trickle of blood warm and not altogether unpleasant, and at the same time she tossed the coffee directly over her shoulder, splattering the hot liquid into Joey's face.

"Ah, fuck!" he cried, letting go of her hair, pawing at his eyes.

Alexa ducked and rolled into the office, and Joey stumbled in after her, waving the knife wildly, slicing at nothing.

From the side of the room, Ezra was a dark shadow along the wall, sweeping in like a wraith, grabbing and jerking Joey's wrist so hard something cracked and the knife clattered across the room. Then Ezra's leg shot out like a piston, connecting with Joey's knee. Another crack, this one louder, and before Joey could scream, Ezra's hand was clamped over the man's mouth, and he was pressing the barrel of the pistol to Joey's temple.

"Looks like you literally brought a knife to a gunfight," Ezra said. "One word, one scream, and I'll be happy to show your brain how to exit your skull."

Alexa pressed her hand to the side of the face, pulled it away and looked at the smear of blood. She stood and walked toward Joey, towering over him where Ezra kept him knelt on the floor. She wiped her hand on his white shirt. Said, "Did you actually think I was smart enough to figure this all out, but dumb enough not to know you'd kill me the second you got what you wanted?" She shook her head. "Francis is going to be so disappointed in you."

"WHERE HAVE YOU BEEN?" Piper said in Alexa's ear.

Alexa had forgotten about the cut on the side of her face, the thin red line that now ran along the back of her jaw and up to her ear, and shifted her cell phone from that side to the other. "Listen," Alexa said, "I don't have a lot of time right now, but I..."

"Alexa, what's wrong?"

Alexa cleared her throat, heard the engines of two vehicles arriving outside. "Nothing. I mean ... I'm fine. Look, I've got to go, but I wanted to call and tell you I'm sorry. I'm sorry for basically disappearing these last two days."

"It's okay," Piper said. "I know work can keep you busy. It happens to all of us."

"Yeah, but this is—" Outside, the sound of a car door opening and closing. "Look, I have to tell you some things. Things you deserve to know. Can we meet for breakfast tomorrow morning at the café? Early. Like, seven?"

A small hesitation, brief, but long enough to cause Alexa's heart to skip. Finally, "Sure. Yeah, of course."

A gentle knock on the door.

"Great. Thank you, Piper. Thank you. I have to go."

She hung up. Before Alexa could drop her truth on Piper, she had to handle the truth waiting on the other side of the motel room door.

After she and Ezra had subdued Joey, Ezra again making fast work of zip ties and duct tape, Alexa had taken the man's cell phone and checked the call logs, choosing the number Joey had called the most in the last couple weeks and dialing it. Francis had answered on the first ring. She had kept the details vague and made her request.

Francis had agreed.

Alexa had driven her Oldsmobile to the run-down motel outside of East River and parked in the back corner of the lot, as always. She'd entered the lobby and was pleased to have found her second-favorite innkeeper behind the desk, only instead of a magazine, this time the woman had looked up from a paperback romance novel when Alexa greeted her. Alexa had slid a hundred-dollar bill across the counter and asked for room 7 and some privacy, because she had some friends joining her. The woman took the bill, nodded, handed over the key, and went back to reading.

Alexa had chosen the motel as the meeting place both because she wanted a neutral playing field and also because of an odd sense of closure she was anticipating by ending this whole mess in the exact place it had started.

Plus, she knew it was a place where people would always look the other way and develop sudden memory loss about anything they might see during their stay.

She'd waited over an hour for Francis and his entourage.

Alexa peered through the peephole in the door and saw one of the two goons who'd been stationed behind Francis's desk during their last meeting standing a couple feet back from the door. She opened the door slowly and stepped back. "Ugh," she said, rolling her eyes. "I asked the service to send someone *good* looking. I want a refund."

The goon ignored her and stepped inside, his eyes doing a quick scan of the room. "Arms out," he said.

Alexa knew better than to protest. This was the endgame, after all, and her compliance was paramount. The last thing she needed was for Francis to think she was trying to pull one over on him.

She raised her arms and closed her eyes and held her breath as the goon patted her down, finding only her wallet, which he placed on the dresser next to the ancient television, where Alexa had already set both her burner phone and the phone she'd taken from Joey.

Ezra had kept Joey's knife to "add to his collection." Alexa hadn't been sure exactly what kind of collection he'd been talking about and had chosen not to ask.

Satisfied Alexa wasn't packing any sort of weapon, the goon moved past her, checking the bathroom for anyone hiding away, and then went back to the opened door and gave the all-clear.

Alexa stayed put in the center of the room, heard more car doors opening and closing. The parking lot was dark, most of the lights busted or burnt out, so when the rest of the group arrived, it looked as though they were slowly being revealed from behind a black curtain: first, the second goon from Francis's office, followed by none other than Michelle VanFleet, her eyes growing wide with shock and confusion when she saw Alexa, and then finally Francis's hulking frame filled the doorway. For a second, Alexa thought the man might have to turn sideways to fit through it. He stopped just shy of crossing the threshold, surveyed the inside of the room for himself, and then greeted her politely. "It's nice to see you again, Alexa. Thank you for meeting with us." As though the meeting had been his idea all along.

He stepped inside and closed the door behind him.

"I am curious," he said, sitting on the edge of the bed, frame sinking beneath his weight so that it nearly touched the floor. "Where's Joey? You mentioned he'd be joining us."

The two goons moved into position on either side of the bed, guard dogs at their master's heel. Michelle VanFleet had slid herself into the corner by the window, unsure what to do. She'd probably been wondering the entire trip why in the hell she'd been brought here, plucked from whatever safe house they'd been hiding her in without a word from her boyfriend. But Alexa could see it in her eyes now, remembered the way the woman's face had contorted with surprise when she'd stepped into the room and found Alexa waiting. Michelle VanFleet was smart, and cunning, and had a cold ruthlessness inside her born of either selfishness or greed or both. She saw Alexa and Alexa knew she understood. Because Michelle knew Alexa was smart and cunning as well. And could damn well be ruthless when it was required.

Michelle VanFleet knew they'd been caught and was trying to calculate just how bad the damage would be.

Bad, if Alexa had to guess. Real bad.

Alexa stared at the woman for several seconds, staying silent but hoping her gaze told Michelle the whole story. *You lied to me. You preyed on my sympathy. And now you're going to wish you'd never met me.*

Alexa looked to Francis and said, "Joey's in the trunk of my car. He was banging around for a while, but he either gave up or knocked himself out."

The room seemed to take in one big breath and hold it. But when Francis only remained silent, Alexa knew he was giving her the green light to explain herself.

And that was when she knew things were going to work out.

She told the story as quickly as she could, filling Francis in on all the details that she knew and adding in what Joey had admitted at the café.

"They did kill Kate Williams," Alexa said. "The journalist who'd been poking around in your business, and who was trying to sleep her way into digging into your finances with Michelle's husband. Which is why you've gone along with Joey's insistence on hiding hide Michelle away for a while so they can work out the rest of their plan. Ruin Adrien's life, so on and so forth. I get it. Hell, I'd probably do the same thing in your shoes. Why not? Reward those who help protect the family."

Alexa moved and leaned against the dresser, so she could face Francis head on. He shifted his weight and the bedsprings gasped their dying breath.

"You know, Francis, when I went to talk with your sister the other night, I found that I really liked her. She's a strong, confident, bold woman. In different circumstances, I'd like to say I could be friends with her. I bet she's a blast at parties.

"Right before she agreed to answer any of my questions, she made a point of stressing honesty. She said she'd be completely honest with me, as long as I returned the favor. That was our deal, and I honored it, Francis. And I know that honesty is something your family prides itself on, regardless of how others might view your business. So what I'm really here to tell you is that while I've been honest with you throughout this entire"—she pointed back and forth between them—"*relationship*, Michelle and Joey haven't."

Francis didn't move, but the two goons on either side of him both turned to look at Michelle VanFleet, who still hadn't said a word, looked as though she was trying to fold herself into the corner, disappear.

Alexa continued, telling Francis what Joey had told her had happened the night Victoria was murdered. How Michelle and Kate had met with the girl at her home and she'd ended up getting knocked unconscious and stabbed to death. Alexa nodded to Michelle. "She was there, Francis. She was right there when Victoria was killed. But..." Alexa looked down at her phone and pulled up the video files Ezra's guy had gotten for them. "I don't know for sure that it was Michelle who killed her."

She stepped forward and sat on the bed next to Francis, swimming through a fog of cologne. She held up the phone so he could see and hit play on the first video. "This was recorded by the traffic camera on the stoplight right before the turn for your sister's maintenance road."

Since the traffic along Blackmill Road had only recently increased to the point that traffic lights had been added, the new traffic cameras mounted atop each were about as state-of-the-art as they come. High-resolution and big sensors to help see better in low light. The video was time-stamped in the bottom left corner with the date of the night Victoria had been killed, and the image on screen showed Michelle VanFleet's SUV driving through the light, her face clearly visible behind the wheel when Alexa pinched the screen to zoom it in. Then she swiped the frozen image over, and Kate Williams was revealed in the passenger seat.

Then Alexa played the second video, which was time-stamped roughly thirty-five minutes later, showing Michelle's SUV heading the opposite direction through the light. This time, it was Joey's face behind the wheel, with Michelle in the passenger seat. Alexa guessed Kate Williams was probably already dead and in the back. "Joey was there that night," Alexa said. "Not only has he known this whole time how Victoria was killed, I think he might have been the one to do it. Whatever plan they had in mind when they got there, Francis, it sounds like your niece fought them off as best she could, and they killed her for it." She looked over to Michelle, whose skin had turned a sickly white. "And I hate to tell you this, sweetie ... okay, that's not true. I fucking love telling you this. If I had to bet, I'd say there was a good chance your boyfriend was going to let you take the fall for this if push came to shove." Alexa shrugged. "Guess he doesn't love you quite as much as you thought, huh? How's that for honesty?"

The woman made Alexa sick. Michelle VanFleet was nothing but a con artist. She'd fooled them all: Francis, Adrien, her two children, and worst of all, Alexa. There was a part of Alexa deep down inside that got giddy at the thought of helping Francis dispose of the woman.

Francis pointed a bratwurst finger to Alexa's phone and said, "How did you get those videos?"

Alexa smiled and slid the phone into her jacket pocket. "I'm really good at my job. Isn't that why you hired me?"

Francis was silent for a beat, then started to laugh, a low rumble that started in his gut and rattled up through his chest. His shoulders heaved and the bed started to bounce, and Alexa had to stand up to keep from getting motion sick.

And it was a good thing she did, because soon Francis's laughter took on a different tone, grew deeper. It morphed from a sound of joy to pained grunts of anger, barometric pressure building to spawn a tornado.

With the same unexpected grace and speed Alexa had seen the man display at his office, Francis leapt off the bed hard enough that the single framed painting on the wall shook and swayed on its hook. He thundered around the bed, knocking his goon aside to tumble onto the abused bed. Francis's figure loomed over Michelle VanFleet, his girth blocking her completely from view. Alexa watched as the man's arm shot up, and she flinched in surprise when Michelle's head was slammed into the motel room wall so hard it punched a hole clean through the drywall. Dust and plaster rained down, and when Francis slammed Michelle's head into the wall again, her skull must have connected with a stud this time, because there was a dull thudding sound, and blood splattered like somebody had stepped on a ketchup packet.

Michelle VanFleet's body crumpled to the floor and Francis turned around and said to his goons, "Go get Joey." Then he stepped over to the door and opened it, pulling out his cell phone. "I need to call my sister."

CHAPTER 36

Alexa's heart hammered in her chest, anticipation threatening to cause her to faint.

It was a quarter past seven in the morning, and the café line was out the door. After a night of restless sleep, Alexa had arrived from upstairs the moment the place had opened, ordering an Americano for herself and an almond milk latte for Piper, and had secured the table in the corner by the window for them. She had sipped her drink and waited for Piper to arrive, doing her best to push away all the doubt and anxiety that seemed to be surrounding the table, growing larger with each ticking second of the clock.

When Piper had come through the café's door and spotted her, she had waved and smiled and politely excused herself around the line of people and joined Alexa at the table, leaning down and giving her a quick kiss on the lips.

Alexa didn't give a shit if it sounded cliché, but the kiss had been like magic, blasting away all the dark feelings and replacing them with the warmest light. With that kiss, she'd felt sure everything was going to work out.

But then Alexa had started talking, launching right into all the truth she'd been keeping inside, hiding from the girl sitting across from her who'd done nothing but bring her happiness, had made her life better in so many ways. She'd explained everything that had happened with the Abatellis, culminating in last night's motel meetup. As she'd said the words, exposed the horrors of her reality over the last few days, the darkness had started to inch its way back in, encroaching on the good vibe.

When the story was over, when Alexa had wiped clean all the lies, she'd apologized profusely, telling Piper how much she hated herself for not being honest with her, for taking their relationship for granted, and, most importantly, for getting involved in something that might have, at worst, put Piper in harm's way.

"I don't care about myself," Alexa had said. "But you … God, if something happened to you because of me…"

"*I* care about you," Piper had said, and then she'd gone still, quiet, sinking into her own thoughts.

That was when the waiting had started, and Alexa's heart rate had risen to dangerous levels as folks crowded into tables around them and the volume turned up on the din of chatter and morning routines.

Finally, mercifully, Piper spoke. "It's over? All of it?"

"Yes," Alexa said too quickly. But she believed it.

Last night, after Francis Abatelli had remodeled the motel room wall with Michelle VanFleet's face, he'd stepped outside to call his sister, Collette. Alexa had given him two minutes and then quietly slipped outside to join him in the dark parking lot, just as Francis's two goons dragged a bound and struggling Joey across the asphalt. The tape over his mouth muffled his protests, and Alexa didn't even give the man a glance as he was dragged into the room and the door was closed.

A mist of rain seemed to hover more than fall through the air, slicking a few strands of hair to Alexa's forehead. She stood next to Francis, who was looking out to the road, which looked lonely and afraid in the night. If somebody had driven by and looked into the parking lot as they passed, Alexa imagined that Francis's figure would have appeared to them more like a monster in an old black-and-white horror show than a man.

"What is it?" Francis asked, as if sensing he already knew why she'd joined him but was going to make her say it. Make her ask.

"I want you to know, I'm very sorry about your niece. From what I can tell, from what Collette told me, she was a bright girl. She didn't deserve what happened to her."

Francis nodded his thanks but said nothing.

"I'm glad we were able to get her some justice."

He turned to look at her then, the mist seeming to part and make way for him. "This isn't justice," he said, his voice low and as soft as Alexa had ever heard it. "This is revenge. This is punishment. Hurting those two in there, that will be cathartic in a way, and a necessity, because *they* do deserve it. But it will be a temporary high. When it's over, and I wash my hands of their blood, Victoria will still be gone, and I'll have to live the rest of my life knowing she's dead because of me. Because of our family's last name." He shook his head. "Justice doesn't exist in this world. I accepted that a long, long time ago."

A car motored by on the road, lighting the front of the

parking lot with its headlamps. Then it was gone and the parking lot fell back into darkness and the quiet resumed.

"I did what you asked of me," Alexa finally found the strength to say.

"You can come by the office tomorrow to pick up your payment."

"I don't want your money, Francis."

He raised his eyebrows. "People don't usually refuse to *take* my money. It's the getting paid part that we tend to have a problem with."

"All I want is for us to be square," Alexa said. "You felt I owed a debt to you—well, now I've paid it. I don't have any interest in anything you do from this day forward, as long as you keep me out of it. As far as I'm concerned, after tonight, you don't even exist. I just want to go live my life, which, if I'm being honest, is something I've only just started to realize how to do. I've got enough fears, Francis. Please don't be another one."

She'd thought of this speech on the drive to East River, had practiced it with the sound of Joey trying to bang his way out of the trunk. In the moment, it sounded rushed, didn't carry as much heart as she'd hoped it would.

But still ... Francis nodded.

"The night you visited Collette," he said, "she called me after you left."

Alexa held her breath.

"She liked you," Francis said. "A lot. She said you showed her more kindness than anyone else since Victoria was found —including me. What you said back in the room, about honesty ... yeah, that sounds exactly like Collette. She's tough as nails and a hell of a lot smarter than me. I think you're right. I think the two of you could be friends."

Francis turned to her and stuck out his hand. "Thank you," he said. "We're all square."

Then he'd turned and headed back into the motel room, leaving Alexa alone and free in the parking lot.

In the parking lot of a fast-food restaurant half a mile up the road, Alexa had pulled into the space next to Ezra's truck. They didn't roll down their windows, didn't say a word. She'd given him a thumbs-up and a smile. Ezra had nodded once and then started the truck's engine and drove away. She'd followed him all the way back to Silent Falls, both she and the Oldsmobile feeling a lot lighter than when they'd left.

Alexa took a sip of her coffee and nodded, saying again to Piper, "Yes, it's over. All of it."

A small, almost pained smile formed on Piper's lips, and she nodded once before turning and staring out the window. And while she stared, Alexa's mind filled with all the loss and heartbreak her story contained. So much death, so many grieving family members left behind: mothers, fathers, young children. Questions left without answers and mysteries left unsolved unless the police managed to put together the pieces. They might come to some conclusions, makes some assumptions, and some might even be correct. But the only people left alive who knew the entire truth would take it to their graves, bonded in a mutual pact of respect.

And Piper. Piper had the answers, too. And with those answers came a choice. Alexa knew it might be an unfair one, but there was no other way. Piper's next words would either end their relationship and potentially threaten Alexa's so-called treaty with Francis, or they would signify the start of something grand, something to be celebrated and shown off and placed on a mantel for all to see. The start of a relationship that, if you were to have asked Alexa from only six months ago, would have seemed all but impossible for somebody like her.

Piper picked up her latte and stood from the table. "It's a nice morning," she said. "I feel like going for a walk."

Alexa felt her heart sink, her stomach roll with nausea. The darkness closed in.

"Go get Barlow," Piper said, and the smile was back. "We can all go together."

The world was bright again. The brightest Alexa had ever seen it.

CHAPTER 37

The next three days felt like clouds moving across an open sky: effortless and uneventful and mostly ignored. With the wild circumstance of the Abatelli and VanFleet disaster behind her, Alexa appreciated the serenity, fielding incoming office phone calls and responding to emails with a lightness that filled her the moment she woke, going about her day as though nothing bad could possibly happen—sunshine and rainbows and all that nonsense. She knew it wasn't true, of course—evil was always lurking, small or grand and any size in between—but for three days she did well at pushing out the darkness and focusing on the light.

Things with Piper weren't exactly normal, but they weren't bad, either. The walk in Collins Park that day they'd met in the café and Alexa had laid all her cards on the table had been a sort of reset button, the relationship not necessarily starting over but certainly taking a handful of steps backward, slowing down enough for them both to reexamine themselves and what they wanted.

Alexa would have to earn Piper's trust again, prove her love and that she could handle all the responsibilities that came along with it.

Which was all she'd ever hoped for. Because she could do it. For the first time in her life since she'd been a twelve-year-old girl, there was no doubt in her mind about that.

There was a soft knock on the Shiffy PI office door and for the first time in three days Alexa felt her stomach sink a bit. A tremor of some unpleasant thing waking inside her. "Come in," she called from where she was seated at her desk. She leaned back in her chair and watched as Colin Wanamaker cracked the door open and stuck his head in, scanning the room as though he wasn't sure what he might be walking into.

"Hi. Got a couple minutes?"

"I said 'come in,' Colin, not stand in the hall like a kid sent to the principal's office."

Colin came in and closed the door behind him. He had a to-go cup from the café in his hand and he set it on the desk before sitting down. Alexa eyed it and saw *Americano* scrawled in Sharpie across the side of the cup. She smiled. "Colin, you don't have to bring me a present every time you want to have a conversation." She leaned forward and picked up the cup. Took a sip. It was good, and she'd take all the free coffee anybody wanted to give her.

"Uh, that was actually mine," Colin said.

Alexa, honest to God, was shocked to feel herself blush. "Oh, shit. I'm—"

She noticed the smirk on his face.

"Kidding," he said.

She laughed, and Colin allowed himself to join in. "Well

played, my guy. Well, played." She took another sip. "But as much as I would love to think this is purely a social visit, something tells me we haven't quite taken our relationship to that level yet. So what's up?"

Colin nodded, as if this conversation was going exactly as he'd mapped it out in his head. A rhythm as familiar as a catchy new song played to death on the radio. "I'm sure you've seen the news."

"I avoid the news at all costs, Colin. Nothing but death and destruction and fabricated despair."

He nodded again, whether because he'd expected as much or because he agreed, Alexa wasn't sure. "We found Michelle VanFleet," he said.

Alexa said nothing.

"Her body and that of a man yet to be identified were found naked and tied together with nylon rope, hanging from the shower rod in a room at a seedy little motel outside of East River. They were ... well, let's just say it wasn't the hanging that killed them."

Alexa allowed enough time for it to seem as though she was thinking about this. "Thoughts?" she asked.

Colin sighed. "Easiest answer is the same old story: she was having an affair and somebody got jealous and got revenge."

Something like that, she thought. "Adrien?"

"Of course that's what we checked out first, but he had an alibi. Turns out his parents brought his kids back home and they verified he hadn't left the house since they'd arrived. So if he killed them, the timeline wouldn't match with what the coroner stated." He shook his head. "It wasn't him."

"Anybody at the motel see anything?" Alexa asked.

"Nothing that helps us. Woman behind the desk said that Michelle and the guy checked in together and she never saw them again."

Alexa almost let loose a smile. Wondered how much cash Francis had dumped in the motel clerk's lap to recite that story. Enough to buy plenty of new romance novels and magazines, that was for sure. "So it sounds like you're trading a missing persons case for a murder case, huh?"

"Not us. It's ERPD's case. But I just wanted to get your thoughts, since, you know, you were kinda involved in this."

Alexa took another sip of coffee and stood from the desk, walking over to the big window that looked down on the street behind the building. She saw Colin's cruiser parked behind her Oldsmobile. Colin didn't stand. Just turned and looked over his shoulder. "My thoughts?" Alexa said. "Jesus, Colin, what a terrifying question that is. If you want a real answer, all I can give you is this: I think there are absolutely good people and bad people in this world. You're one of the good ones, Colin, and contrary to some people's opinions, so am I. But what actions are deemed good and bad, well, I think that's a lot grayer of an area than people understand."

The room was silent for a full thirty seconds, and when Alexa turned from the window, she saw that Colin had stood and was leaning against her desk. He eyed her for a beat and then asked, "What does any of that have to do with Michelle VanFleet?"

"Everything, Colin. It has everything to do with it."

Maybe Colin understood, maybe he didn't—Alexa would bet that he did. The kid had climbed up several rungs of her trust ladder lately. She had faith in him now, where previously she'd had very little.

He stood from the desk and headed to the door, stopping before reaching out for the handle. "You know you're on the sheriff's radar, right? He doesn't trust you at all. First, the thing with the Anthony Romano, and now Michelle VanFleet ... you seem to keep getting involved with people who end up dead."

"And what do you think, Colin? Do you think I'm a killer?"

Alexa gave the guy credit, because Colin stayed silent for a few seconds and considered this. Finally, he gave his answer. "No," he said. "I don't. Like you said, you're one of the good ones, and I believe you."

"Thank you."

"I also believe you're keeping a lot of secrets," Colin added. "But I'm trusting that they're all for the right reasons."

The kid was smart, his finger right on the pulse of reality.

"For the record, I don't trust Sheriff Byrd either," Alexa said. "So at least he and I are on the same page."

When Colin left the office, Alexa walked back to the big window and watched below as he appeared on the sidewalk and rounded to the driver's door of his cruiser. Before pulling the car door open, he stopped and craned his head up and looked at her window, caught her watching him. Alexa smiled and waved. He waved back.

One of the good ones, Alexa thought again. Then she went back to her desk and drank her coffee and tried to chase that good feeling from the last three days. Wanted to hold on to it for as long as it would let her.

AUTHOR'S NOTE

Thanks so much for reading **PREY NO MORE**. I hope you enjoyed it. If you *did* enjoy it and have a few minutes to spare, I would greatly appreciate it if you could leave a review saying so. Reviews help authors more than you can imagine, and help readers like you find more great books to read. Win-win!

While the Shiffy P.I. series can stand on its own, Alexa first appeared in a couple books from my Lance Brody series. If you like supernatural mysteries, I hope you'll give them a read.

If you'd like to stay up-to-date on what I'm working on, there's a link on the following page where you can sign-up for my newsletter, and as a thank you you'll receive a free book starter bundle. And...

If you'd like to check out my Patreon page (patreon.com/ mrobertsonjr), I'm offering lots of perks, early-access to projects, and behind-the-scenes content to supporters.

THANK YOU to the following Patreon members for your support:

Chris Cool, Deana Harper, Debra Kowalski, Diane Benson, Diane Porter, Judi Josephson, Karin Anderson, Kathy Oudinot, Lisa Fazalare, Lorraine Meyer, Lynette Stone, Marilyn Aiken, Martha Gilmore, Mike Gagliardi, Rebecca Curry, Robert Bray, Steph, Tami, and Tanya Wolf.

You guys rock!

-Michael Robertson Jr

For all the latest info, including release dates, giveaways, and special events, sign up for the Michael Robertson, Jr. VIP Readers List. As a Thank You, you'll also receive a FREE audiobook and ebook. (He promises to never spam you!)

http://mrobertsonjr.com/newsletter-sign-up

For early-access to books, behind the scenes content, and other perks, join Michael on Patreon.

https://patreon.com/mrobertsonjr

More from Michael Robertson Jr

LANCE BRODY SERIES

Dark Choice (Book 7)

Dark Holiday (Book 6)

Dark Rest (Book 5.5 - Short Story)

Dark Woods (Book 5)

Dark Vacancy (Book 4)

Dark Shore (Book 3)

Dark Deception (Book 2.5 - Short Story)

Dark Son (Book 2)

Dark Game (Book 1)

Dark Beginnings (Book 0 - Prequel Novella)

SHIFFY P.I. SERIES

Prey No More (Book 2)

Run No More (Book 1)

OTHER NOVELS

Cedar Ridge

Transit

Rough Draft (A Kindle #1 Horror Bestseller!)

Regret*

Collections

Tormented Thoughts: Tales of Horror

The Teachers' Lounge*

*Writing as Dan Dawkins

Follow On:

Facebook.com/mrobertsonjr

Twitter.com/mrobertsonjr

Instagram.com/mrobertsonjr